T0207961

YESTERDAY'S SUNSET

A time travel romance.

Glenda Reed

YESTERDAY'S SUNSET
A time travel romance.

iUniverse books may be ordered through booksellers or by contacting:

iUniverse
1663 Liberty Drive
Bloomington, IN 47403
www.iuniverse.com
1-800-Authors (1-800-288-4677)

ISBN: 978-1-4917-4961-6 (sc)
ISBN: 978-1-4917-4962-3 (e)

Print information available on the last page.

iUniverse rev. date: 01/22/2015

Chapter One

Kelly was following a group of Americans around an old castle. Her mood was excited. Drummond Castle had always been the one that Kelly had been in love with, ever since she had been 14 years old and she had studied it in high school. It had fascinated her with all the nooks and hiding places it had, the stories of knights and clan wars and priest holes. She had always remembered the long hall with all the family portraits. She had dreamed about them long after her medieval classes had ended. After this class, she had longed and dreamed about a trip someday to England. Just thinking about it made her shiver with excitement. Her mother had told her that they could start saving now and maybe when she graduated from college, she would have enough money for a trip to England. Here in Chicago, there were museums galore, but nothing ever came close to her expectations of Drummond Castle in the North of England.

When she finally graduated, she had saved three thousand dollars. The three thousand dollars was only the start. After she counted up all the gifts from graduation, she had twelve hundred more dollars to add to it.

Her trip was going to finally come true. She made plans with her mom and got a passport. She went out and gathered up literature for her trip. She studied everything from cover to cover. She got an International Drivers License. She got a new suitcase and she began to pack. Day by day, she would add something to it and her date of departure was set for July 1st. She was 22 years old and had made her mind made up. She wanted to go to Drummond Castle and walk those halls. She had two huge books from the bookstore about the castle. She had devoured them like a thirsty animal in the desert.

Her suitcase had ten rolls of film in it and a new camera. She had new clothes and new shoes and most of all, she had knowledge. She had a plan and knew exactly what every day had in store for her.

Finally, the day came and she was driven to O'Hare Airport. She got out and gave her mom and dad a long last hug. She turned and walked into the airport. She was on her way to a dream that she had had since she could remember.

Kelly checked in her bags and walked to the gate. They were about to load the plane, she grabbed some chips and a Coke, got out her boarding card, and got in line. Once on the plane, she got seated and waited for her next stop. London, England.

Chapter Two

The trip was a smooth flight and she had her breakfast an hour before they landed. She was so excited to at last be there.

Looking out the little window, she saw the sun coming up and the trees and houses coming into view as the plane got lower and lower before it landed.

Eight o'clock in the morning in England. She was tired and it was such a scary feeling to be all alone in a big place like this. Kelly said to herself, "Okay, here I go." As she got into the big black cab, she relaxed, sat back and closed her eyes.

The next thing she remembered was the driver opening her door in front of the Lancaster Thistle Gate Hotel. It was a big hotel and it was all white. Her bags were sitting on the sidewalk and a porter came out to get them.

"What is that across the street?" she asked the porter as she moved her hand towards a wall that went so far she couldn't see the end of it.

"That is an art show. The artists show their paintings for about two miles down the avenue," he answered her. "You can get a good bargain over there. While you are here, you should go see all the art hanging there."

"I will." Kelly picked up her carry on case and purse and went in to register.

It was 8:15 a.m., so she took the elevator to her room, got in a hot bath, and went to bed. She needed a nap badly. Three hours later, she woke up and felt like she needed to eat something before going to see the castle. It was already 12:30 p.m. and she knew the castle closed at 5:00 p.m. so she had to hurry with a sandwich and drink and get started on her adventure.

She met two girls in the restaurant named Sherry and Elaine. They were so friendly. They were from England. They talked and got to know each other pretty well. They asked her where she was going today and she told them she had just arrived and was on her own for the first time on vacation. They ate together and then they went with her to the castle. They had told her they had not planned anything for today and asked if they could go with her. She agreed and off they went. She was surprised to have made friends already and was glowing with pleasure as they left the hotel. She knew they loved her accent and she loved theirs.

They talked and by the time she got to the castle, she knew a lot about them. They were a little older than her, but they had a day off today and even though they lived in London, they still had never seen all the castles or taken all the tours. It was going to be a great day for all of them. They worked in Safeway and were not married, but they had boyfriends. They wanted to know if Kelly had a boyfriend back home in America. She told them not a serious one, but a lot of good friends that she hung out with.

About an hour later, their cab pulled up and she saw the first glimpse of her childhood dream. It was overwhelming and she gulped as she got out of the cab and paid the driver.

At the front door, she paid a fee to see the whole estate, inside and out, also including a short film about its history. Her day was going perfectly. She was so happy. Inside, the first thing she did was get in line with a group of tourists and follow them on a guided tour.

The guided tour started in the Gallery Hall. She told her new friends that she had goose bumps. They laughed and giggled at Kelly. Kelly told them she had studied this castle in depth and already knew a lot about it. But she said she was most excited about the Gallery and the long dead ancestors of who knew who that she was about to see for the first time. The shivers came up and down her long tanned arms and goose bumps replaced the chill bumps.

"I wonder why I'm so cold," she said to Elaine.

"I think it is cool and nice in here, but I'm not cold," Elaine said.

Kelly was straining her head to listen to the typical English woman give her speech. The lady was pointing her tourist stick at the faces and calling names.

The girls and Kelly followed the rest of the group and listened to her talk about who they were and how they died and who they killed and what war they fought in and what castle they were bound to.

Kelly was silent. As one of the pictures looked straight at her, she tried to think why this man looked so familiar to her. She backed up and took a second long look. His wide smile and bright blue eyes just made her smile, too. He looked like a young Spencer Tracy, but much more handsome. She turned her head to a right angle and looked into his eyes. Her heart felt a gut wrenching sadness. She quickly backed up and the wall behind her felt cold to her back as she leaned on it. The name on it said Sir Jamie Drummond, first Earl of Drummond Castle and the year 1600.

Sherry came running back to Kelly and asked her why she had not followed the rest of the group. She couldn't answer. There was a blockage in her throat. Sherry reached out her hand and when she touched Kelly's shoulder, she blinked really fast and it felt like she had been in a trance before. She shook her head and all of a sudden she was back to where she should have been all the time. The name, Jamie, made her heart beat fast but she had no idea why.

"What happened?" Kelly asked.

Sherry said, "I noticed you had slowed up and there seemed to be a certain painting on the wall that had all your attention. So I came back to get you. Also, I have a friend here that I want you to meet. I was so surprised when I saw Arthur that I rushed back to find you. Come on, let's go."

Kelly turned to leave and she heard a voice say, "Come back to me, please."

She stopped fast and turned around. "Did you hear that?" Kelly asked Sherry.

"What did you hear?" Sherry asked her.

Kelly thought that maybe her mind was playing tricks on her. So she shook it off and grabbed her new friend's hand and then went on to join the group for the turret visit.

Up on the battlements she could breathe the fresh air and she immediately felt very good again. She could see for as far as the eye could see. Trees and rolling hills and, in her mind, somewhere she though she saw a horse and rider coming up the path towards the big castle. She stared ahead and she saw that the horse had on armor. The rider had a metal suit on and she could not see his features at all. Kelly took Sherry's hand and said, "Look over there and tell me what you see."

Sherry looked straight at the area she pointed to and she said, "I see the most beautiful grass and trees and hills that could have been painted right out of a medieval painting. I love it here and I can not believe that I have always lived in London and never visited the castles at all. Have you a famous place in your state that tourists come to all the time and yet you might nave not ever been there?"

"I have never been to the Field Museum and people come from all over the world to visit the scientific things they have on display there," she answered with a thought that she was sure to be reminded of some day.

The local guide was saying that there had been many battles planned and organized from the high point of the castle. Seeing all around gave the laird of the castle the advantage on approaching armies. There had been many big wars through the years and the castle had stood proud and strong through it all. Never had it fallen to an enemy army. There had been fires shot over the tall rock walls and arrows a plenty flying through the air. But Drummond Castle had never fallen.

Kelly had been in a trance seeing all that she heard like it was real to her. She could almost feel the crisp air and she could see the horse flying up to the bridge when she heard her name being called quite loudly by a man. She turned around and Sherry was touching her on the arm and a young man was standing beside her staring into Kelly's eyes. In an instant, Kelly thought that she had been transported through time and back again.

"Oh, hi," she said, "and who is this handsome man you have by the arm?"

Sherry smiled and her eyes sparkled like she had a secret that Kelly needed to know. "This is a friend of mine and he saw us getting out of the cab and decided to join us for the tour, too. Only he couldn't find us when he got his ticket and came to the front of the castle."

Sherry was quick to introduce them and ask him to join the group. His name was Arthur. He was a chemical engineer student at the University of London. He hung out with these girls sometimes because they all went to school together. He was still in school, but didn't see his friends very often anymore, so he jumped at the chance to spend the day with them.

This new girl was enchanting. He just loved Americans. Their accent was so charming to hear.

"Let me take our new friend around a bit. I know this old castle inside and out, because I did a paper on it a long time ago. It is so old and has a long history of kings and queens visiting here. I would like to walk the halls of the Gallery. I love it here. So many faces and through the long centuries, so many changes in dress" he said.

"I love it, too," Kelly told the cute guy. "I studied it in school in Medieval History. I have been saving my money for five years to be able to do this trip and visit the castle and I'm so excited I can't stand it," she said.

The rest of the girls came back to them then and they all took off following the tourists in front of them. The group of new friends went through the castle from the front to the dungeons. They loved every moment. When it came time to head back to London, they all went to the cab and Arthur got Kelly's hotel name and phone number for future use.

"I am so excited," she told Sherry. "I just have the feeling he will be calling me. He is so good looking and he is too smart. I hope he really likes me and not just my accent," she told her friend laughing. "You know, he had me saying all kinds of things so he could hear the Chicago words and how I said them."

"I know and he did like you. I know him and he does not have a girlfriend and he is so into his degree that he never took much time out for girls at all."

Kelly began to wonder how a long distance relationship would work when all of a sudden she heard a voice say, "Please don't leave so fast, stay a while and visit with me. Please."

She looked all around and she was shocked to see no one. Not a soul in sight. Where had that voice come from she wondered. She looked at the girls and saw they were sharing a joke and all of them were laughing so loud she knew they had not heard anything. She looked for Arthur, but he was gone, also. Kelly was stunned to hear a man's voice and not be able to see this person. Where was he? She kept looking and then she put out her right foot and climbed into a cab. It didn't take anytime until they were back in front of the hotel she had begun to think of as home for the next few weeks. She realized how tired she was and said a quick goodbye.

Kelly got into the elevator and disappeared to her room. She put her things away and laid down on her bed to think about her day. She was still trying to figure out the voice she thought she had heard. It was a mystery to her. Maybe she just thought she had heard that male voice speaking into her ear. But what about on the battlements when she saw the horse and rider coming towards her? She had had so many dreams about the castle that she put it all down to her studying the castle and movies she had seen about medieval England. She fell asleep so quickly she never had time to come to a conclusion about anything.

Chapter Three

The phone was ringing in her dreams and she opened her sleepy eyes and looked around to get her bearings and find that noisy phone. By the time she got to it, the stupid phone had stopped ringing. She stood up and stretched out her kinks. She opened the heavy drapes at the window and stood looking down on a busy little street in London. This was a dream she had for so long. It was hard to believe it was finally real.

Kelly ran a hot bath and was just about to step in it when she heard a knocking on her door. Reaching for her robe, she quickly wrapped it around her body and opened the door. To her surprise, Arthur was standing there with a huge bunch of flowers in his hands. She was shocked to see him so early and to see those flowers made her speechless.

"Hello, Kelly," said her new acquaintance, Arthur.

"What are you doing here so early? And why didn't you call?" All at once she realized that he had called her. It was him she heard when she missed the phone earlier.

"I tried to call, but you didn't answer the phone," he replied to Kelly with a smile on his face.

"I wondered who that was. Since I'm just a tourist, I couldn't imagine who could be calling me. I guess it could have been my mom, but it is still too early in the USA for her to even be out of bed."

"I wanted to take you to breakfast, if you will go. Then we can get to know one another better," Arthur told Kelly.

"Okay, but let me have thirty minutes to get ready and I will meet you in the restaurant downstairs."

All the time she was getting ready, she was going over mentally how cute he was. She wanted to get to know him better. This was the sure fire way to get close to him. Kelly didn't know how she got so lucky, first meeting the girls and then Arthur. How lucky could a girl get? In her favorite country, visiting castles and finding friends left and right. Her day was sure to be another exciting one.

By the end of the first week, they had been together six times. They had gone sightseeing on the big red double decker bus and gone through the changing of the guards at Buckingham Palace. Arthur had taken her to the pubs and to Stratford on the Avon where Shakespeare had lived and written his stories. They had grown close to each other without even noticing it.

When Arthur left her at her door each night, she felt terribly alone and missed him more than she could imagine. After all, he was a stranger six days ago. She would get a quick kiss on the cheek and he was gone.

In her room all alone, she would wonder where he would go and would he miss her or was she mistaken with the camaraderie they had shared each day and evening they had been together.

The days passed in a blur and soon it would be time for her vacation to be over. The thought gave her chills. She now knew she did not want to go back to the States.

One evening, Arthur took her to Piccadilly Circus where they ate at an outside restaurant. While he was studying her face, he noticed that something was wrong.

"What is on your mind?" he asked her gently while he reached his hand and took hers in his.

"I'm going to have to go home soon and I know I'm not ready to go yet. My money is still good and I have been trying to figure out if I could get a room in a bed and breakfast around the area. I didn't want to tell you, but it is so sad to think about leaving you. I would like to stay a while longer. I have grown so close to you in these past few weeks that I will miss you more than I could have imagined."

Arthur was listening with his heart in his hands. "I know that I have been waiting for you to tell me. I knew it was coming. I could see it in your face lately. It scared me, too," Arthur said with a bittersweet smile in his eyes. He was wringing his hands and she saw the fear in his eyes now. "I knew you would have to go home soon, but it hurt me to think about it."

"Can I ask you something?" Kelly spoke softly. "Do you want me to stay?"

His eyes lighted up immediately and the words came tumbling out of his mouth. "Oh how I wanted to know that if I asked you to stay, you would feel the same way." He reached over and took her hands in his hands and looking up to her face spoke these words ever so slowly. "I think I love you, Kelly, and I never want you to go back to the States. Do you hear me?"

She sighed and then told him, "I don't want to go back either, Arthur. I will stay. I will call my mom tonight and tell her the news," she said.

"Kelly, will you marry me?" The words were out of his mouth before he knew it and he lowered his head in shame. He had not even thought this to himself before this very minute. He was shocked to see her big smile.

"I know we just met a few weeks ago, but it feels like we have known each other for so long. I have no fears about the future and I have always been the kind of person who plans for the future, since I was ten years old. I saved for this trip for years. And now I see what must have been in the stars for me and you, my new friend, all those years ago." She smiled and shook her head. "Yes, I will marry you and I will marry you today if you ask me to."

His heart was thumping in his rib cage and his heart was beating in his ears. He was so happy he could hardly believe her words were real.

Together they got up and walked over to the convent gardens where they spent the rest of the evening planning their future. Planning her phone call to her mother, planning where she would get married, when she would get married, whether they would wait for her parents to come over or whether they would get married immediately.

Chapter Four

Kelly's mother and father were worried about her new boyfriend at first, but after a few phone calls and speaking to Arthur on the phone, they relented and got busy planning the trip to England to their daughter's marriage. They were both very shaken from the first, but they knew their daughter was too smart to fall for a line and took heart that she had the common sense to call them first.

They arrived early one morning in Gatwick at 8:30 a.m. and Kelly and Arthur met them in Customs. They had a car and made the long drive back to South Hampton in easy conversation. Together, they all enjoyed each other.

Arthur was smiling when he helped them out of the small car. Kelly had found them rooms in the same hotel she had been staying in. Her mom was so tired, she wanted to go to bed and have a little rest. Then they would all get together and talk. Kelly helped her get her bags to her room and then said goodbye to both her mom and dad. Together Arthur and Kelly walked down the long hall to the little bar on the first floor.

They ordered coffee and took their cups to the outside lounge area. It was chilly so far today, but they sat in the corner and were sheltered from the wind. It was a sunny morning, but the chill was still in the air from the night before.

"You know, it has only been four weeks since we first met, Arthur, and I can hardly make myself believe that we just met for the first time a very few weeks ago. It just doesn't seem like the usual relationship to me. I feel like I've known you all my life, even when I was a kid. Do you understand how I feel," Kelly asked as she lowered her head.

Even though they had talked about this before, it still made no sense to her at all. She knew she really loved him. She knew she wanted to stay in England and she knew that he loved her. Those three things kept her going when she got to thinking about this wedding that she wanted to happen. She already had a date in mind.

Now that her parents had gotten here, she was sure that they could plan a wedding to remember forever. She loved England. She loved everything about her new life, but she had to find a job and get to work. She had to make her share of money to feel supportive to Arthur. He had already mentioned to her that she did not need to work. He wanted a family. He wanted children. He had spoken to her of things he told her he had never thought of before. Like children. He had never even met a woman he thought he could love, let alone marry. So this was a new thing for him, also.

They had a lot to talk about, even though they had been talking for three weeks now. Every day brought a closer feeling to them and their plans were getting made without haste. Her parents' arrival was the beginning of this future between Kelly and Arthur. They were both so happy. She had to kiss him. Kelly reached over to him and put her hand on his cheek. He leaned in toward her and she said, "I love you" to him in the sweetest voice he had ever heard.

"I love you too, Kelly," he said to her.

After they had coffee, they went to his apartment. She had already put into motion a moving plan. Since she had only her clothes, it was going to be so easy for her. She still was living in her room in the Thistle Gate Hotel for the meantime. She did not want to make any mistakes, so she kept their relationship purely together in spirit only. They had never discussed sex, but they had a strong tie that was binding them together. They both felt it. Some nights, it was hard for Kelly to say goodnight to him. She wanted to bring him in and make long sweet love to him. She had never had sex before. She was still so young. And that appealed to Arthur a lot. She could tell. He was so proud to have a woman all his own. He had told her many times before.

Arthur had let her go shopping in Harrods for some new things for their room. She had bought a new comforter for his big bed and some new curtains for their living room windows. He called it the parlor. She loved the English words. He had often spoken of a lorry until she asked him what a lorry was. When he said a truck, she had giggled hard and he asked her why she was laughing so hard. She told him lorry was a new word to her. He looked surprised, but he knew from her laughter that she was telling him the truth.

The days went by in a blur. August in England got colder faster than at home and Chicago was no match for the dampness here. Everywhere there was mold and mildew and she could smell it in his apartment every time she was there.

She had plans for that apartment. She had already cleaned it thoroughly several times. The Clorox had removed the damp feeling and the smell was gone. Arthur had mentioned to her that he loved the way his place smelled now. He wanted to know what she had done. When she told him, he could not believe it. A little Clorox does wonders for just about anything she had told him.

Chapter Five

The miracle wedding was coming up soon. Her parents had to go home, but not before they made the wedding plans in full. They had found a quaint little church to get married in and paid the fee for the service. Her parents had given her money and all the time they had to give her on this trip.

This morning before they went back to the States, Kelly and Arthur had asked them to spend the whole day with them. They wanted to take her parents out to the castle where they had first met. It seemed appropriate that they should go back there with her parents and she loved that castle so much she could probably go there every day if she had time. Just to visit those halls and look at those faces in the Gallery. Every time she remembered the Gallery, she had goose bumps. She could see those eyes and hear that voice that said, "Come back." She heard it all the time. Although she never told anyone, it haunted her day and night. Her heart felt like it was breaking and she had to get into something exciting to get it off her mind. The words echoed in her ears. The sound of the accent was weird. It did not sound like any of the English people she had met so far. It was like a mixture of English and French and somehow they blended together to make that accent.

They met at the little coffee house in the hotel and rode in one car to the castle tour. Kelly was so happy all of a sudden. When she sat down in the back seat with her mother, she put her hand on her mom's arm and said, "Oh Mom, I'm so happy that you get to see this place before you leave to go home. It is just like I thought it would be. It's so old and the halls echo with sounds I can't explain. It almost feels like it is calling out to me. I don't actually hear any words, but I hear sounds in my mind. What do you think it can be?"

Her mom just smiled and looked at her. "I think you have loved those castles for so long that you are in tune with this one unconsciously and don't even know it," her mom said in a hushed voice. "We don't want anyone to think we are crazy, so let's keep this to ourselves, okay?"

"Sure, Mom, but when we get there, can you tell me how it makes you feel?"

"Of course I will. But by now, I will be expecting something to happen and, if it does, I will tell you with my eyes, okay?"

"Great," Kelly said.

They drove into the parking lot and parked the little car. Kelly would never get used to those tiny cars. At home in the States, they had one, but not as tiny as this one that she had been riding in with Arthur. It was called a mini. And a mini described it perfectly. Arthur gave everyone the tickets for admission to the castle grounds. They walked in line and as, she got closer, she had goose bumps.

Then she heard it again. "You are back." She shook her head. The voice said, "I have been waiting." Kelly felt herself getting nervous. Her hands were shaking. "Calm down, you know I can feel the tensing in your mind and body each time I speak to you."

Now Kelly was getting scared. They had not even gotten in the front doors and she felt like there was a cold snake crawling up her arms and upper body. She checked to see if the rest of them had noticed. They had not. They were too busy looking at the turrets and the beautiful flower gardens on the path inside the gates.

Her feet were moving unconsciously. She was heading towards a side entrance. She didn't even know that the rest of her party was not following her. She reached out and moved the old vines that were growing up the side of the castle. She had no idea why she was standing there all alone. She turned her head to find her mother and then she heard it, almost like a man was standing right beside her. Her head jerked back. Her hand moved of its own accord. Then she felt a cold metal handle in her hand. She pulled on it. It opened up a door that was so hidden by the vines that it groaned with pressure while it tried to open. Finally she had enough room for her little body to squeeze through the opening.

It was dark and her feet felt a wet damp slick slime on the rocks beneath her. She tried to see ahead of her, but it was too dark.

"Look to your right," a voice said to her mind. She could not help but look and saw a pitiful excuse of a candle hiding in a hole in the rocks. "Pick it up," the voice said. "You left it there so you could get back in and not be seen leaving the castle at night. Can you remember?" Then she was trying to find a way to light this candle. But they didn't have matches back then she told herself.

Here she got scared. How can I light it she thought in her mind?

"You know how," the voice said.

She was shivering by now with fear and cold. Her hands were shaking and she said out loud, as if she really thought someone was there, "Can you do it for me?" She waited to see if she had really been hearing a person talking to her. All of a sudden, the candle burst with a flame.

"Pick it up and follow your heart's desire. If you do, you will begin to remember me."

She obediently picked it up and started to walk forward. The passage was very thin and very slick. She had walked a few paces when she heard her mother call her name. It was like she was in a trance. She cleared her head and ran carefully back the way she had come. The candle went out and she reached her hand up to the hole where she found it and put it back.

The next thing she saw was her mother's head peeking in the opening of the doorway. She was out of breath and her mother noticed it right away.

"What on earth were you doing in there all alone?" Her mother had a worried look on her face.

Kelly just told her that she had seen it and was wondering where it might go, so she walked on ahead of them, since they were enjoying the scenery. She had already seen the gardens and she didn't think it would matter if she checked out her new find. "It was a passageway into a long deserted area of the castle," she told her mom. Her mom just looked at her and wondered if she was telling the truth. "Really, mom, I was just exploring. That's all."

She did not tell her that her stomach was churning and her eyes and arms were aching. Why, she had no idea.

As they walked toward the entrance, she heard a male voice say, "You'll be back." She rubbed her head and her eyes and kept walking.

Arthur was picking up their separate tour tickets. "Here is yours," he said to Kelly. She reached out her hand and took the ticket between her fingers. At once it felt hot to her. She checked it out and then put it in her shirt pocket. Her mom noticed the quick movement of her fingers and asked her what was wrong. Kelly just changed the subject by saying, "Mom, here is yours and dad's tickets. Let's get going. I am so excited to be here again. Do you remember when I did all that studying on this castle in school, Mom?"

"Yes, I do remember and you loved it even then. I can understand how interesting this must be for you to be here, Kelly."

They walked into the line of tourists and started the tour. The Gallery was the first stop, because the long hall had quite a history of landowners who were Barons and so forth. Kelly took an instant interest to one particular Baron, who had been a penniless knight and third son of one of the richest landowners around. His name was Robert Kirk. He had a blond mustache and blond curls on his head. His hair was trimmed and neat. His eyes were as blue as the sky. Kelly wondered who had painted this portrait of the Baron Kirk. It was articulate in every stroke. The colors were a blend of pastels like Kelly had never seen before in a painting, especially one that old. It had been taken care of through the years because it still looked like it had just been painted yesterday.

Somewhere in the background, a lute was playing, soft and soothing, and the melody was enchanting. All at once she was in a scene from the past. All around her were green trees and flower gardens and three little puppies running all around her skirts. She looked down and saw ruffles of pink satin and ribbons flowing down her shoulders where her bodice fell off her arms. Her skirts were full and her underskirts were making a loud rustling sound as she felt herself running with the puppies. She stopped and took a good look around. All at once from the front doors of the castle looming in the background, she saw a man come rushing out the door towards her. Who was he? She just thought she was dreaming and so she let herself go with the flow.

She went toward the man and he picked her up and twirled her around in circles. She studied his face. He was the man in the picture she had been looking at.

"Kelly?" She heard her mother speaking to her and all her attention went towards going back to her mother's voice.

"Yes?" Kelly said, as she realized she had been day dreaming about the man in the picture. She looked all around her and no one else seemed to find anything out of the ordinary at the moment.

"Nothing," her mother said. "I just thought that you were not feeling well, because you got all pale and looked like you were about to fall down in the midst of all these people. Are you okay? Do you feel okay, Kelly?"

Her mother was worried about her. Kelly could see it in her face.

"I'm fine, really I am, Mom. Tell me what you think about the character in this frame," Kelly said to her mom.

"I think the artist must have been this man's friend, because it is the best of them hanging here in the hall."

"Mom, look at the colors and the blend. It is magnificent, don't you agree?"

"Yes, it is." Her mother spoke up all of a sudden because the other tourists were moving toward them and there was a lot of chatter amongst them.

Again, Kelly wondered what had happened to her, but the spell was broken when she once again glanced at the portrait on the wall. It was as if he was smiling at her, at her alone. She gazed at him until she felt she knew every line in his face, every angle of his jaw and the piercing stare from his beautiful blue eyes.

As the group moved up the stairs, Kelly found herself thinking about her daydream. He was gorgeous and he made her heart beat fast. She remembered that and it felt really good. Arthur was holding out his hand waiting for her to take hold of it when he finally had to say, "Kelly?" She had to think quickly because she did not want him to think she was going nuts on him.

"Yes, I hear you, Arthur, but I'm having so much fun today that I guess I was daydreaming. What do we do next?"

"Come back to me," was what she heard. She looked at Arthur's mouth and he had not spoken a word. She turned her head around and looked everywhere, but there was only a group of six ladies deep in conversation on the other side of the room. Kelly wanted to know who that was. Why was she hearing voices when she couldn't see anyone around? It was a question she was keeping to herself for the time being.

They spent the rest of the day having lunch in the small quaint sandwich shop on the grounds and then they stopped in the souvenir shop. Kelly bought a huge post card of the castle and a gallery photo of all the previous Barons and Baronesses of Drummond Castle.

In the afternoon, they toured the bedrooms of the castle. Once they reached the top floor where the tour was about to begin, Kelly saw a door open on its own. She stared and it opened wider. She walked over to the open door and looked inside the beautiful room. She saw a picture hanging on the wall and instinct made her move inside without thinking to tell anyone else.

She walked over to the bed and stood looking up at the girl in the painting. She choked back her breath. It was her. The picture was of Kelly. But the title underneath said Amelia Kirk and was dated 1634, wife of Robert Kirk at Drummond Castle.

Kelly stood still. The door opened and in walked Robert Kirk. Kelly tried to act normal. Robert said, "Amelia? Are you ill?"

She tried to speak up, but her voice was quivering. Finally she saw the concern in his eyes and she said, "No, I'm fine."

She searched his face for recognition in his eyes. All she saw was concern, so she said, "I need to lie down for a while if you don't mind, Robert. I'm just very tired."

He looked concerned and reached for her arm to lead her to the bed. She shivered when he touched her and walked slowly to the bed. "Thank you, Robert. I'm sure I will be better after I rest a while."

Robert looked at her so funny, like he could tell there was something different about her. "You don't sound the same, Amelia. Are you sure you are okay?"

"Yes, I'm okay." Her hands were shaking. She knew something was wrong, but what? She must be dreaming again. She decided to clap her hands and that would wake her up. She clapped them together hard. Nothing happened, except Robert looked at her as if she was a stranger.

"Amelia, whatever is the matter? Darling, you know, I think that you need to see the doctor."

At once, Kelly calmed down and tried to smooth this over. "My hands were itching and I clapped them to stop the itch. I'm so sorry if I startled you, Robert. Now please leave me so I can rest."

He looked down and walked out of the room, closing the door behind him. Kelly was frightened. Where was she? What was going on? She did not understand. She looked out the window at the landscape and knew something strange had happened to her. She heard horses, she heard chickens, she smelled horse manure and she was scared.

Kelly laid herself down on the high bed and closed her eyes. Just for a moment, she thought she had gone back in time. She fell asleep quickly and when she woke up, she was still in the same room and on the same bed. Her mind was going crazy.

She heard footsteps coming up the hall. Then the knock on the door came. It was Robert. He asked if he could come in and get her for dinner. She didn't say a word. She pretended to be asleep. He quietly opened the door and stepped over to the bed. She turned over and he reached out his hand to wake her. She felt the touch like electricity run through her body. She quivered and opened her eyes.

How she got to the floor without waking up surprised her. She was being hovered over by her mother and Arthur. "Let's take her home," they were saying to each other.

Kelly spoke up and said she was okay and that she had not slept well the night before. She was sure she had fallen asleep because she was really tired. Both her mom and her dad were looking at her. They realized that she could very easily be tired, so they helped her up and they went to the car park to head back home.

"We saw a lot today, Kelly. I just love that old place. I can see why you have always been so partial to it," her mom said.

"Yes, Mom, I have had two trips out here and each time I love it more. I hope you had a nice day. I might be coming down with something, because I have never felt like this before. I feel bad that we have to leave early, but there is a lot more to see and we can come back if you want to."

Chapter Six

After her parents had gone to their rooms and she got back home, she rested for a while. Arthur was worried about her, but she promised her husband-to-be that she was really okay. He went to work and Kelly lay down again. It occurred to her that she had never in her life laid down so much before.

Her mind was confused about what had happened today at the castle. Strange feelings had come over her both times she had made the trip to Drummond, almost like it had known she was coming. She knew that was foolish thinking, but it was sure a mystery right now. Even her heart knew what was going on, because she had felt stirrings that she had never felt before, when she was in that corridor all alone and heard a voice that sounded so familiar to her mind, but not really to her ears.

Kelly had to forget the strange things now and take care of her family. They were almost ready to go back to the States. She really felt better, so she got up and dressed and went to the hotel to go to dinner with her mom and dad. Arthur had a nighttime job and was at work, so they had the evening alone together one more time before they left.

The pub they went to was heavenly. It had the best fish and chips pub meal she had found since she started checking out the restaurants.

The food was so good that evening, Kelly kept her conversation on the future and her parents were quite happy.

"I have had a wonderful time here and I wish we could come back for the ceremony, but it's just impossible to do that with our jobs the way they are. If we even could get more time off, we wouldn't really have the money for another trip like this one. Arthur is just the greatest guy. I am so happy for you," her mother said. Her mother's smile was huge.

Kelly felt so good right now that she did not know how to express herself to them. Everything is turning out for me, she thought. Kelly put the castle events out of her mind for the time being.

After dinner, she stood up and stretched until she felt the kinks leave her body. "What time is your flight, Mom?" Kelly asked as they walked down the street together.

"We have a cab coming at 9:30 and the flight leaves Gatwick at 11:30, arriving back in Chicago at 4 o'clock. It feels like we just got over jet lag and now, when we get home, we have to go through it again," her mother laughed.

"Since you won't be coming home to get your things, I will look over everything and, if I find anything I think you might need, I will mail it to you," Kelly's mom told her while she was going through her purse looking for something.

As they strolled up the steps to the hotel, Kelly thought about how it would feel to not be able to see her parents for long stretches of time. She knew she had really grown a lot in the past few months since she had arrived on that plane in England all alone. She had made new friends and she was about to be married. She had spent many agonizing nights thinking about this and she was sure her life was moving forward in the pattern she wanted. She had chosen right. She left them with big hugs and many kisses and took a cab back home.

On the way home, she had laid her head down and was resting her eyes when she heard that voice in the back of her mind. It was saying come back to me, come back to me. It gave Kelly a headache and she straightened up in the back seat and looked at the lights as they drove through the quiet dark night towards her apartment with Arthur. She tried thinking about Arthur and where he was and whether he would be home when she got there and drove the words away for the meanwhile.

The cab pulled up and Kelly paid him and got out. She gathered up her shopping bag and purse and scarf and had gone up to the door with her key in her hand, when she heard Arthur coming behind her.

"Hey! Wait up!" he called to her.

She stood back to let him get the key into the lock and help her into the apartment. She went to the standing floor lamp and flicked it on. The apartment looked warm and cozy to her at this moment. Her thoughts of being alone left with the sound of Arthur's laughter. The conversation turned to their day and they talked into the wee hours of the night. Kelly was as content as a bug in a rug, as they would have said at home. So she repeated it to him. Arthur loved her American slang. He had even picked up a few himself. At work, he would throw out a new one every now and again and his coworkers would love it, calling him a cradle robber and telling him the only reason he hit on her so quick was his love for the American language.

Arthur loved Kelly so much that he had forgotten about his life before she came into it. He did not want to remember it, so he didn't give it much thought anymore. His wedding was coming up soon and he couldn't wait.

Kelly spent most of the morning getting her things together for the wedding. Arthur had gone to the little flower shop around the corner from their flat to get her bouquet and she was alone in the apartment, when she heard the voice saying, "Come back to me."

This time, she did not have time to be bothered with it. Leaving her thoughts of voices in the castle, she got busy and got out her wedding dress. She had found the perfect dress in a little shop in town and purchased it just last week. Her parents had given her the money before they left and she bought it. It was cream color with a lace bodice. It had an empire waist and a very tiny stain bustle in the rear with ribbons hanging down to the floor. Her sleeves were puffy and covered in seed pearls that had been dyed white, beige and cream colored. It was too beautiful.

Kelly loved it the moment she had laid her eyes on it in the store window. It was the empire waist and a big sash made out of the same lace that covered her bodice that took her breath away at first sight. She thought it looked medieval and it took her breath away again when she saw the little buttons on the lace cuff that went up to her elbows. She thought she had seen a wedding gown like this before at home, but she could not remember where.

Standing outside the little quaint shop, she could see herself in the dress dancing away the night. She tried to look closer to see who she was dancing with, but his face was not clear. She must be daydreaming about her wedding dance with Arthur. This was a very special time in her life. She felt like all her dreams were coming true.

All at once, she heard the music in the background. It was the lute again, playing a melancholy song, one she had heard before. But she didn't remember where she heard it either. She knew it made her heart jump with a happiness that she remembered from other times in her life when she was surprised with something that she could not put a name to.

From there, she went limp and sad. The music stopped and the man in the window was gone. She felt like she had lost her lover. Her mind was reeling with this new incident. She had to get herself together and she didn't understand what was going on anymore.

She walked away that afternoon and never looked back. Weeks later she had gone into the shop and bought the dress for herself. She remembered the shopkeeper telling her it was antique and that she had purchased it from an estate sale. Kelly had wanted to know where it had come from and the lady didn't know exactly where it had come from, but she had a date on the style of gown if Kelly wanted it.

At the moment, Kelly was worried that it would fall apart from age and was afraid to purchase it. But when she left the shop and walked 10 steps away, her heart told her to turn around and go back. She did it and that was the end of the dress. It belonged to Kelly now.

"I think if you are very careful with this gown, Ma'am, it will hold up fine for you. I restitched all the seams when I got it and I sewed the buttons on with new thread. I made a few changes and fixed a few holes here and there and it is as good as new now," Eileen the shopkeeper told her as she turned around to walk out of the shop with her wedding dress.

"Thank you so much for the dress. I just feel like it was meant for me. I love it so much. The color and style are a favorite of mine. I wish I knew where it had come from and who had worn it before," she said with a wistful sound to her voice.

The shopkeeper thought that the dress belonged to Kelly. From the first time she had gone in to see it, she watched her feel the fabric and watched her eyes as she searched it up and down and a thought came into her head, one that she had not known was coming. This dress was hers. She knew it. She felt it and she knew the girl knew it, too. It was as if it had been made for her alone.

A few hours after Kelly had taken the dress and gone home, she thought she heard a man's voice say, "You did a good deed today." She had searched her shop, but there was no one there. She was all alone. But she knew she wasn't alone. She had heard the voice. Where it came from, she did not know, but when she heard an aristocratic male voice like that, she knew there was something going on here that maybe she did not want to know about. She hoped that girl never came back to her shop again. It was too much for her and she knew it.

Kelly heard the key in the lock and knew that Arthur was back. "Here is your wedding bouquet, my darling," he said to her back as she was taking the perfect dress off the hanger. When she turned around for him to see it, he sucked in his breath and then he let out a whistle that told her she had made the perfect purchase. "It's absolutely beautiful, Kelly. My goodness, where did you find this dress, anyway?"

"I found it in a cute little antique dress shop in Piccadilly," she told him. "When I first saw it, I knew it was for me. It felt like I needed it and when I tried it on, it was a perfect fit, almost like it was made for me. But I knew it was not in too good of a shape, so I questioned the lady about the strength of the dress, being as old as it was. She told me what I wanted to hear. So here it is. Don't you love it, Arthur?"

He did and he told her so. He made her so happy. Sometimes she wondered how she had lived so long without him by her side. But that was a long time ago and this was her new life. She was going to make it the best.

Chapter Seven

The day was a perfect day for a wedding. The sun was shining and the breeze was blowing gentle ripples down her arms as they got into the cab and proceeded to the church. He held her hand and had many thoughts running through his mind as he looked out the window.

He had been single and on his own for so long that this change was welcome to him in so many ways. There had been something so familiar to him about her when he had first seen her. He had run that through his mind so many times when he was alone at work or alone at home. It felt right. From then first introduction to last night, Kelly felt right in every way. Like a new pair of gloves, she fit perfectly in his life. Her personality and charm and wit were choices that he would have chosen if he could have picked her out of a catalog.

They liked the same food, they liked the same kind of people and they even had a love for the medieval times. She had read extensively and he had wanted to, but had not had the time. The castle had drawn them together. Arthur had told her many times late at night when they were sitting in front of the fireplace how he had seen her in the great hall and when his friends had seen him and mentioned her to him, he could not wait to meet her.

It was her wedding day, a very special day. She was stressed by a lot of things. Things she did not understand. Why did she hear voices? What was wrong here? Ever since she went to the castle, things had been different for her. Things she heard, saw, and felt were things that couldn't be happening, but were.

The day she had sat on the corner of her bed and held her new dress to her chest, she had smelled a sweet perfume on the fabric. When she checked more closely, it was gone. Then when she placed the sleeves up to her arms and twirled all around her room, her fingers felt like they were not hers and when she looked in to the glass at her reflection, it was not her face she saw, but one that looked like her, only younger and slimmer. Then she looked closer at the faced and it shocked her at how close it looked like her. The young girl was crying with happiness because she could feel it in her heart. It was another wedding day and the girl had on Kelly's dress, Kelly's wedding dress.

All at once a well groomed young man walked into the room. She turned to him and flew into his arms. As they stood there, connected together, she heard sounds of people running and screaming. Both of them turned visibly pale to her eyes. Whatever was coming was very frightening to them. She could see the girl shaking and the man turned her face towards him as if to shield her from something bad.

Robert and Amelia knew who had killed them and why they had to be killed. It all happened so fast, but in the back of their minds, both Robert and Amelia knew that after Robert's father had died, they had heard talk in the castle about his uncle, the Earl of Brentwall. He was a wicked man with evil in his heart. Everyone in the castle stayed clear of him, even his own brother, Robert.

There was speculation that he had something to do with his brother's death, but everyone was afraid to go any further with accusations. His father had died from some kind of poison, they did know that, but they could point their finger at no one because there was no real proof.

As for Robert and Amelia, there had been other threats. Amelia's herb garden had been torched late one night, a week before the wedding. Someone had cut all of Amelia's flowers in her flower garden the same night. Someone did not want Amelia to have her own flowers for her bridal bouquet. The week before, they had let horses run through her garden.

But Amelia had saved some of the smashed flowers, some of the smashed rhododendrons for her bouquet, and amidst the plans for the wedding, they had put aside all the rumors, thinking only of the wedding day and their happiness beyond. Now in the back of her mind, she knew they should have paid more attention to the goings on in the castle.

Then she saw the door break open and she saw the intruders come rushing in. They grabbed for her and he held on tight to her body. Then she saw them fall down and she saw blood everywhere. People were laughing and they dragged the two bodies out of the room. As they were pulling on his body, she heard him say, "Come back to me, my darling. I will always be your protector. They cannot kill us. Let them try. We will always be together, forever." He was trying to look in her face, but he fell forward and

Kelly knew that what she had just seen was a scene from something terrible that had happened to two other people in some other time frame.

She did not mention this to another person. She quietly tried to forget it ever happened to her. And in the days to come, she did forget it. But every time she tried the dress on, the sleeves had a different feeling to them. The lace on the sleeves had the smell on them and it was not her perfume she smelled.

There were more weird things, but they seemed to fade and she felt like she might have been dreaming some of them, because as time passed, they dimmed so much that she couldn't be bothered to think about them anymore. So she forgot them entirely, except when she accidentally rubbed her fingers on the old lace on the sleeves of her gown, or when the smell of perfume invaded her room of its own accord, shocking her memory back to another time.

Today was special and as they waited for the cab, they held hands and smiled to each other. As the big, shiny black cab drove smoothly around the bends and into the city center through the morning sunshine, Kelly was looking out the window at all the little homes and flower gardens they passed by. The roses and gardenias were so plentiful here. She made a mental note to have a garden like that some day. She wanted to live amidst a million flowers.

She was wondering how her life would proceed from today on. She knew it was what she had always wanted; a family like her and her parents had shared together.

If her day was any more beautiful, she couldn't imagine it in her wildest dreams. And as dreams go, she had had a few lately. Strange places, strange clothing on people and voices that had a sound that she couldn't identify. It was a rough version of the English heard here, but it was so hard to understand in her dreams that she forgot them as soon as she opened her eyes in the mornings. They drifted back and forth in her conscience from day to day and she would blank it out.

Knowing that dreams are not to be bothered with in the daylight hours kept her memory at bay. Driving along, her thoughts returned to her wedding gown and how she had found it and how it had beckoned to her from the small antique dress shop window. It was so beautiful. It was glistening in the sunbeams and dancing across the prisms of the old fashioned glass in the window. The golden threads wove a spell of enchantment to her eyes, leaving her no other choice than go to in and touch it. When she had touched the door knob, an electric current, stronger than anything she had ever felt before, hit her and the sidewalk had jarred. She had lost her footing and slipped in the door like a thief, falling against the door at the same time.

The saleslady inside the shop had seen her outside and had felt compelled to show her the dress, before she even got her breath back from an electric tingling that had raced up and down her arms and before the lovely young girl had even asked to see it.

As the city passed by her cab in a blur, she prayed a quick prayer to God above and thanked him for her life as it was today and her wedding day, even thanked him for her beautiful gown. They were getting closer and she was getting very nervous. Her hands were shaking so hard that she moved them and started to trace her sleeves with her fingers.

Just as she got to the satin insert above the lace, she had a chill race over her entire body. Once again, she heard a male voice in the background of her mind. It was trying to calm her down. The voice said, "It will be okay this time. Don't be frightened, my darling."

It was so soothing that she shut her eyes and relaxed. Again she began to rub her finger up and down her arms and again when she got close to the satin insert, she had a violent chill. It shook her teeth. She at once moved her eyes toward Arthur. He saw nothing unusual she could tell, because he didn't even notice her looking at him. He was lost in his own world, a new world for him, she supposed. A world with a wife. The shaking stopped when she moved her hands down into her lap.

"This dress has a mind of its own," she said to herself. And then she crossed both her arms, hugging herself tightly. The chill went away. Both the fear and shock of the feeling bothered her. She wondered what had just happened.

She was staring at the dress sleeves. She could see where the seamstress had altered the dress at the elbow. She could see the cream color of the dress was different from the beige color or the lace. The lace actually looked older than the other part of the dress. There were small patches of a darker color on the lace. It was a stain of some kind.

"It was your blood, my darling." The voice seemed to come out of nowhere. "It will never happen again. Forget it and go on with your day. I am waiting."

She was also seeing another pair of hands in her lap. She looked harder and she saw a shaking pair of hands. They were grasping hands. Hands that she felt were not her own. Kelly blinked her eyes so hard that her head jerked backward.

At the motion, Arthur spoke up and said, "What is wrong, Kelly?"

She let her eyes close for a second and then she said, "Nothing. I guess I'm having the jitters before the wedding." Then she laughed.

She reached out her hand and picked his up and held them tightly for a second or two. Then he relaxed and smiled back at her, a tender smile, a smile she had always dreamed of. All at once she wondered where that notion had come from. Then she heard the voice again. "It is my smile, Kelly, and you have dreamed of it and me."

Her eyes shut voluntarily and the voice continued to scare her by saying, "The dress feels familiar too, doesn't it Kelly? Come back to me and let our time be again as it was back then."

Whoever that was, Kelly considered it a minute and then she started to talk nonstop to Arthur, hoping this would put the sound of that voice out of her head. This was her wedding day and nothing was going to mess it up for them. If she needed to chatter on, okay, then she would. It worked and there was no more crazy voice in her mind at the moment.

The cab pulled up and stopped at Redding Square, where the old church stood beckoning them to enter.

"Kelly, it pleases me that you chose our church to do this in."

Kelly picked up the heavy gown and reached for the door latch. As the cabby opened her door, she scooted to the edge of her seat and put her feet on the ground. But as she stood up, she felt suddenly very dizzy. She grabbed onto the cabby's arm and held on tight. Arthur saw her and hurried over to take her hand. "Whatever is wrong, Kelly?" he questioned her as she began to weave back and forth.

"I don't know," she thought, but did not speak a word. Her dress felt so heavy and she heard a sound when she picked it back up again, a sound she recognized from somewhere. She could hear the fabric dragging the ground and she felt more than heard a person behind her pick it up and carry it for her. She turned her head and there was no one there. She thought she was going crazy at that very moment. Then she heard that soothing male voice, "Don't be frightened, Kelly. What you are hearing and feeling are sounds of your past, sounds that remind you of another time and another wedding day that belonged to you and me. You have found the dress and you have found your home long ago when you did the tour of Drummond Castle. Come back to me at last. Your wounds have been healed now. I'm waiting for you at Drummond Castle. Please come back to me."

Kelly fainted dead away. Arthur dropped down on his knees to the hard gravel driveway and caught Kelly as she fell head first towards the cold ground, thinking that he was glad she wasn't going to hit the gravel. His knees were hurting badly as he felt the weight of her body fall into his arms. The look on his face was one of shock. He could not imagine why she fainted away like that. Whatever was going on, he wanted to stop it because it was his wedding day. He had waited long enough to find the perfect girl and now that he had, he wanted to get married and go on with starting a family.

He was staring into her eyes and finally she flicked them open and he saw a startled look in them. He could tell she had not a clue what had just happened to her. Her head began to turn left and right. When she saw him, she smiled and he knew she was okay.

"Kelly, what happened to you just now?" Arthur was so upset and his voice showed it.

Kelly replied, "I'm okay now, Arthur. I don't know what happened though. Help me get up so we can brush off the dirt. I don't want my gown ruined. It has been through so much already," she said with a sad look in her eyes.

"What do you mean?" Arthur asked her in a very quiet voice. Surprise was written all over his face. He heard her say the dress had been through so much and he had no idea what that meant. She had just brought it home three days before. "What did that mean?" he wondered to himself.

"I think the dress was so heavy that it pulled me down with the weight of it. I was also too warm in the cab, so I think that is what happened to me, Arthur." She reached out a shaky hand and touched his face with a loving look in her eyes. He felt like she might be right.

The cabby and Arthur helped her get her footing and they brushed off the beautiful gown. Even to Arthur's fingers, he felt electricity run through his hands. He lifted his hands away from the dress and it stopped immediately. He looked at it and then he thought he must be imagining it, so he moved forward holding onto her hand.

They walked straight to the front doors of the church. There were people seated all over the whole interior of the cathedral. They had not come for Kelly's wedding, but were praying and lighting candles. The cathedral was open 24/7. They had services three times a day.

Kelly's wedding was a private affair in a chamber off the main hall where vespers were being held at the moment. People were allowed to watch or even come in and sit down if they chose to.

As she lifted her feet to walk into the hall, she noticed that everything was the same as before. Nothing had changed. The old stained glass windows were as beautiful as they ever were. The silence in the place was eerie. It was as if she had been here before. Many times. She could hear the priest chanting. When she looked around for the priest, he was gone. Or maybe he was never there in the first place. She decided not to ask Arthur, because this may have been one of the times she could not understand. One of the many things that were strange and she was not ready to think about that again today. Not today.

Her premonition of being there before was real. She saw flowers and she heard voices that she knew with her own eyes she should not be hearing. She closed her eyes and shook her body very easily until she felt like she was okay to proceed ahead with the wedding ceremony.

On the steps where she was stepping up to the altar, they had put flowers on each step, three steps and six baskets of flowers. Kelly wanted to ask who had donated them, but she kept quiet about it.

The old stone steps had a vibration to them as she stood there. She turned to Arthur and asked him if he felt it. He shook his head yes, but said nothing. She saw a strange light in his eyes. He almost looked like another man. Not Arthur. She thought about it and wondered where this was going, when all of a sudden, a priest walked in front of them and the ceremony began. When she turned to look at him again, he was indeed Arthur.

Her mind had been playing many tricks on her for some time now and, even though she was upset by them, she had begun to accept that there might be something going on that she could not explain. So she didn't think about it anymore.

They had practiced this two other times, so it went perfect today for them both. The music was beautiful and when he kissed the bride, she was on a high. They said their words at the right time and they became man and wife.

Chapter Eight

They were married now and a new life was looming on the horizon. Kelly had the most beautiful smile on her face and Arthur was grinning from ear to ear. They turned and thanked the priest and walked to the door to find their cab for the trip home. This time to their home, not Arthur's home, but both of theirs.

Kelly held onto her bouquet in her lap as they rode the short distance home. She was staring at the flowers so hard that Arthur had to ask her where she was. She did not even hear him. In her mind, she saw a girl with a bouquet in her hands and a little bee buzzing around it. They were yellow and white daisies and it was also another wedding day.

She was in a large green courtyard. There was another man there, too. He was dressed in a gold and black outfit that she was shocked to see. It was very different and she stared at him. He was so handsome. He had big clear blue eyes and blond hair. His hair was long and he had it caught back at his neck with a gold tie. His pants were black and he was stunning to the eyes. He had a cheerful smile and he was beaming at her. He knew her. She could tell that she knew him, too.

Then she felt a touch on her arm. When she looked up from her bouquet, she was looking at Arthur. She was shocked again and to hide it, she laid her head on his shoulder and said nothing. It must have been enough, because he did not say anything else. He just held her hand until the cab came to a complete stop and then he adjusted her gown so she could get out of the cab.

Arthur paid the cab and they walked slowly up the steps and into the cheery little apartment. The wedding day was coming to an end. They had pictures to last for the rest of their lives and they could not have been happier. Arthur got the special bottle of wine he had purchased a week earlier at a small liquor shop on the main street. When he looked in the window of the shop, he had felt a strong compulsion to go right in. He had not been thinking about buying anything, least of all a bottle of wine. He had just been out for a pub meal and then back to work. But this shop had pulled on him and eventually he could not fight the temptation, so he went in the door. As he opened the door, a little bell tinkled at the top announcing that he had come in. A wise older gentleman had come from the back of the shop to help him. He remembered thinking that the man was way too old to be working there at the time, but then he started a conversation and Arthur was drawn in like a spool of silk thread.

The man said his name was Jeffery Roberts. His voice was soft like satin and it mesmerized Arthur for a few minutes. While he listened to the man, time stood very still. Arthur was not sure when he left the shop, how he knew that, but he did. He also told Arthur that he had just the perfect bottle of wine for him. At the time, Arthur had not even asked for wine. His mind kept questioning the fact that he did not want wine and why had Jeffery brought up the topic of wine.

"Sir, why do you think I need a bottle of wine?" Arthur questioned the wise old man who was looking like the man who had swallowed the golden goose.

"I remember you telling me that you were getting married soon," was what he told the startled Arthur.

"No, I did not tell you anything like that," he snapped back to the man.

The shocked look on his face told Arthur that maybe he had hit a raw nerve. Arthur was thinking back to when he had first walked into the shop. He certainly did not remember telling him anything. He only remembered the man talking to him, but what if he did? Maybe he would be nicer to the man.

"Well, as a matter of fact," Arthur continued, "I am getting married in two weeks." He smiled.

"I have a special, very old bottle of red wine that would be perfect for you and your new wife," he replied. "I can sell it to you for twenty quid. Oops! I'm sorry. I meant twenty pounds," he corrected himself quickly.

Arthur said, "I haven't heard anyone speak of quids in many years. I had almost forgotten we called the pound quid in earlier times." I'm not a big drinker, but it would be nice for us to have at home after the ceremony, he thought to himself. He took the bottle out of the old man's hands and gave it a good look over. The bottle was indeed very old. Arthur could not help but ask Jeffery how he came to have this bottle of wine.

Jeffery almost spoke like a machine. "It was in the wine cellar and we found it late last night as we cleaned out a new space for a new arrival that should arrive this afternoon. And when I saw you look in the window outside, I had a feeling that you could be the one I would be able to sell this bottle to."

Jeffery was watching Arthur as he spoke and he made his case with very little effort. Arthur felt his hand go into his pocket and pull out some money. It was odd for Arthur to do that, because being a non-drinking man; he normally would have never even entered a spirits shop in the first place. For him to be reaching for his money was shocking to Arthur's mind, which told him that he did not want to pass this opportunity up. Even as weird as it felt, he had to buy it.

Arthur had had enough surprises for one day and he took his wine and left the little shop. Walking away, he had a feeling that he had indeed purchased a special bottle of claret wine. He wanted to check the date on the bottle, so he stepped over to a wall where the people were apt to walk around him and not bump into him so he could take the bottle out of the beautiful gold leaf box the old man had placed it in.

With his back against the building wall, he pulled the bottle out and tried to see the label so he could check the date on it. It felt warm in his hands. It was a dark red like wine he thought subconsciously and it had bubbles on top of the liquid. The cork, or whatever it was, was so strange that Arthur had never seen anything like it before. It was almost like a seal, but not quite. It was obviously sealed up long ago, but the cork was not the right word for the way the wine had been sealed. There was no date visible to his eyes.

He saw some numbers and saw a rhyme like a love potion might have on it in the French Quarter of New Orleans, but he had no way of reading it because it had disappeared many years ago. "Wow," he thought as he walked on to his office. "I just got the deal of the century today and was not even looking for one."

He unconsciously looked down at his watch on his arm and it hit him that he was three hours late for work. Where had the afternoon gone he wondered to himself. "I surely did not stay that long or did I?" Now it seemed that he couldn't remember too much about the purchase itself, but that he had paid twenty pounds for bottle of wine worth three hundred pounds. How had he gotten so lucky? He just felt good and, when he walked into the office, not one person commented on his being late. That was odd, too. He had finished up and taken the bottle carefully home to hoard until the wedding night.

Kelly was waiting for him to get glasses and had seen him wander into another place while he was looking at the bottle.

"A dime for your thoughts," her voice penetrated his thoughts. He looked up and smiled at her beautiful face. She was all smiles and her eyes were looking straight into his.

"Oh, I wasn't thinking anything in particular, but I have been secretly hiding this bottle of wine until tonight for us to toast our new life with," he answered her.

As he held up the bottle, she gasped out loud. "Wherever did you find any wine so old?" she asked him in a breathless voice.

"I was walking one day and came upon a liquor shop on a little old side street and when I looked in the window,

I was compelled to go in and buy it. It was a strange day, but I think we got ourselves a good deal here, don't you?" Arthur waited for her response.

"It's so old, Arthur. Does it have a date on it?"

"No, I have already searched for one," Arthur told her and then he started to try to figure out how to get it open.

Finally, the bottle popped open and the wine dribbled over the side of the bottle when he poured them each a glass full. He sat the bottle down carefully and got a chill racing through his body at the same time. He made the sound of a cold wind coming out of his mouth and Kelly moved over beside him and put an arm around her new husband, carefully rubbing his arms.

"Are you cold?" she asked.

"I just had a chill, but it is gone now," he said. "Here, let's make a toast to the future. May it be long and happy and healthy and may we have many children," he said with a giggle in his voice.

She took her glass and toasted his. They took a long sip and each one had a short vision. For Arthur, he was not surprised, but let it happen. He saw them together in another place. He was not sure what was happening, but it felt good and right, so he relaxed and let it go on. He was so happy. It was a happiness that he had never felt before, a different place and a different time was in front of his eyes. Kelly was there. Although she appeared to look different, it was her. He was sure of that. She looked like a different person. He felt like he knew her and he felt a love so strong it hurt.

Kelly also saw a different place and time. It mellowed her thoughts and she felt a love like she had never felt before, also. It felt like a surge of electricity slicing through her body. It shook her. It rocked her. It took her to a place she had been before, but had forgotten. All at once, it came back to her. Pink shades of glistening pyramids were dancing in her eyes. It left her body cool. It warmed her heart. It made her shiver with anticipation. She was stunned with the eagerness she felt for this man.

At almost the same time, they both put their glasses down and neither one of them spoke of what they had just witnessed. The look in each of their eyes spoke volumes. No words were needed at this time. They were anxious to make love and it showed in both their eyes. The eagerness to finally be together got the best of them. They walked over to the fireplace and turned down the fire and went toward the bedroom, arm in arm. Time passed and the visions would pass, too.

Chapter Nine

Outside Kelly could hear the birds singing to each other. The night was gone and it had been a beautiful one. They had talked and made love until the early hours of the morning, when they had fallen asleep.

Arthur also heard it and he was remembering how she had been so sweet to touch and he was surprised when he figured out that she was still so innocent to the male-female role. She had been a virgin and he had wanted to ask her how she had kept herself so pure in this time and age. Girls her age were just not innocent anymore. He wanted to tell her how much he loved her and the fact that he was the first man to make love to her made her all important to him.

He just laid there so comfortable that he did not want to break the mood, the first morning of his new life. Together they had reached the stars last night. It was stunning to remember how in tune they were to each other's needs. Each one gave and took until there was nothing more to reach for. They had fallen to sleep in each other's arms as comfortably as if they had been doing it all of their lives.

The night had flown by and when they began to stir, Arthur said, "Kelly, my dear love, come with me and let's look at the first morning light together, because it is still early and with you by my side, we will begin the day together."

Kelly thought to herself that they would have many years like this. It felt so good to be there with him, married, together, never to be alone again.

Kelly moved to his arm, reaching out for him. She took his hand and they walked a few steps to the open window and pushed it outward. The fresh air was still full of dew and the morning air was fresh to breathe. The birds were frolicking in their nests and it was a sight to see.

Kelly loved the feeling of mornings here in England. They had a different feeling because they were always wet. Rain was something she loved, too. So England had always made her happy. The grass was so green and the heat was not like at home. It felt good. Warm sunny days were not to be taken lightly here. The first thing she had noticed was that people went to the parks and laid around reading and enjoying days like this one. Where she came from, people did not do that.

She was staring out over the hills and wondering what was there, maybe another old castle or maybe a monastery. She could picture the black hooded figures of the monks going about their daily business and praying. It seemed to take her back somewhere and as she felt it, she quickly turned around.

All at once, she saw Arthur standing there. He was smiling at her. He thought she had been admiring the beauty of the morning, but he was wrong. But this time, she stopped the past from coming to her.

Arthur moved to the kitchen. It was time to make the coffee. Kelly wanted to help, but he told her to sit down and he was going to make breakfast for her. Kelly told him she was hungry and asked for pancakes and sausage. He was glad to oblige her wishes. He got out the pots and pans and started breakfast. A special one, their wedding breakfast.

After they had eaten, he told her he wanted to take her to Arlington Park. It was so close they only had to walk a couple of blocks. She said okay and they got ready and walked down the sidewalks holding hands.

There was a special seat there in the park and he took her right to it. They sat down and he told her he had a surprise for her. He reached into his left back pocket and pulled out a large envelope. Kelly stared at it. When he opened it, he handed it to her. She made no move to take it.

Kelly was so happy that she had not even thought about a wedding present. She had not gotten him anything and was very reluctant to accept it.

"I have nothing for you. How could I be so selfish and not think about a wedding gift for you, too?" She had big tears in her eyes.

Of all the things he might have thought she would say this was not one of them. "Don't be silly, Kelly. I did this for my new wife and I want us both to share in this experience."

"Okay, so I'll be quiet and listen to my new husband," she said with a twinkle in her eye. Her smile was enticing and it was not the place for that kind of a look.

Arthur had tickets for the United States and was taking her there to see her parents. Also, he had never been there. He wanted her to be surprised, so he put it in her hands and sat back down and waited for her to open it. She really felt bad. As she looked down at the envelope, she had no idea what he had planned for them.

Gently she tore open the sticky flap. Her fingers reached inside and took out the tickets. At first, she was shocked and then she saw the destination.

"Oh, my God!" she nearly screamed. "You are taking me home for a visit." The tears fell now, hot and heavy. She cried and cried. The thought that he had spent so much money to make her happy made her shock turn into happiness. "When do we go?" she asked him.

"We leave next week," Arthur said. I have already bought new luggage and I know we will have a great time. You know I have never been to the States. Maybe I won't ever want to come home. Will I like it?" he asked like an innocent child.

All the rest of the morning, he had a million questions for her. She tried to answer all of them. She had no idea he was so excited for this trip, too. She made a remark that took him back a step, but then he broke down and laughed so hard that he had tears in his eyes, too. Only his tears were ones of joy.

"I bet you bought this for yourself. Not for me, but because you want to go there, too. Is that why you married me, you sinister, sneaking, plotting man?" She was laughing, too. "You planned this from the beginning, from the first time you heard my Yankee drawl."

She got up and raced around the bench. She hit him in the head with the tickets and he got up and ran after her. He grabbed for her and, as she jumped back, he fell down. She dropped to the ground, also. Together they laid there. Both of them were out of breath from playing.

"I don't know what to say. It is so hard to believe, Arthur, that you planned this just for me. My head is spinning and I'm so happy."

Kelly could not believe it. She was going home at last for the first time since she had come here for a vacation many months ago. Her life had changed a lot since then, but she missed home off and on. She never mentioned it to Arthur, because she was happy wherever he was. And it was in England for now. But a short trip home would perk her up and she knew it.

They gathered up their things and left the park. The day had been glorious and she wasn't ready for it to end. They walked the few blocks home, unlocked the door and went inside to their own world. They lit the fireplace. As they sat down in the floor in front of the fire, it occurred to Kelly that the flat always had that cold feeling to her. She would want to light the fire and Arthur would say it was warm in the parlor. To her, it felt cold. Cold all the time.

There were times when the cold surrounded her and she had heard the voices. There were times when she actually thought she had seen a man in the flat. Things had never really been too good for her. The best times were when he was home from work and they were together. The day she tried on her wedding gown, she had seen more than she wanted to. This was another reason why the trip home would make her happy.

"All I can say is thank you, Arthur." Kelly wanted him to know how much she appreciated his gesture and the trip was just the best thing for her right now.

She had thought about these strange things in the dark of the night when she was alone in her little room in her bed.

She had had times when she felt like she could not take this forever. She really wanted to, but she had times when she was so scared that she had thought about going home for a break to see if things would change when she returned to Arthur and the flat.

Chapter Ten

A week later, it was time for their trip. Arthur took out the tickets and they checked the times and began to pack. Kelly phoned her mother and told her the good news. She told her that she wanted to bring the film from their wedding day and develop it there in the States. She wanted to use the one hour photo and share the beautiful day with her parents. Since they had had to return home before the wedding, this was the best that she could do. Her mom was excited and told her she would pick them up in the afternoon. Arthur told Kelly the flight left Gatwick at 10:00 in the morning, arriving at O'Hare at 4:00 p.m.

With everything all packed, they had a quiet little dinner together and got out the special bottle of wine. They toasted the trip and went to bed to dream about the day to come. Right before Kelly went to that other world between asleep and awake, she heard the voice again. In her almost asleep state, she managed to pull the covers up over her head. The voice was still there. This time she heard him say, "Please don't go so far away. I have waited so long for you to return to your home. Come back to me, please come back."

Just before she went to sleep, she thought if she could figure this out, she would slap him in his mouth, whoever he was and wherever he was.

The morning came early. It was an hour and a half to Gatwick. They ate quickly and headed to the airport. Parking and getting to the right terminal was a job in itself. Since Arthur had never gone to the States before, he was so glad she had traveled and together they got to the right gate in time for their flight.

They settled down and eight hours later, the arrived refreshed and excited to see her parents again.

Exiting the plane, they saw her parents standing there in the gateway. Kelly ran towards her mom and they clasped each other in their arms. "Oh, Kelly, I'm so glad to see you. While we are getting the bags, tell me about the wedding."

All the way through the airport, Kelly talked and talked. Her dad and Arthur were also chatting away. They got into the car and headed for her home. Kelly wanted Arthur to see where she had been raised and to meet all her friends.

Once they got home and got unpacked, Kelly and Arthur told her parents they wanted to take them out to dinner. In their room, Arthur asked Kelly questions about the restaurants in the area. Finally they decided to go to Outback Steak House. Arthur was a big steak man and was ready to go quickly.

They arrived and were seated. Arthur was shocked to see such a big restaurant. In England, the places to eat were few and far between.

During the meal, a friend of Kelly's saw her there and came over to see her. "Oh, Kelly, I have missed you so much," Patty said to her long lost friend. They hugged each other and Kelly asked her to sit for a while.

They were engrossed in conversation when Kelly heard the voice in the background of her mind. "Kelly, please come back. I can't feel you anymore. You are too far away." Kelly shook with cold chills, but kept up the conversation.

Patty's husband came in looking for Patty and saw her sitting there with Kelly. He came over and introduced himself to Kelly's new husband. They were engrossed in conversation when Larry asked Arthur what he did in England. "I'm the editor of a magazine called London Home & Gardens. I rewrite and edit the magazine articles as they come in for each month. I love what I do and I have been told that I am very good at it. I wanted to get Kelly a job there, but so far I haven't had anything come up in a field that she could do easily."

Larry told Arthur that he was a mechanic on a huge farm and his day was spent also doing what he loved, fixing machinery and tractors and anything with a motor in it. They at once became enchanted with each other. They joined them for the meal and the evening was a pleasant one that Kelly would remember for years to come.

After they paid the bill and started to leave, Patty and Larry asked them over for cocktails the next night. Kelly cleared it with her mom first, in case she had made other plans already. The time was set and they were excited to be able to show Arthur around Chicago a little bit at night.

Back at her parents' house, they were full of questions for Kelly and Arthur both. The rest of the night was gone before they knew it. Kelly and Arthur retired to their bedroom and both were very tired. Kelly had just laid her head down on the pillow, when the voice came again. "Where are you, Kelly?" was what she thought she heard.

Kelly put that out of her mind and went to sleep, giving it no more thought that night.

Chapter Eleven

Springtime was so beautiful, but late coming this year. The wind was blowing fiercely when they went out to the car. Arthur wanted to find out how it felt to drive on the other side of the road. He jumped into Kelly's father's car and started the motor. When it got warm, he blew the horn for Kelly to come on out.

They drove all around and then went to the mall. Arthur was shocked to see how big the mall was. Compared to the shopping in London, it was a monster. He loved it. They ate out for lunch and Arthur felt like he would love to live here, too. He was thinking about asking Kelly how she would feel about staying here and him getting a new job. It sounded good to him at the moment. His thoughts were far away and he had a lot to think about before he mentioned it to Kelly.

The week wore on and Arthur fell in love with the big city lights and action in Chicago. He was daydreaming about living here with Kelly and her family. One thing he had missed in his life was the presence of the parents he had loved. They had been killed in a car accident ten years before and he had to go on with his life. It had been so empty for so long. He had always felt the love between his parents and when he lost them, he decided that he was not going to have a relationship like that because it never lasted and the pain was too great. For years, he had immersed himself in his private life and grown to be a solitary man. When he met Kelly, he was shocked to feel what he was feeling.

He had met her and instantly felt a warmth he had not felt for so many years. As they grew closer, he felt it must have been meant to be. Her world was so much nicer than his. There were people to love here and a family like he had once had. If they had children, he wanted them to have this. So with this in mind, he asked Kelly to take a walk with him. They had been here for a week now and with each new day, he wanted this life for them and today he was going to ask Kelly what she thought about his idea.

The sun was shining brightly and the daffodils were in bloom. It was a perfect day to discuss the rest of their life together.

"Kelly, I have been thinking about something and I want to run it by you and see what you think, okay?"

"Sure, Arthur, go on and break it to me slowly. Do you want to go home? Are you getting bored with all this excitement we have been through since we arrived here?"

"No, Kelly. That's just it. I love it here and I forgot how it felt to have family all around you and the happiness it brings to the soul. So, I wondered what you would think if I asked you to move back here and begin a new life with a family that I have missed for so long that I had almost forgotten how it feels."

Kelly was surprised. She did not say a word. She just stared at him. He thought he was getting negative feelings here and he spoke up quickly so as not to upset her.

"Look, Kelly, if you want to go back to London, we can. I just thought you might like to be here around your family and I love them and feel so close to them after just a few meetings with them. I'm sure I just miss my own parents and want to transfer my feelings to yours."

Kelly almost cried. She did love England, but everyone knows there is no place like home. "I think it would be a miracle if you wanted to do that, Arthur," Kelly said softly. Then she hugged him so tightly he had to move her back.

"So, when do we tell them?" Arthur asked with stars in his eyes.

"Tomorrow will be good," Kelly replied to her husband, whom she loved more than ever right at this moment. She grabbed him and kissed him in the mouth in front of everyone in sight. He was choking with laughter and she was, too.

Between them, there was a feeling of contentment, a feeling of uniting and loving. Kelly told him that she wanted nothing more than to make him happy. It was then that she heard the voice in her head say, "What about me, Kelly? How can you forget about me? I'm still waiting for you, Kelly, and always will be."

With that, she was even more sure than ever, because if she came back here she would forget that castle and the things that she could not explain to herself. That gave her more reason to be happy.

The move was explained to her parents and they were delighted. They could not be happier for the couple. They were crazy about Arthur and having Kelly home again made their life complete. They had often talked about their grandchildren and how far away they were from their daughter. If she continued to live there, they would not have enough money to travel there often and it made them so sad. This was good news.

They wanted all the details and how long it would take them to get everything done and move back to Chicago. They talked and talked and the next day, Kelly and her mother went out apartment hunting.

The cost was a fraction of the cost in Europe. Arthur was impressed when they took him there to see what they had found and ask his advice and his choice of places to live. He loved the first place, because it was near the river and ran outside of town. He would have to use the Ell to get to town and to work, but it was perfect for them. They paid the deposit and prepared to go back to London to sell everything and move back to Kelly's hometown.

On the plane back to London, the voice was there in her sleep. "Thank God, Kelly, that you are coming back to me. I knew you would not leave me now that we have found each other and it was always meant to be that way."

She tossed and turned and her mind finally went to sleep soundly for a couple of hours during the flight home.

Chapter Twelve

Arthur was lying in his bed feeling all cozy and warm. The trip back had been easy for both of them. Kelly had gotten up and tucked the blanket all around Arthur and kissed him on his cute little nose when she was ready to go out for some scones for their breakfast. They had gotten home late and with the time difference, they were really tired. Arthur kept saying that he didn't feel this way when they went to the States before. Kelly had to remind him that when you go that way, you arrive in the afternoon and then after you eat, you get a good night's sleep. But then when you come back across the big pond, you travel all night and get home early in the morning, making for jet lag that doesn't go away so easily.

Arthur patted her back and gave her a hard pull forward and she fell on top of him giggling, the covers going everywhere. They both were laughing so hard that they almost fell off the bed.

Kelly pushed herself up and said, "Take a nap and I'll be back with some warm scones and clotted cream in a flash."

She turned up the heater and got her coat and headed out in the foggy morning. She had only walked about one block when she had a feeling that someone was behind her and closing in fast on her. Turning around very quickly, she saw a man right behind her. She stopped to see if he would keep walking and pass her up. He was very close and she thought that she knew the face. She was stunned when he opened his mouth and nothing came out. She looked at him. He was unable to speak to her.

"Who are you?" Kelly asked the man in front of her. She saw eyes of sky blue. She saw a smile that any girl would die for. She saw blond hair falling down his neck and she saw the ribbon in the back.

Again she spoke to him. "Hello. I'm sure that you can hear me. What is the problem here? Do you know me? What do you want?" She was totally irritated now. What kind of man would stop in front of a girl and then stare and not speak to her? She wanted an answer.

All at once, she noticed the shirt he had on was so old-fashioned that it belonged to another era. It belonged to another time, not here in today's London.

So many strange things kept happening. She was back in England now and she could feel it. Whatever it was, she didn't like it at all. She looked at the buttons and she saw that they had to be looped to shut them. She was certain that she had never seen anything like that shirt before. It had a high collar and was edged in silk of all things. The buttons were black and shiny. Why was she looking at his attire so closely she wondered to herself? What was so different about this man that she was not afraid at all and wanted to force him to talk to her? What was the attraction here? She needed to hurry and get the bread and get back to Arthur.

All at once, Arthur did not matter anymore. This man was attracting her so strongly that she wanted to grab him and hold him close to her body, rocking him like a little baby, soothing his fears away. His fears? Kelly thought she was freaking out. What was this all about? What was she doing? Her hands were clutching him and her fingers were running all around his face. Like someone drowning, she was pulled to him. He smiled at her and all at once she was clutching at thin air.

Kelly was shaking and trembling all over. Her hands were cold and she wondered if anyone had seen her strange actions there on the sidewalk. Looking left and right and placing one foot in front of the other, she slowly moved forward. As she put her bag on her shoulder and her hands in her pockets, she knew that something had just happened to her that she could never explain in a million years.

She walked very slowly at first. Then she got her momentum going and moved on down the street to her destination called Mallory's Bakery.

She went in and Maureen waited on her. She noticed Maureen looking at her like maybe she was in pain. "Good morning, Kelly," she spoke in that delightful English accent.

Kelly loved these pastries and forced her mind to go where it belonged, to the bakery and all the goodies she saw in the glass cases.

"Hi," Kelly managed to get out.

"When did you and Arthur get back?" Maureen made conversation.

"We got home late last night and this morning we had nothing to eat in the flat. So I ran down here to get his favorite scones. Please tell me you have clotted cream today. I am dying for some. We don't have anything that good in the States."

The salesman in her smiled and she reached into the cooler and brought out a new bottle of that sweet English clotted cream. Kelly just couldn't believe her luck this morning, a strange encounter on the sidewalk and now good luck for Arthur, his favorite breakfast.

Kelly selected six scones and paid for them. She left the bakery with a wave of her hand and a promise to be back again soon.

Maureen just stood there and stared. All the time she was talking to Kelly, there was a man standing behind her. He was staring at Kelly and he acted like he knew her, but he never said a word. And when Kelly left, he walked out behind her. Maureen was about to run out and call her back, when the man turned around and looked at her. It seemed like his eyes were telling her to mind her own business. Maureen was stunned and immediately went back to her job selling scones. His face was beautiful. She kept thinking about him. All through the day, he came back and forth in her mind. Maureen was shocked to think that Kelly did not know he was there. As the day went by, she began to think she needed to phone Kelly. She asked her boss for an hour off and went to the pay phone. She began to search for Arthur's number in the huge book. Finally finding it, she put ten pence in and made the call.

"Hello," a man's voice answered.

"Hello," she replied and then went into her conversation. "Is Kelly available?"

"Yes, I'll just go get her. May I ask who is calling?"

"Yes, this is Maureen from the bakery. Kelly came in this morning and got some scones and I just wanted to ask her a question."

"Of course," he told her so politely. "Kelly, the phone is for you," he called to her.

"Coming," Kelly said as she walked to the parlor to take the call. "Hello," Kelly said.

"Oh, hi, Kelly. It is just Maureen and I wanted to check and make sure that you were all right. When you were in here this morning, I couldn't keep from noticing the gentleman who seemed to be with you, because he stood right behind you all the time we talked. When you left, he followed you out. I went out to see if you knew he was there and he turned around like he knew I was there and gave me this cold look as if to say for me to mind my own business, but I was terribly worried about you."

Kelly heard her and she knew that she had seen the same man that Kelly had seen that day. She thought to herself that she had better think quickly on this one. Arthur was listening and Maureen was worried. Kelly was a smart girl and she started to talk all at once about a cake that she forgot to order, hoping that she could give Maureen a silent message, hoping that she would understand that she could not talk in front of Arthur.

Maureen stood there and listened and then she said to Kelly, "Okay, Kelly. I will write that order up right away. But the man I saw, did you see him, too?"

"Yes, I did. Thank you, Maureen. I'll be talking to you soon. Cheerio now."

Maureen hung up the receiver and went back to work. She was still as confused as before, but she caught the message that Kelly could not speak then. She put it away in her memory bank for another day.

Kelly put the phone down and saw Arthur's questions on his face. So she tried to put it down to the cake that she had wanted to order and had forgotten.

"My birthday is coming soon and I wanted to order a special cake. The bakery was really busy and I guess I just forgot to finish my order. We got to talking about the trip and I told her we were moving to the States and we just forgot about it."

Arthur felt like there was something else, but he didn't say a word. Later he mentioned that he was going to work and give them the good news. His leaving wouldn't directly hurt them. They had more people than work some weeks and so he was glad that he wouldn't be causing a problem that might cause him not to get a good recommendation with whatever he decided to do in the States.

It was cool outside, so he gathered up his coat and briefcase and left Kelly home alone. At first she was just grateful to be alone. Then she had time to think about this morning and her experience. She was sure that the man she saw had followed her inside the bakery and that the lady saw him caused her a bit of alarm. She thought that she was the only one who was able to see him. Because he had said not a word, she was almost positive he was the ghost that was tormenting her daily now. Being back in England made her fearful that she was where he wanted her to be. There had been too many circumstances bring him to her for her not to believe it now.

Kelly took a quick shower and called her mom to say hello. She told her that Arthur had gone in to give his two weeks notice. She also told her that they were placing the flat that he owned on the rental list and had hired a company in

London to sublet for them. Arthur had not wanted to sell the flat that he had inherited from his parents. Not many people actually owned their own homes or flats in the UK. It made good sense to her to keep it. It would be a valuable asset to them years down the road.

After she had a snack, she went out to get boxes so she could pack up the things she wanted to go home with her.

"Thanks and we will deliver these tomorrow for you," the salesman told Kelly after she picked out the size she needed to pack.

"Thanks to you and I'll see you then." With that done, Kelly went to the pub and had a sandwich. She always loved the pub lunches. She was sitting alone in the Boras Head Pub when all of a sudden, she felt like she was not alone. When she turned her head, she saw the same man standing at the end of the bar. He was hard to see. She thought it was because it was dark inside the bar. Then, as she watched, he faded out of sight. She looked all around to see if anyone else had seen him. It appeared that she was the only one who saw him.

That ruined her lunch, so she paid the check and headed home. Walking made her head clear, but there was something about this man that wouldn't go away. She tried to forget it and walked a little bit faster.

Putting the key in the lock, she finally relaxed and let her mind be at peace. She got a cool cloth and lay down on her bed. She put her feet up on the pillows and drifted off to sleep.

Arthur came in and saw her asleep and left her there while he made supper.

One thing that she wanted to do now that she was back home, and before they moved away to the States, was to go back to the castle where she thought all the strange voices and other things she could not understand had begun.

She told Arthur that she was going to get lunch with her friends and she would be home before he got back from work. Of course Arthur said it was okay and that was all she had to do. Her plan had already been made, so she carefully got herself dressed and warm. Then she called a taxi. She had the taxi meet her at the bakery. She was going to leave from a place where no one would know her and could not ask any questions.

Walking down the street, she had second thoughts, but then if that was where it had all started, why not go back to see if she was right or not. She had already called the taxi and he was there when she rounded the corner. She got in and told the driver her final destination.

On the drive out to the castle, she was trying to remember the first time it had started. It was when she had seen the portrait on the wall in the castle. She could hardly remember because since that day there had been so many times and so many different occurrences that she had a hard time separating them in her memory.

The driver broke through her concentration and told her that she was probably there way too early. "I don't even see the guides' cars and if I remember right, this place opens its doors at 10:00. You have over an hour before anyone will be here. Will you be all right alone here?"

"Yes, I will be fine. Don't worry about me because I love it here and I feel right at home. There are so many things for me to see outside that I will enjoy myself immensely and I don't want you to worry about me, okay?" Kelly told him.

After he drove off, she walked around to where she had seen the door behind all the ivy and it was still covered in it. She moved a hand full of ivy from around the door knob and she heard it start to creek open. She jumped back. It swung open like it was waiting for her. She stepped inside the dark passage. She could smell the mold and mildew and she felt wet air going down into her lungs with each step she took into the darkness. It was so dark that she could only feel around and, touching the wall, she cringed at the slime she came in touch with. Two steps inside the passage, she remembered the oil lamp she had found the first time she had visited this place quite by accident. She was moving her fingers all over when she found it. "Ouch." She cursed herself for not being more careful. The nail or whatever it was had punctured her finger. She could feel the blood running down her hand. She immediately held her hand up to slow the blood flow. It was just too dark in here. She decided to turn around and go back the way she had just come.

Two steps later, she felt so lightheaded that she leaned against the dark wet cobwebs and slick rock wall for just a second, long enough to squeeze the finger again to stop the flow of blood that seemed to be dripping down her shirt and pants at the same time. When her right shoulder touched the slimy wall, her feet slipped right out from under her. Her body went down and her head hit something hard. She saw stars and felt herself spinning in a vortex, like nothing she had ever experienced before. She was going so fast and it was all black. Darkness overcame her.

In the distance, she could hear a man's voice calling to someone to come quickly and help him. She heard him say he had found Rebecca. She could remember wondering who Rebecca was. Then it got all black again. She felt nothing and heard no more voices.

Chapter Thirteen

The Earl of Dunraven was walking back and forth, clasping both hands together and pacing so fast that the doctor thought maybe he needed some medicine.

"Please calm yourself, Lord Dunraven," he begged the man for the tenth time since they had found his Lady in the field laying face down in the dirt. "She will be fine, I promise you."

"But how did she get there," he asked himself over and over again.

These past three months had been so hard on him with his wife gone and no one knowing anything about her disappearance and the knowledge that someone had kidnapped her from her own home in front of the servants' eyes. The talk was that she heard someone calling to her and she went out in the buggy to the fields behind the castle alone to see who was calling her name. No one else heard a voice, just Rebecca.

When Lord Dunraven came home that evening, no one could find her. They searched the land for days and never found a thing. He collapsed in the chair and remained there for hours until his servant and trusted friend came in and took him to his room. He had helped him remove his clothes and had lit a warm fire in the fireplace. Then he helped him lie down in his big bed. Just being there alone was more than he could bear. He changed rooms later that week and had not been back in there since.

"Hurry and get her in the house!" he screamed to all of them. With no time to waste, they got her undressed and checked her body for any accidents that might have happened to her and finally Matilda, her Lady's maid came running in and ran them all off except for Lord Dunraven. Together they got her into the big bed, propped her up with huge pillows and placed warm soft blankets all around her. Her face finally turned pink again. Her eyes were open wide and she had a blank look about her.

Kelly kept thinking she was dreaming. She looked the room over more than twice and then just closed her eyes, hoping that she would wake up and be at the castle waiting in line for it to open up. Those were the last thoughts she had. Sleep conquered her again and she relaxed and fell into oblivion.

The Earl was pacing back and forth. Shively, his servant, was going to make him eat something soon. He had not eaten in a couple of days because he was beside himself with worry about Rebecca.

"Sir, please let me get you a cup of coffee," he begged. "You need to sit down and eat and rest now that we have her here with us again. She will be waking up soon and you don't want her to see the worry and the new lines in your face. It will upset the mistress greatly. So let me take care of you for a while and we will come back to her room and wait for her to wake up. I want to bring some warm soup for the mistress to eat when she wakes up, too."

The Earl looked into his wise old face and knew he was right. He would leave her long enough to eat and change his clothes so that when she wakes up she will see her husband all clean and happy. To him it made sense and so he leaned over and placed both hands on her sleeping body to give her a kiss.

Shively took his master to the dining room and pulled out his chair to seat him. The dining room had been empty for many weeks now and Shively only wanted things back the way they had been before the mistress had wandered off and gotten lost, or whatever had happened to her. To Shively it seemed strange that she had ever been found and his mind wanted to know where she had been. But today, there were no answers to anyone's questions. Shively was going to make certain that the Earl was taken care of before he got ill.

"Thank you, Shively. This bread is good. I have a hunger that I have pushed back for so long that I forgot how it feels to satisfy the hunger and now I am ready to eat. Anything you bring me, I will eat, Shively. Bring me more."

The smile that went over his servant's face made his day. "I want some meat," the Earl's big booming voice came after his back as he went back to the kitchen to get more food for him.

Sitting there, he felt his heart beating. He was calmer now. He knew Rebecca would wake up and his world would be good again. Just remembering how he had let things go on the grounds gave him worries. He needed to get Rebecca to wake up and show him that she was okay. Then he would get back to the problems he had before she had turned up missing.

The servants needed to settle some personal problems that they had brought to him a month ago. He needed to make sure that the meat was brought in and cured for the long cold winter months. The cooks were already making lists for him to take to town. Getting supplies was his and Shively's major mob in the fall months. They would go into town and it would take Shively and three men a good week to pack it all up for the trip back to the castle.

He had not wanted to go when he was searching for his wife. He had not listened to anyone who said that there were things he needed to do and he had put it all out of his mind. He was waiting for someone to find her. He took men out in groups for days after she had gone missing. He searched the woods to the north of Dunraven Castle. He sent messages to all of his uncles and his neighbors to the east of Dunraven Castle. No one had heard or seen anything. Everyone was looking for her. There were search parties out. The Earl of Dunraven had sent his knights out two weeks ago. They had not even returned to him yet.

Chapter Fourteen

He ate until he was satisfied and then he went up the stairs to get some clean clothes on before he went back to the chamber where he had left her. The door between the sleeping chamber and the dressing area was open a crack and he peeked into the room. He saw her and she was looking all around the room like she wanted to find something. Her eyes were going back and forth. Then she reached out a hand from under the warm blanket he had put on her himself and rubbed her eyes. He watched her from the corner of the massive door that he was standing behind and she seemed to be lost in thought.

He watched her closer. She tried to sit up and she closed her eyes and began to retch. HE raced to her side with a bucket. She grabbed it just in time. Whatever they had fed her came up. She was so embarrassed. She felt her face turn red. Then she looked up at the stranger. She saw passion in his eyes for her. How could that be? She had never seen him before in her life. She looked again. He had bright blue eyes and had a beard that hid everything else. The beard was gold and yellow. He had blond hair. He was beautiful, like a man in a magazine she had seen somewhere before. He was staring at her and she stared back.

"What?" she asked him. "What do you want from me, sir?" she asked in a soft voice.

At first he was shocked at her language because he had never heard that voice before. He looked at her before he spoke and then he said, "What do you mean, Rebecca? I want to see if you are well and I want to make sure that you are warm and fed and, most of all, I am so happy you are found and back where you belong."

"Huh?" she just grunted. "I need to make something clear. I'm not Rebecca is the first thing and the second is I want to know where I am and how I got here. Can you answer that?"

He just looked at this woman and spoke not a word. He didn't understand what she meant. She was his wife and Lady Mistress of Dunraven Castle. What was wrong with her? And that voice, he most certainly did not remember that. He was really confused now. He pulled up a chair and gave her a wet cloth to wipe her mouth with. When she did not reach out to take it, he made the motion to wipe it for her. She grabbed his hand and took the cloth.

"Please don't touch me until you tell me where I am!" She spoke in alarm.

The Earl put his hands in his lap and said to her in quite a matter of fact voice, "You are my wife and this is our home. You are in Dunraven Castle, madam."

The shocked look could have not been more clear. Even a stranger would have seen the look in her eyes. It was like she did not believe him.

Kelly cleared her voice and spoke again. "I am Kelly to you, sir. I do not know this Rebecca and I found a door in the wall where I made the first mistake I guess, but I opened the door and stepped inside for a short minute. When I reached to turn on a light switch, I cut my hand. That was when I saw all the blood running down my arm and I went to steady myself. The next thing I remember was waking up here. Who are you kidding anyway, bud?"

"I do not understand you, madam. And what is a bud?"

"Listen to me, buster. I don't care who you think you are, I known who I am and where I am and its time you came down off your high horse, mister, because I want to get out of here now!"

The look on his face was one of pure shock. Automatically, his right hand went to his head. "What kind of talk is that? I have never heard you shout before," the Earl replied to his distraught wife. He was beginning to shake and he lowered his hand to his lap. He looked at her and he noticed a strange look in her eyes. She was the same woman, but there was a difference. Her voice and her motions were fast and not very proper. Her language was strange, too. He sat there very quietly and just looked at her.

"My God! Did you hear anything I said? I want out of here. What in the hell are you looking at?" she screamed at him

He blinked and said, "Madam, I have never heard you swear before. Please will you just remain calm and I will ask Cook to bring up a tray for you. You must be hungry," he said while staring at her face, trying to establish a connection between his Lady and this very odd woman.

"Like I said, buddy, my name is Kelly and I came here to do the tour of the castle and the next thing I know I wake up here in this bed. I am a married woman and you are not my husband," she retorted to his shocked expression.

The Earl did not know what to say. He knew who she was. What he did not know was how to handle this lady and make her feel better about being found and brought home where she belonged. He was so worried about her and he could not understand her words and the way she looked at him. He was so puzzled. If he could get her to go back to sleep, maybe she would wake up and everything would be all right. And buster! What in the world was a buster? Hell! That was not a word he had ever heard her say and buddy was another odd word.

"I am going to take my leave of you right now," he spoke so calmly to her that she finally realized that she had to get herself together.

She said, "That will be fine. But when you come back, I might not be here, sir."

The Earl just looked at her and turned his back and walked out the bedroom door.

Kelly had to think. She looked all around her. The room had the look of a real castle. But who was she kidding? She knew when she cut her hand and she knew when she had fallen backwards and hit the floor.

The door came open and in walked a maid with a tray. All at once she felt the hunger pains. She relaxed and took the tray. The food was terrible. She pushed the tray back.

The maid curtsied and asked if there was anything she could do to help her relax and change into a day dress. Kelly thought it was a strange thing to have someone help her get dressed, but she said, "Yes, that would be nice. Can you tell me what your name is?" she casually asked as she watched the girl tidy the things on the dressing table. For the first time, she noticed all the things lying around. A very old hair brush with a golden handle and bristles that she thought would tear a girl's hair out. A long handle on a mirror had a shadow on it and so she did not see it very well from her position in the bed. But it was so beautiful that she could hardly tear her eyes off it.

The girl turned around and looked shocked. Then she asked her in a voice that sounded like she was afraid, "Ma'am, you don't know me? I have been your personal maid for the past year! My name is Matilda. Please tell me you know me, Ma'am. I don't know what I would do if I lost you and your trust, Ma'am."

Kelly took the words in and knew she had to act right then. If she was to get away and back home to Arthur, she had to be able to think and then she could make the right move and leave this castle for good this time.

"Matilda, can you tell me how old you are? I must have hurt my head when I fell because I am having trouble remembering everything about home and names. Can you understand what I mean?"

Matilda looked at her mistress and bent her head down so she could not meet her mistress' eyes. "Yes, Ma'am, I am twenty-two. I have been with you since I was twenty-one. My mammy died and I came in the house to be trained to help you in all your needs. Are you okay? Is there something I can do to help you right now?"

Kelly was thinking. "Yes, please find my clothes and help me dress. I want to go outside and take a walk."

Matilda said, "But we need to feed you, Ma'am. Let me dress you, okay?"

Matilda went straight to the wardrobe and opened the mahogany doors where she pulled out two or three different dressings and laid them on the high bed where Kelly was beginning to sit up. "Matilda, please open the window for me."

"Window, Ma'am?"

She looked so scared that Kelly spoke up and said, "I mean that I would like some fresh air, Matilda. Can you do that for me?"

"Yes, of course I can do that. But the word you said was one that I don't understand, mistress," she said with her eyes downcast. "What was it that you said?" she asked her mistress with a real curiosity in her eyes that Kelly had to answer.

"I meant that I wanted wind in my face and it came out wrong." Wow, Kelly thought, I better watch my words or I'll never get out of this weird place. Poor Arthur, he must be worried sick by now. And hell is not the first curse word he has ever heard either, I would bet my life on it. That stuck up old Earl. I would bet he is not an Earl either, Kelly told herself as she got up and went to get dressed.

"Oh Mistress, please let me help you. The Earl will punish me if I don't help you and you get hurt or ill again. You must tell me where you have been and how they found you, Mistress." The girl went on and on and Kelly thought it must be a real good actress in the making because she was getting in all the right words and actions were true to the nature of this girl that she had just met. What a situation. Kelly wondered what would happen next.

Then the door burst open and in walked the Earl. "Rebecca, are you sure you should be up just yet?" He questioned her thoroughly as if she might break in two if she got dressed.

"I am fine." Kelly had decided to play along with them until she could get out of the castle and then she would have to find a way to get back to London. Her plan was to get to a phone quickly and call Arthur to come and get her.

"Sir, may I ask you a question?" Kelly said to the Earl acting man in front of her.

"Of course, my dear," he said with real concern in his voice. "What do you need?"

"Could I possibly use the phone?"

"My dear, I don't know what you want. A phone? May I ask you what a phone is? Are you okay, my dear? You seem to be asking and speaking words we don't understand."

"A telephone. Is that so hard to hear? A phone to call my husband to come and get me."

The Earl looked at her hard and then he motioned for everyone to leave the room. "I'll call when she needs you back here to get her ready for the dinner hour. I want her to take dinner with us in the dining room tonight," he told his servants as they left the room. He had seen the tray was still full and he wanted to get her to eat.

Kelly went over to a hard wooden chair sitting by the bed. She let herself all into it. She felt defeated and very unsure of what was going on in front of her very own eyes. Finally, she spoke up again to the man who kept repeating that he was her husband. She looked up at him and noticed that he was standing very rigid and had both arms folded in front of his body. He was also staring at her. She wondered if he had finally decided to let her in on the joke. That is what it had to be, a big joke.

The joke might be on me, she thought as she remembered dreaming about a man who looked exactly like this beautiful man in front of her. But who was he? And then she remembered the man in front of Maureen's bakery that day. She tried hard to bring it back but all she could get was the blond hair and the blue eyes part of him. He had been tall, too. So was this man called the Earl? Earl my butt, she said to herself. A grin spread around her lips and she saw him looking at her.

"What is the smile about?" he asked her in a strained voice.

She could tell he was very nervous about something and she knew it had to be her. My God, why can't I go home or wake up or something, she was thinking to herself.

When he spoke, she listened and was surprised at the tenderness in his voice. His eyes betrayed his face because she could see worry there and she had not seen it before. Her first thoughts were to ask him some questions and let him know she thought it was a game he was playing. Or maybe, she thought, it could be a play. Whatever was going on, she needed to have some answers. If she could stay calm, she might be able to get out of this mess she had landed in when she had fainted in the entrance to the walled up door she had accidentally found.

"What time is it?" she asked him in a very controlled voice.

"It is almost dinner time and I thought you might like to dine with us tonight."

She was impressed with her control and went on to ask more. "Are you sure you want me to go downstairs and eat with all of you?"

"Well," he said as he moved toward her chair, "I would like to ask you if you could tell me about the time you were gone. You know, I almost died myself at the thought of losing you. I thought you were dead and I had no idea how to go on and the worst part was I didn't know how to find you. Did you know we were looking? We were searching day in and day out and no one knew what to do next. We did not know where else to look after a few days. Please tell me what happened to you and who was responsible for it. I want more than anything to get them and make them pay for kidnapping the Lady Rebecca. Please inform me of the incident so I can prepare to get my men together to search for them and make them pay with their heads."

She was listening, but she did not want to hear all that because it was not true and she was not the famous Rebecca he kept insisting she was. "Pay with their heads?" she asked. "What do you mean with their heads? Are you a murderer, sir? Am I in a murderer's home right now? Do you kill people? I'm sorry, sir, but I am totally lost in this play and all I really want is to go home. Please, sir, can you help me?" Kelly almost had tears in her eyes this time and he saw it.

"No, my dear, I am not a murderer. But someone has to pay for taking you and you should want me to find them. I am also confused by all of this. Can't you tell me more? If you can't talk about it yet, I fully understand and I will wait until the appropriate time and then we will discuss it. Is this going to be all right with you?" He waited for her to answer him. She said not a word. He had been so surprised at her wording and her lack of feeling for him that he was thrown back to the time when she was gone and he thought he might not ever see her again. It was a dismal time and he never wanted to go through that again.

If it was time she needed, it was time she would receive from him. He loved her so much and it hurt so bad not to see the love in her eyes that she used to have for him.

Keep calm she kept saying to herself. Don't let him get to you. She was very quiet, but her mind was working overtime. To be sure of her next words was what she wanted to concentrate on now. She remained very quiet.

Thinking fast, finally she replied, "May I please get ready to go to dinner and then we can talk more after we eat?"

He seemed pleased that she would talk about anything at the moment and so he answered her, "Yes that will be good. Get ready and I will send Shively to get you in about an hour."

She wanted to ask who Shively was but she wanted to know what was going on first so she kept quiet as he walked closer to her and reached out his hand for hers. At first, she did not move a muscle. She let him grasp it and he took it to his mouth where he kissed her hand gently and dismissed himself from her presence.

Chapter Fifteen

Her mind was working fast now. As she stood up, the door opened again and in came the maid, or rather her maid, Matilda. She just wanted to laugh. Just think she told herself, I have a maid. She smiled and went on with the farce she had been thrown into by some freak of luck, or not really luck, just a real weird, freaky thing.

"Mistress, I am here to get you ready for dinner this evening."

Kelly smiled her best smile and went forward. "What's for supper?" she asked Matilda. The maid just turned around and stared at her.

"Supper, ma'am?" she questioned Kelly.

Oops, she had done it again. Kelly knew she had to be careful or she might never find out what was going on. "I'm hungry and if you know what we will be eating, maybe you can tell me?" She left the question hanging, waiting for Matilda to answer her.

Matilda looked at her and then she said, "Why do you sound different, Mistress?"

"Please don't call me that," Kelly said to her new maid.

"But Mistress, what else would I call you? It wouldn't be right for me to call you Rebecca. It is not my place to do so. I could get sent back to the servants' quarters. And I love you so much that I would just die if I could not help you in your bath and dressing. Am I not pleasing you, Mistress?"

Her eyes showed pain and Kelly immediately spoke up, "No, Matilda, but I thought if we were such good friends and you cared so much about me, well I wanted to give you a gift and the gift is to call me Kelly."

Matilda looked at her and said, "But Mistress, your name is not Kelly. Your name is Rebecca."

Kelly was getting tired of playing this game, but she went on for Matilda's sake, especially since she had started this whole thing about calling her by her first name. "All right then, you can call me Rebecca from today on," Kelly told her. Kelly saw the look in her maid's eyes and then she went on to say, "At dinner, I will ask the Earl if I may give you the gift of first names between us." She saw Matilda's smile come back and Kelly knew she was playing the game well.

Just as she got herself together and Matilda convinced her that she had to do something with her hair, she realized that at dinner tonight she would not know a person there and she was keeping in the back of her mind the idea that if she could get out of the castle doors, she could find a phone to call Arthur to come and get her.

Every once in a while she let her mind think she was Rebecca and she was in the Dunraven Castle and the blond man might really be her husband. Then she thought again and got worried that maybe she was going nuts and got a sinking feeling in the pit of her stomach. She would shake her head and Matilda would say, "What's wrong, Mistress?"

And she would answer, "Oh, it is nothing. I think I am getting a headache is all."

That was when she would try to be Rebecca again, but that was just until she could unravel this mystery she had fallen upon when she hit her head in the castle gateway.

The knock came on her door. They were being escorted down the winding rock stairs to have dinner with the Earl of Dunraven. Kelly could not imagine why this was happening unless she was dreaming. So she went on with the plan.

She walked down the long hall with the long dead ancestors hanging everywhere. All at once, she stopped and stared at the same picture she had seen in the castle on her first visit. It was her!

Matilda stopped and turned back to her Mistress' muffled scream. "What is wrong now, Mistress?" Matilda was frightened by the horrified look on her Mistress' face and took her in her arms and tried to stop her from weeping.

"It looks like me!" Kelly said too loudly.

"Why wouldn't it look like you, Mistress? The Earl had it done just this past summer solstice. Have you forgotten how many long days you sat and I waited for the painter to get it right? Your back ached and your head ached and you quarreled with the Earl each day until he finally gave you a week break from sitting for the painting," she said very surprised at her reaction to the painting that she had seen so many times before.

"But it looks new, Matilda. The last time I saw it, the painting was over four hundred years old and hanging in a castle that was only a tourist spot."

Matilda looked shocked at Kelly's words and tried to come up with something to make her mind go to the wonderful feast that the Earl had ordered for her for tonight. "Oh come now, Mistress. Maybe you had a knock on the head and you will remember tomorrow, okay?"

Kelly just looked at her and started to walk down the remaining length of the hall to her first meal in the castle. She tried to imagine what she might taste tonight, but then she thought she might also get to the bottom of this mystery tonight and nothing could be better than that. So she pasted on a smile and walked into the biggest stone room she had ever seen.

The Earl stood up and made a motion for her to sit down beside him. His manservant, Shively, pulled out her chair and helped her get seated. The table was a good twelve feet long with benches at one end and some huge chairs at the end where they were seated. She looked all around the room. The fireplace was twenty feet in length and the flame was three feet high with crackling logs making a warm, toasty hall for their dinner. She felt like all eyes were on her and she tried to be friendly all the while asking questions that she had to think through before she opened her mouth, which was hard for Kelly to remember to do.

For Kelly, the next hour was trial and miss. She answered any questions put to her and delayed the others by saying that she needed to think about it and her memory was fuzzy. Fuzzy caused a murmur all around the table. Who would have thought the tiny word was foreign to them at that table. Not Kelly of course. She saw the men and women looking at each other like she had three heads. Then she asked them straight up what their problem was anyway. That did it again. She guessed that the lady of the house had better shut up. She did. She lowered her head and all the time she was looking for the door she could use to get away to the world she had left somehow.

She had been served mead to drink. She had been so thirsty that she gulped down the swallow and then she gasped for breath. She had never tasted anything so bitter in her life. Everyone was staring at her and she guessed that she had surprised them again with her 2006 manners.

She politely wiped her mouth and asked for some water, saying that her throat was hurting and the wine made her choke. Everyone was once again looking at her like she had three heads!

"Please don't worry," she said in her voice that she could tell many of them did not understand. "I am just so tired and now could we please have some food to go with the drink?" she asked the Earl.

He looked at her and shook his head. "You are supposed to be the one who tells the cooks when to serve, My Lady," he answered her.

Kelly had to think again and then began her play acting. On television, she had seen movies from this time period, so she mimicked one and clapped her hands and asked the man nearest her to begin serving. He turned and went out of the hall.

While she waited, she searched the faces of all the people at the table. Where on earth did they all come from? They were dirty and there was a stink in the whole room of unwashed bodies. She saw ten dogs chained at the fireplace. This was the biggest fireplace she had ever seen or even imagined. It had to heat the entire hall and with the heat and the bodies and the dogs, it made her sick to her stomach.

There was straw all over the floor. It had bugs in it and they were biting her feet. She was scratching and just miserable.

In came the food. It was meat but she did not recognize it. "Will you serve the Earl first?" she asked the man holding the tray that had to weigh at least a hundred pounds. She was wondering what it was when she heard someone say, "I want the ox tail."

Ox! Gross was what she thought. But she had to admit that it smelled good and it looked good. She must be starving.

"I had a light meal of cheese and bread served at the noon hour and we are having this big meal as celebration that you are finally home again where you belong," her husband spoke into her thoughts.

She just hoped he could not see the revulsion on her face from the smell and the wine.

"I'm sorry the mead hurt your throat and next time I will weaken it for you until you are back to normal. I purposely had them get the mead that you favor, My Lady. Maybe we need to get a different bottle and make sure that it is not gone bad by some trick."

She stared at him. He honestly believed she was his wife. How could this be happening? She was just exhausted from all the strain of playacting and wanting to get home.

Vegetables came next. She had never seen such a procession. Trays and trays and she did not recognize any of them. She waited for her turn and asked the Earl to please show her the potatoes. That was all that she wanted. He was shocked and insisted that she try the mutton, also. She shook her head and they piled her plate full of odd looking food. She actually tried to eat some of it because she was really hungry. But it tasted so strong and the only thing she ate that evening was a few different types of fruit. She had cherries, figs and an apple that she cut up and put in her pocket when no one was looking.

The minstrels came in and then a magician. She was entertained and tried to not think about where she was and what was really going on. Throughout the evening, she had figured out that the Earl and his family were all seated by the fire and the help and his men at arms that protected the castle (she thought) were further down the table. They all had weapons strapped to their bodies. Bows and arrows that she knew would cost a mint in an antique shop on Piccadilly. Hatchets that you could imagine coming at you hanging from their belts, knives so long that it scared her to see them, and more. She shivered to think that she was in the great hall with the meanest men she had ever come across in her life.

"I think I would like some fresh air, sir," she told the Earl. "Could that be arranged?" she asked again. He did not even hear her.

All of a sudden she thought, if I am asleep I would not be able to taste this wine and food and maybe if I try to touch the Earl and he agrees to take me outside, I can figure out a way to escape these nuts. Either I am really here or I am asleep and I need to wake up. With that thought she reached out her hand again and tried to touch the man she was praying was a figment of her imagination or a dream so real she needed something to happen to wake her up.

He turned to her and took her hand in his. Oh God, she thought it felt real. She grasped his hand and asked him again to take her outside. He complied and took her by the elbow and lifted her off the bench and they started towards the huge double door that had a massive knocker on it. It had a long piece of steel that slid back and forth to let them open and shut the door. It was so huge that she knew she could not get out that way without someone to open the door for her. What a setback that put in her mind.

If, and only if, it turned out that she had been kidnapped by these strange people or whatever she found out was going on, she was truly tired of playacting and felt the need to escape now. But how could she do it? She had to make a plan and maybe if she could find a way to be alone for a while, she would be able to leave by herself and no one would notice she was gone for a time and that would be great.

They reached the door and she was right about the opener. It took two of his men to slide the bar open. What a protection they had in those days was all that she could think of. He escorted her outside arm in arm and they walked into the courtyard. She was reacting to the difference because she felt him stiffen up and let go of her arm and he was asking her if she was okay and what was wrong. She only stared.

She saw chickens and she saw pigs, but most surprising were the amount of horses standing tied to a long rail to her left. To her right, she saw a castle gate. Huge and imposing even to her memory of castle entrances. It must have been fifteen feet wide and thirty feet high. The stone walls all around her made her think she might be in danger and that was a hell of a dream. She asked the Earl why the gates were closed. He looked at her and shook his head. He could not understand what had happened to her, but he knew she was not right anymore. She must have been hit in the head, what else would cause this damage to her knowledge of the castle that she had been born in, where she had chosen him as her husband on that day her parents had given her that castle and all the lands around it as a wedding present, and where she chose to be married. They had been friends and fell in love at an early age. He had been Earl of his own castle, but she had asked him to please let her remain in her home and he had given in to her pleas. Now he was shockingly disturbed that she could not remember why she had been kidnapped or where she had been taken or even her own home. She did not remember anything. He was so worried about her. He took her in his arms and she stiffened up immediately. He released her and looked down into her eyes.

"Do you remember me?" he asked her. He was not ready to hear the words, but he knew he must.

She lowered her head and she spoke the very words that he did not want to hear. "I am not too sure. You seem familiar to me, but I can't say I remember you like I guess I should if you say we are married." She shook when she got through because she knew she was lost somewhere and she did not know where in time she really was. Her mind must be playing tricks on her, lost in time was a trick and a joke, not real.

Being lost in time was not her idea of a joke. Her next thought was to ask the Earl. So she did. "Please, can you tell me one thing?" she asked.

"Anything, my love," was his answer. He waited for the question that he hoped he could answer for her.

"What is the date today, sir?" she wanted to know.

He was surprised and thought that was an easy question to answer. "Today is Sunday, my love."

"No, that is not exactly what I wanted to know. I want to know the date and the year." She watched his eyes to make sure that he did not think she was a nut or a witch. She remembered that in those days they burned a witch at the stake for any little odd thing that someone would charge her with. Her fear was real. He saw it in her eyes and tried to calm her.

This is an easy question he thought to himself. "November the fourth and the year is one thousand six hundred."

"Sixteen hundred! Oh my God! Where am I?" she cried out loud. "You don't expect me to believe this, do you?" she cried out to him.

"Why do you think I would like you to remember, Rebecca?" he asked her.

"Because I am from the year two thousand and six," she replied to his hurting eyes.

He did not want to upset her any more so he took her gently into his arms again and tried to soothe away her fears.

"Look, I can prove it to you," she said, "but you won't believe me, will you?" she asked with doubt that he would be able to understand her trying to explain this one.

She pushed herself away and while she was looking into those baby blue eyes, she remembered the figure behind her the day she went to Maureen's bakery. It was the same man. But how did this happen she wanted to know? She remembered seeing this face once before when she was getting the wedding gown on at home the day of her wedding. What did it all mean? Oh lands sake, she thought. I must be having a breakdown. I will wake up and be at home, and soon I hope. She did not say this out loud, but she knew that the Earl was waiting for an answer.

"Okay, just let me go back inside and if you will take me to my chambers, I will show you something that will make you believe I just might be telling the truth. Is that a deal?"

He looked at her and said, "What is a deal?"

She started to laugh out loud. He stared at her until she started to calm down and then he said it again, "What is a deal, Rebecca?"

"Well, it is sort of a compromise between two people and one of us has to listen to the other one's explanation of what we are talking about. There, does that make sense to you?"

"Not really, but can you tell me why you are using words I have never heard you use before?"

"That's all part of the reason I need to see you in private, now if you please."

"Then proceed and I will follow you to our chamber." He sounded thoroughly disgusted with her and she wondered if she tried to make a point with the things she had in her pocket of her blue jeans back in the room if he would really listen or just let her ramble on and then leave the room convinced that she had lost it all.

"But after you show me what you have, I want to talk about the abduction and I want to know who it was. Do you understand that I cannot let this go unpunished, Rebecca?" he said in a stern voice.

Now she was in a spot. What on earth could she tell him to make him happy? She didn't have a blooming clue what had happened to the real Rebecca and all she really knew was that everyone there seemed to think she was the lost Rebecca. And she was not that person. How was she going to get through this question and answer game he kept playing? She didn't know the answer to that one yet.

He banged on the doors and they automatically opened to let them in. She had been aware that there were at least three men in the dark shadows all the time and they had to be bodyguards. They went in and a few seconds later she heard the others come in.

"Please tell me, Earl, that we are not being watched. Because I know they were outside and are always close enough to us to even hear our conversation. Can we have a private time alone, the two of us, just to talk?"

"You have always been watched and you never complained before. Maybe if you hadn't left the castle unescorted, this kidnapping wouldn't have happened. And you know perfectly well that ladies are never left alone, that they cannot protect themselves and that this is my job as your Lord and the Earl of Dunraven, My Lady?" He was a little perturbed. She could tell it and now she had to calm him down and then she would share a secret with this strange man who consistently called himself her Lord.

"I don't need to be scolded like a child," she exclaimed to his temper that he was not hiding from her anymore.

He bowed to her and took her by the upper arm and led her up the winding stone turret stairs.

Chapter Sixteen

Once in the turret, she told him to have a chair. He seated himself and then she went about trying to find her old clothes. She searched the wardrobe and then she looked under the bed. She saw a closet of a sort and moved things around until she saw her blue jeans sticking out from under some old rags. She grabbed them and went to sit on the bed.

She searched the pockets hoping that she still had the small pink pill box with the aspirin in it. She felt it and then the fingernail clippers fell out on the cold stone floor. The Earl saw them and went to get them for her, but she was faster. She grabbed for them and picked them up first.

"Here," she said. "What do you think of these?"

"What are they? You must tell me because I have never seen anything like that before!" the Earl said.

"Where I come from we use them to clip our nails and keep them neat and clean, which I have noticed you must do with soap. Am I right?" she questioned him.

He held them and turned them over several times. Then he handed them to her and told her to show him how they worked. She took them in her fingers and cut her thumb nail back a little. She had always been so proud of her beautiful long nails. It was then that he saw the nail polish. It was pale pink and that may have been why no one had noticed them yet. But now he had and he needed an answer to how she got the color on her nails. He wanted to know if her nail had been hurt and if they were sore. She almost laughed, but held herself in check. She explained that in two thousand and six, ladies got manicures and also got pedicures. This brought out more questions. She tried to answer them all, but was really getting tired of the whole idea of explaining her way out of this. All she could hope for now was to go to bed and wake up in two thousand six.

Kelly just sat down and looked at him. "Let me show you my medicine that will stop a pain anywhere in the body."

He was so curious that he moved over to the bed and sat down beside her. She was a little jumpy now, but he was behaving, so she showed them to him. Again he fingered them. She asked him if he had any pain and he told her that he hurt his side jousting just this morning and he pulled the material away from an open sore. She knew it was a blade that had made that cut. The cut was red and inflamed and she was certainly surprised to see the big man sitting there with that horrible open wound on his body. He never showed her that he was in any pain. This was a great way to show him how it might work and it would be to his benefit if he would agree to swallow them. But that might prove to be a very hard thing to accomplish with this Earl who was so in charge of everything and everyone.

He just looked at them and then he said, "How does a person do this? How does it work? I have never heard of anything like this before. I'm not sure if I should believe you because you keep talking with such strange words and now I see this white pellet called aspirin."

"They are not pellets. They are tablets in my world. They are pain killers."

His face showed a whitish color. She knew he was very disturbed by the words, pain killers.

"Try it. It will be a blessing to you because it will stop the pain you must be in right now." Kelly kept talking and kept watching his face for a hint of understanding. She saw her opening and jumped in. "Please let me do this for you and then you will be more comfortable and we can talk more, if you like," she sort of begged him.

"Tell me how to do it."

"Okay," Kelly said almost too quickly, because she saw him stare at her face for a few seconds. "Can we get some cool water to drink?"

He stood up and went to the door. When he opened it, she saw two men standing there in full warrior get up.

"I guess they are the guards to watch over me tonight," she said in a nasty way.

"Yes, Rebecca, and you know how that works. You never once complained before about my protection of you. Why are you so different now?"

The guard came back with a bucket of clear water and a dipper to drink with. She took the dipper and dropped the aspirins in the water. They dissolved fast and she said, "If you drink this, you will believe me. But I will drink some, too, so you know that you can trust me."

He just looked at her and then he said, "I have always trusted you, Rebecca. Don't you remember that at all?" The Earl took the dipper and drank the mixture she had prepared for him. "I do not think you would poison me, Rebecca, but then you say you are not Rebecca. So what I would like to know now, my delicate fragile flower, is who are you? The expression on your face also tells me that you don't remember the little flower at all either, am I right, Rebecca?"

He was getting worried and if it took all night, he would get to know who she was and then maybe he could talk her back to him and the life she had shared with him for the past ten years. The first seven, she was a child and then the next two, they had courted. They had been married for a year now and he wanted her to remember that before the evening ended that day.

The taste of the drink was bitter, but he smiled at her, showing his trust in her in his glowing eyes. She watched him drink it and she was excited to think about how he would feel when the pain went away.

"Let me clean the wound for you. It needs to be stitched together. I am finding it hard to understand how you could carry on all your duties with an open wound on your body that really needs to be tended to immediately."

He could see the concern on her face. It made him have hope. But his next question might shatter it all. He had to think how to put this question to her and how to make sure she was not going to feel like he was putting her down. "What do you mean, Rebecca, when you say stitched up?"

The Earl had a vague notion what she meant, but the Rebecca he knew and loved fainted at the sight of blood. She was absolutely no good at all in a circumstance that required any kind of healing or curing of any kind of wound or illness. He had witnessed her faint on two different occasions and one was on a hunting trip. He had killed a wild boar and the blood was all over the ground where the boar had fallen. When he jumped off his mount to get his trophy, she was looking very pale to him. Then when he took out his knife to clean the animal for food for the castle, she had fallen off with no warning, not even a scream had come out of her mouth, just a thud. When he turned around at the sound, he saw her and rushed to her side. He picked her up only to have her open her eyes and look up at him and then faint again when she saw the blood on his hands.

He would never forget that, because that is when he discovered her fear of blood. After that, she never accompanied him on any kind of hunting trips again. He wanted her safe from her fears.

Now he was stunned and he had to let her do what she wanted, just to see if she could. It was very unnerving to hear her keep repeating that she was not Rebecca, when he knew that she was. Something was not right here, so he had to investigate deeper to find out what had happened to his Lady when she had been kidnapped.

He had been so lucky to get her back. But what was going on now was incomprehensible. He wanted and needed to know what had changed his Lady so much. Their life together was very important to him. He had discovered long ago that life without her was not worth living at all. Alone was not a word he cared for and his main object was to keep her safe and happy.

"Let me doctor you, please," she said in a soft sweet voice.

It almost sounded like his Rebecca again. She was becoming needy. That was how she always was before the kidnapping happened. But what did she mean by doctor?

"Go ahead, Rebecca."

"I told you that I am not Rebecca," she almost screamed at him.

This was not the Rebecca he knew, not at the moment anyway. "Okay. Please tell me who you are then," he said in a calm quiet manner, leaving her to stare at him like she did not know who he was at all.

"I want to, but I know what you will be thinking if I do. You must think I am a nut case already."

"Please tell me. What is a nut case?" he asked her very politely.

She smiled and then it occurred to her that the slang she liked had slipped out again. She told him, "A nut case is a person who is insane or crazy."

He blinked, but there was no recognition of these words on his face either. So she replied, "Please take care of your wound before it becomes infected and you wither up and die."

"Infected? Wither up?" he questioned.

This time she laughed out loud and moved over to where he stood and started to unbutton the strange closure on his tunic. She had heard tunic in the great hall, so she know she had the right word this time. He relaxed and asked no more from her. He would let her do whatever it was she wanted. This was a kind of experiment for him, for her to prove that she could care for this wound which had been open and bleeding and hurting him all day long. This was something he must see for himself.

She asked him to get her some very hot, boiling water, some white rags and any kind of medicinal healing herb he might have in the castle. He was astonished again because she knew that in his kitchen she had an herb garden and she grew all kinds of healing herbs. What he did not understand now was why she denied knowing these things.

He opened the door and sent Shively to gather these things. She also needed a needle and a strong thread. Needles he had. White cloth he could find. The herbs for healing were no problem either. Shively came back with all that she had asked for.

She tore the cloth into three pieces and took the hot water and fussed that it was not boiling. He had never heard anyone say the word boiling before. But he kept quiet. She asked for some kind of soap. The Earl sent for it and when it came, she washed the wound.

When she touched it, he realized that the pain had almost disappeared in his chest. He was shocked at first. Then he told her the pain had lessened and he wanted to know where she had gotten the white things she called aspirin.

Her laughter was such a happy sound. She told him that she would try to explain, but it was as hard for her to tell him as it was for him to hear it, because she was not sure what had happened here and she had to find out a little more before she accepted that fact that she might not be where she thought she was, that maybe the explanation might make him change his mind about her.

At this he shook his head and reassured her that nothing could ever stop him from loving her and wanting to protect her for the rest of their lifetime together.

Kelly was probing inside the deep cut and the blood was flowing freely. The Earl said not a word, but he watched her face and the way she chewed on her bottom lip. Rebecca had never done that before. He watched her eyes as she looked at the wound. While she was cleaning it, she muttered under her breath how she wished she had some antibiotics and a few band-aids to keep out the damaging germs. He still never opened his mouth. Whatever she was doing was something that his Rebecca could not have done.

He was very surprised when she had finished cleaning the wound that she had wiped the blood off the side of his body where it had run. Then she wanted to know which of the herbs she should use to keep out infection. He honestly did not know what infection was, so he asked her to explain exactly what she wanted the herb to do. Then he knew which one to give her. Together they worked out the problem of understanding each other's needs and all went well.

"I am very surprised that you can do these things, Rebecca, because you must remember that you were not even able to look at blood before," the Earl said to her.

"I am not Rebecca. Can you please call me Kelly?" she asked in a subdued voice. He listened to her request, but he was not sure that he could to what she asked.

"Why do you insist on being called Kelly?" he wanted to know.

"Because I am Kelly, and now we must get into a conversation where you are not going to be pleased with my answers. But you must admit that I am very different than your Rebecca, am I right?" she wanted to know. There seemed to be pleading in her expression and in her eyes.

"I am ready to hear whatever it is that you want me to hear. But I cannot make myself call you Kelly. Surely you must know if I do that, everyone in the castle will think that there is something wrong with me." He tried to make her see the problem that it would cause.

She did see the rumble that it would cause in the castle with the servants and the guards. So she decided to compromise. "Okay, here goes. I will pretend to be your Rebecca, but you need to remember that I am not her. You will treat me as if everything is the same and I will do the same for you. But we both will know that it is not." Her commands were heard.

"You have yet to prove anything to me. It is very hard sitting here and looking at my dear wife and have her tell me that she is not the same person. I do not understand this at all. And while we are talking, I think I will need another of your aspirins when my pain comes back. Now that you have cleaned my wound and not become faint at all, I must admit that there is something different here. What are you going to do now that you have it all cleaned and have placed herbs inside the gaping hole?" he asked her. It appeared that he had come to terms with her name now.

"I am going to sew you up. It is going to hurt very badly, so I want Shively to get me a piece of leather to put between your teeth to bite on when the pain is unbearable," she told him.

"My dear, there has not been a pain that would make me cry out that I can remember in my whole life span. I will be able to withstand whatever I must to get this healed. You may start now. I have asked Shively to bring Yarrow Root for you to put inside the wound. It is healing and will begin to make me whole again within hours of the stitching, my dear."

She listened, but she was not sure that she should put anything in that big hole. She wanted to sew him up first and then rub it on the outside of the wound, but he would not hear of it. So she began to sew him up.

It was very hard to pierce his tender, red, blotched skin on his chest, but she pushed the needle through and kept going until it looked like it would heal without even a slight scar. She had made about twenty stitches, tiny ones, and then she rubbed more Yarrow Root on the outside as well as she had on the inside. She only prayed that it was the right herb and that he wouldn't die, because then they would burn her as a witch at the stake. She had visions of it happening to her. She had a chill. When she opened her eyes, he was still there watching her facial features as they contorted with each horrible thought she had had.

Her Earl leaned back in the big chair. He looked very calm, but she knew he was no such thing. She knew it had to hurt, but he had made not a sound. It occurred to her that she had just thought of him as "her Earl." What a stupid thing she thought mentally. He is not "my Earl." Then she wondered if he had another name, besides The Earl.

"Sir, can you tell me what your name really is?" she asked him. "I have never heard anyone call you anything but The Earl."

"My name should be on your lips and in your heart and I find it hard to believe that you cannot remember my name. I have always been called Jamie by you since you were a child, my dear." He watched her expression. It was not recognizable to him at that moment. She asked if she could call him Jamie and he told her of course, that she had always called him that in the privacy of their chambers. She smiled at that. Somewhere in the back of her mind, she could almost see her as a child running after a boy and calling out, "Wait for me, Jamie." But then it faded.

She had seen it on TV many times and she knew he would die from some strange ailment if she did not help him. She wanted to know how long he would have gone without having it seen to. She asked him, "Sir, when were you going to get this taken care of? If you had waited and not let me see it, you might have died from an infection," she told him quite matter of factly.

"I have been more concerned about you and I had not had time to see to it yet. I would have, of course, had it cleaned and taken care of. I had not had time yet to see to it. You are foremost on my mind these days, my Lady."

She had yet another surprise to show him, so she attacked quickly while he was so at ease finally.

Her key chain had been in her back pocket. She pulled it out to show him. He was amazed at the thing. She told him what it was for. "This is my key to my flat where I live with Arthur. This is the key to the car. And this is the key to my safety deposit box in the bank." She handed it to him. He turned it over and over and then he asked her what was the thing around the keys. They had plastic covers on the end of each one. She told him it was plastic and that it let her know which key fit which lock.

He was studying them and then she took the attention from the keys and held up a piece of paper that was in her front pocket, also. It was her library card and it had her name on it. "Look," she said, pointing to the name. "Kelly Kirk. That's me. That is who I am. Not Rebecca."

She waited for his response and when he spoke, he was clearly disturbed. "Let me hold it," he said. She handed it to him. He asked her, "What is a library card?"

She thought for a minute, but when she started to try and tell him, he spoke up first. "I have an extensive library here with five hundred or more books, but why would I need a library card?"

To tell the truth, it was a good question. So she answered it to the best of her ability, considering her position here.

"In my time, we have libraries with millions of books and people borrow them to read and then bring them back. You have to have a library card to get in and out with the books you want to read. Can you understand now?" she asked him. Probing his eyes did her no good, either. She did not know if he understood or not.

"It seems so odd to me, but I will think on it. And plastic, what is that made of?"

She could not answer that one. So she casually said, "I don't know the answer there, Jamie."

"Where do you mean? You said there. Where is there?" More confused now than ever she tried to get him to go to bed.

She thought that tomorrow was soon enough for these questions. She was tired, too. And he had to be exhausted. "In the morning we can talk more. But I am really from two thousand and six, Jamie."

The Earl loved hearing her call him Jamie again. There was just one thing that was not right yet. Her spoken word was different. She sounded like she was from another place.

She spoke with a strange accent now. He had a lot to think on and so he bid her goodnight and thanked her for the healing she had performed on his chest and shoulder.

Jamie stood up and asked her leave of his presence.

"Jamie, I need to ask you a favor if you will listen. It is something I need to do around here to feel like I am at home again."

"May I ask what you mean? What is a favor, Rebecca? I do not recall hearing that word before."

"I need you to let me change something that has become hard for me to bear."

"Whatever you need," he replied to her statement.

"May I give Matilda permission to call me Kelly?"

The Earl cleared his throat and before he spoke she grinned from ear to ear. "I'm so sorry. I meant to ask you if Matilda could begin to call me Rebecca. It will make things better for me, I think," she answered his questioned expression.

"But I don't know a Kelly. I only know Rebecca and that is who you are, to me that is," he replied. "Can you please try to remember your name in the presence of the castle servants, Rebecca? It is very important to keep up the continuity that you had before you were kidnapped and if you really believe you are someone else, I will try to understand, but they would have you burned at the stake as a witch. And I could do nothing to help you at all."

"Yes, I will give Matilda a command to call you Mistress Rebecca. But it is very improper for the servant to call a Lady by her first name. And Matilda may find it hard to do this. It is very hard to change the way a servant thinks. You must always have the control of the household servants, my Lady," he answered her finally.

Kelly felt a shiver run all over her body. "But I have proved to you that I am not Rebecca. You saw my nail clippers. You saw the aspirins and you told me they worked on your pain. What else can I do to prove to you who I am?" She was really frustrated now. She wanted him to know who she was and she wanted his help to go home. How was she ever going to get home if he did not believe her and would not help her? The problem was still there and the doubt had been planted in his head. Kelly decided to let him think on it and approach the time switch tomorrow. She heard him going down the turret steps one at a time, like he was thinking on what had just transpired between the two of them.

Kelly was so tired and the high bed looked so inviting to her. Her fingers were aching and she looked at the cut. It was deep and it had a red streak running up towards her wrist. She was scared now. This was all she needed, a case of blood poisoning in whatever year he had told her it was. She decided to go to bed and worry about it in the morning.

She had a secret silent hope that she would wake up in her bed with Arthur and she has just been dreaming all along. But now she thought that if this was a dream, it was a detailed, vibrant motion picture of a dream. With sound, touch, smell and taste and all included in Technicolor vision and stereo sound.

She laughed as the door opened and Matilda came in to dress her for sleep. This still was bothering her so she told Matilda that she could leave and that she would dress herself. The shocked look on her face made Kelly think and then she said, "Maybe I do need you after all. I don't feel too well tonight." She showed Matilda her finger and the maid went into a lecture about how she needed to get some salve for her. She then raced out the door for the kitchen and the herbs that she needed.

"God," Kelly said out loud. "Please let me wake up and be home. I'm getting tired of all this medieval stuff."

Matilda came right back and dressed Kelly's whole hand and then dressed her and brushed her hair. Kelly thought it was a good thing her hair was long, because if she had a popular bobbed hairstyle, Matilda and everyone else in the castle would have gone mad trying to figure it out.

Matilda twisted it up and tied a beautiful silk streaming ribbon around it and she looked good.

Chapter Seventeen

She was running down a steep bank. The wind was blowing through her hair. The mist off the sea was blowing through the air and her hair felt wet. The salt smell off the ocean was everywhere. Behind her, she heard someone calling to her. She was laughing and running so hard that she did not see the clump of rocks ahead of her until she tripped and fell, rolling towards the sea. Footsteps were behind her and a man yelled, "Rebecca, are you okay? I'm coming. Hold on."

He fell over the rocks, too. They landed face up laying in the pebbles at the edge of the water with the waves rolling in right on them. When she looked up again, she saw Jamie and he was covered with sand and water. She reached out her sandy hand and they got up and shook off what they could and then they both laughed so hard that they had to hold onto each other to keep from falling down again. It was hard to keep their footing in the wet sand, but they finally got back to the top of the embankment where all this started.

Jamie wanted to take her back to the castle where her parents could make sure she was not hurt in any way, but she wanted to play with Jamie and refused to go back. So they raced to the stables where he sneaked in and got a feed sack for her and one for him. There was no one in the stables so they climbed up to the straw and hay and laid down the sacks and huddled together for warmth. Just to be together made Rebecca and Jamie so happy. They were holding each other when she heard horses coming up the path towards the barn. She grabbed Jamie and said, "What if they find us here." Jamie had the same thought, but he answered her in a way that she forgot to be frightened. "No one saw us come in here and no one will see us leave. But we have to be quiet and wait for dark. I hope your father isn't missing you yet."

"I told him that I was going to the beach to collect shells so he knows where I was going. But if he looks for me, he will be very mad if he cannot find me," Rebecca said.

They got dry and when dark started to fall, they went out in the evening air and hurried back to the castle. Sight unseen, they crawled under the gates that had been dropped down for the safety of the castle folk. The guards were on the battlements so they had to be careful not to be seen. Jamie knew where there was a crevice that he and the other boys had used to get in and out of the castle after sword practice each evening. They crawled under it and were safe. When they saw her father coming towards them, they acted like they had been grooming the horses. Her father was grumpy and they could see it in his face.

"And where might I ask you have you both been all afternoon? Your mother is furious and you are not to go out of the castle again without a guard beside you all the way. If you disobey her again, you will be punished. You will be made to sit in the solarium and do needlepoint until your fingers fall off. Do you understand this warning from your

Lady Mother?" he asked her with a fury she had not seen before.

"Yes sir. I told her I was going swimming and she said I could go. I took Jamie with me for a guard. Why am I in trouble?"

"It is dark and we thought you would return earlier. We sent a search party out to find you and they came back with no knowledge of where you might have gone. Did it not occur to you to come back in a timely manner, Lassie? Now you have to go to your Lady Mother and explain yourself to her, not me. And as for you, Jamie, what do you think you are doing keeping my daughter out until the sun sets and no one can find either of you? Have you an answer for me, Lad?" he asked in his Scottish bur that had attracted his daughter's attention since she was a tiny lass. She could sound just like her father when she had the notion, too. He had always felt partial to her because she was so beautiful and looked like his Lady wife. They were comparable to a sunset and fresh breath of air. His family meant everything to him and his daughter would not be sneaking off with the young knight anymore.

Rebecca had begun to weep and her eyes told him that he had hit the mark. She was chasing after the young laird, but her Lady Mother would not allow this anymore when he told her what he had seen when he found them together this evening, so happy and smiling up at each other. She began to cry.

She was thrashing around on her big bed. She was moaning and crying out openly. Where was Jamie? Where had they taken him? She wanted him and she could not find him.

Matilda came rushing into the room. Kelly felt rather than heard her calling her to wake up. She opened her eyes and then she realized what was wrong. She had been dreaming and she was so sad. She had lost Jamie.

"Oh, my word!" she said to Matilda. "I'm so sorry. I guess I had a nightmare."

Matilda looked at her and asked the question that Kelly had known was coming. "My Lady, what is a nightmare? I might not have heard you correctly, but I thought you said you had a nightmare."

"I had a bad dream," she told Matilda. Her maid didn't get it, but she let go of it and tried to make her Lady comfortable again. She tucked her and fluffed her furs all around her and then she gave her a small drink of cool water and left her to sleep.

Matilda did not know what was going on. These new words she kept speaking to all of them made her very nervous. She saw the Earl's face when she said words they did not understand and she was worried that something had happened to her when she was missing and her Lady was not ready to talk about it yet.

The dream had her on edge. It seemed so real. She could feel and could smell it. Where had the dream come from anyway? Her past? What past? She was who she was. She might not know what was going on right this minute, but one thing she was sure about was that this was a real castle and she was trapped inside with people who thought they were living in the year sixteen hundred.

There was no way to explain to her maid. So she just got quiet like she was sleepy. Her mind wandered back to the dream and she let herself go back to the place where the handsome man had been a young man and they had just been caught sneaking back into the castle after dark.

"Let's get together now and work on this tapestry. It has many angles and I want to show you a new stitch," Rebecca's mother spoke in a stern voice. Rebecca hated needlepoint and all that fancy lace tatting her mother's ladies taught her. She was never any good at it. Kelly was worse. She had been trying to get outside the castle all day long and no one would find her mother so she could get what she wanted. She wanted to meet Jamie to see the summer solstice. They had planned all week long to sneak out when the parents went to the ritual.

Everyone had been talking about the summer solstice. They knew it was coming and all the grownups would be planning their night at the fires, so she thought that Jamie could take her, too. They watched the servants gathering wood for the fires for a week now. It was a splendid thing and they intended to see it this year.

No one needed to know where they were going today at dusk.

What fun, she thought. Jamie might even kiss her again. Those kisses had been so exciting. He fumbled and she was scared, but they soon found the ecstasy in the stolen moment.

They were bound together. She knew she wanted to have Jamie forever and he loved her so much that it was all the talk around the sword activity each day. The young men laughed and joked and called him a knight in love and when he was thrusting that sword at them, they had to be on guard, because he went after them with no sympathy at all. Jamie was the best swordsman out of all of them. It just made him better and he knew that they were jealous of him.

The sun was going down. Everyone in the castle was out on the hill west of the castle and the fires were roaring. Rebecca saw her mother and father holding hands down by the fire. They were gazing into each other's eyes and Rebecca knew that was what she wanted when she was betrothed. A man who loved her mightily. A man who looked at her the way her father looked at his Lady.

Her heart swelled from the look in Jamie's eyes and she knew he was the one. He took her hand and took her away from the erotic scene in front of them. He did not want her to see the lust and sex that would come next. The dancing had already started and so he said, "Let's go beyond the tree lines and I can hold you and we can dance the dance of mating."

She smiled and they walked away. No one saw them go. No one expected them to be outside the castle gates at this time of night.

Jamie took her and they danced the dance of soul mates. Their souls joined together as the stars watched from above as the two young people moved in motion to the universe.

Chapter Eighteen

"Let me help her."

She heard the masculine voice coming from somewhere near her. Kelly opened her eyes and there he stood. Jamie. The same one she had been dreaming about all night long. She looked at him and smiled.

"What's all the fuss?" she questioned her maid. "I am awake and I guess I'm still here, right?" She was hoping that she was dreaming. But by now, she had begun to know that what she was living through each day was much too long to be a dream. And she was getting used to the world without a bathroom, no newspaper and no pizza.

She stretched her arms and then she felt the pain in her hand.

"What is the matter? All of you look like I have died and been brought back to life again." She murmured under her breath, "I wish I had a bacon cheese biscuit and three hash browns."

"What, My Lady?" the Earl asked her. "What were you asking for? I will certainly get it for you in haste, My Lady."

Oops! I did it again she told herself. "Oh, Jamie, I was just mumbling. I don't know why I'm still abed this day." She thought she was talking strangely. Her brain told her

125

not to get too much into their language because when she did wake up or whatever happened, she did not want to be home and speaking like a lady from the seventeenth century. Even if she did believe now that she was truly there.

Her hand hurt and Matilda had said her body was hot to the touch.

"Do I have a fever?" she asked in a hushed voice. "If I do, then give me the aspirins, Jamie."

He looked at the maid and he noticed that she was looking bewildered by the things Rebecca was saying. "Please keep quiet, Rebecca, and I will take care of it for you when Matilda leaves us."

"Okay, you blond hunk of a man." It came out before she could stop it.

Matilda said, "What is a hunk, My Lady?"

All at once, Kelly knew she must have a high temperature and that her mouth was speaking and her mind came in to help too late.

"Matilda, please leave us alone for a minute because there is something I need to ask the Earl."

Matilda curtsied and left them alone.

"I'm sorry, Jamie, but it comes out and I forget to smother all the things that I knew in my time and it is so hard to remember that I can't talk freely like I always did before I woke up here."

He said that it was all right, but that Matilda might talk at night to the other staff and he wanted her to know how dangerous it could be to her life.

"Let me see your hand, Rebecca," he said as he reached out for her hand. When he touched her, she felt it again, electricity all through her body.

"Did you feel that, Jamie?"

He looked at her and said, "Yes, but I always did feel the pull of your nature to me since we were children, Rebecca. Do not tell me that you had forgotten the love that we shared, because I could not bear it. I will always feel it and throughout eternity it will remain. You and I belong together. Why do you look so surprised? The gods on the summer solstice matched us and we have always felt rather than shared the intense binding between us. When we were young and determined to be together, we first felt it. We have always known this, Rebecca."

She looked into those blue eyes and she knew from her dream that she did indeed know it. She may not have always known it, but she knew she did now.

"I need two aspirins, Jamie."

He went to her blue jean pocket where he had seen her get them before and handed them to her.

"You know, the cloth of those pants as you call them is not something I have ever seen before, Rebecca. I have no answer as to where they came from, but I am trying to take our story into my mind and I do know that the aspirins made the pain leave my body. Now I have another question for you. What are the metals in pants? And I also want to know why you had on men's clothing when you were found."

"Jamie, those are blue jeans and where I come from, all women wear them everyday. The metals are how we keep them closed. It is called a zipper. Bring yourself over here and let me show you."

He did and when she pulled the zipper up and down a few times, his expression changed. He said, "I do not know how this works and I have never seen anything like it before, but I admit to you that you are certainly different now that you are back."

"I am different because, although I resemble Rebecca, I am not her. I am Kelly. I seem to know a lot about us. I don't know how to explain it, but I feel the essence of us in my heart and, although I am as puzzled about this transformation as you must be, I will try my best to make it fit me. Until you admit that I am not Rebecca. Then when you do, I must ask you to please help me return to my time some day. Is this too much to ask? She waited a moment to let this question sink in and then said, "Jamie, I need to go home some day."

He did not know what to say, but in his heart he knew there was something different about this woman. "How do I do this aspirin?" he asked her.

"Please get me some water and make sure it is from the water I had boiled just for me," she told him. "I must always have my food cooked very well done and my water boiled."

He nodded his head and went to the door and told the maid to fetch his Lady some cool water from the batch she had boiled for herself, and not to forget it ever. She shook her head and started down the turret stairs.

"My Lady, I am boiling sage leaves, marigolds and a small amount of basil for your wound. I will sew it into a bag and you will place it on your wound. First I will apply some of the potion on your finger and then you must do the rest."

Kelly knew the herbs were all she had. It was a scary thing. Her fever went down and her finger healed nicely. She was ever thankful. Her husband had come in and seated himself by her bedside.

"Let me see how you are doing today." His smile told her all.

"Can we talk about my going home?" she asked him.

He did not speak. He just lowered his head and she knew he was not ready for this yet. "My Lady, I have no idea how to perform such a task. Do you know how we can approach this?"

Kelly had not really thought about it too much and now she was at a loss for words. She did not remember how she got here.

"Can we take a walk down to the door in the castle wall where the gardens are located?" she asked.

"Why, yes Ma'am, we can, but what is it you want to accomplish there, my Lady?"

"The last thing I remember is falling in the passageway. That is where I hurt my hand, Jamie. That must be the passage between my world and yours," she told him.

"Tomorrow when you eat your food to break your fast, I will certainly take you down there. I think you might be sorely disappointed." He was praying that he was right in believing that there was nothing there but a secret door that they had sealed up a few years ago.

"Tell me about this so called world you talk about so much. I would like to know more, if you please."

She had known this would come and she had also known that he would not understand anything she could tell him. She promised him that tomorrow before she went back that she would share her world with him. Tonight, she was to join him back in his chambers. When he first mentioned this to her, she was not sure she could do this. She had never been with another man before Arthur. Her thoughts went immediately to poor Arthur. She worried about her disappearance and his reaction to her being gone. But here she was and she must stay until she figured out what to do.

Chapter Nineteen

He had eaten beside her and then he had dismissed the jester and took her hand, she knew she was about to share the night with Jamie.

In his chambers, she had her maid there to finish her hair and dress her for The Earl's pleasure. Kelly was taking it all in and her acting tonight must be perfect.

"That will be all we require tonight, Matilda," the Earl said as he escorted her to the outer chamber where she went to her room.

The huge bed reminded Kelly about the king size ones at home. But this one had been handmade and it had been in this castle for over one hundred years. The steps leading up to the bed were hand carved and looked like solid cherry.

"My Lady, let me help you into our bed. Tonight we have a lot to share. History being one and loving you until the sun arises in the east. Let me take your night dress for you."

She let him take the thing she had been assuming was a bath robe and her body had been cleaned by Matilda earlier in the evening, just for her first night back in his bed.

"Do you not remember what you told me the day of our wedding? Until the sun arises in the east."

She thought about it and it sure sounded like something she had heard before. Maybe she did say it four hundred years ago. She laughed out loud.

"What is so funny, Rebecca?" he asked while watching her face.

She took a chance and said, "I wish we could have a pepperoni pizza tonight, my Lord."

He knew it was a joke, but he had no idea what she had meant by the word pepperoni. "Please do explain, Rebecca. Let me laugh with you as we always did before this terrible kidnapping happened to us."

She said, "I used to eat four pizzas a week in my time, Jamie. I would like for you to taste one, but I do not k now what the spices were and you probably have never heard of them in this time. So you are sure out of luck as far as the pizza goes, but for the rest of the night, I might have a few tricks to show you." Please remember that I am not the Rebecca you once knew," she reminded him before she took him into her arms and kissed the blue eyed man of her dreams from the night before.

Their lips fit together like jam and bread. Her heart was beating fast and she knew every part of this man like she had known him before tonight. They shared their bodies and they shared hearts. He held her and she knew she had been there before, in those arms and in love. He lay beside her and he told her his feelings. She felt his heart beat as he made love to her. She shared the same intimate inner beating of her heart. Together they reached the stars and back again. When he said her name, he knew in his world that she was not the same woman he had married and he also knew he would accept her and take her as Rebecca, if she would let him. He would ask no more questions.

He knew what he wanted and he knew where she was, in his arms where she belonged forever. His next sane thought was how to accomplish this and keep her happy. He wanted to know what her heart said now. He wanted her to tell him that she no longer wanted to go home, but that she would rather stay here with him. He wanted to hear her say that she loved him and she longed to remain here and to never hear her say another word about the strange world where she said she came from. To tell the truth, he wanted to tell her he really did believe her, but he was afraid to mention it again.

He knew that her absence would leave a hole he could never begin to fill. How could he ever lose her now? The words hurt him and she felt it in the way his body tensed up all of a sudden.

"What is wrong, Jamie?" she tenderly asked him. She leaned up on his chest and saw tears in the big man's eyes.

"I don't want to let tonight end," he replied.

"Jamie, you must know now that the Rebecca you once knew never acted like I did tonight. That had to be the proof you needed to understand that although I do not understand what happened or why I am here, I am not your Rebecca. I want to be, but it is not like I can choose. What I need is to figure out how to get back to my time. But if I can't, you know I will be forever happy to be your Rebecca from Sunnybrook Farm," she giggled.

"Sunnybrook Farm?" he asked. "Where is Sunnybrook Farm?" She could tell that he was thinking hard. "I have no recollection of anywhere with that particular name, Rebecca."

He was still thinking. He started to scratch the back of his neck, which was a sure sign that he had lost her subject line again. Kelly was about to die. She stifled her amusement and then she told him where Sunnybrook Farm might be found. Jamie was waiting to hear.

"It is a book I read when I was very young. It is no place really, just a made up name from my time."

"Okay, I see another one of your, what did you call them?" he said while scratching the back of his neck again. "Oh, I remember. You call it a joke," he said. Finally, he laughed with her. "We won't be looking for that place today, will we?" he asked her with that dimple on his chin popping out. It had been one of the things that she had liked about his face. He was very handsome and the dimple had set a look about him that she would never forget. "Let's go," he said to her and reached out his hand to help her up from the breakfast table.

"Oh and where are we about to go today?" she asked.

"Only to see the side door in the east wall of the castle. Do you really not remember where it went to, Rebecca? Think hard. We used to run there and go down to the beach through the long tunnel that was used for pirating in the days of old. It was our secret hideaway. There is a room carved out in one of the wider spots. That is where our fathers found chests of gold when they were young. We would take blankets and bread and cheese and go there with a bottle of wine from the dungeons. It was our secret. There was even a hole in the top of the cave and we would burn wood sometimes, but only when our fathers were out hunting. Do you remember any of that story yet?"

In her mind she knew that had to be the reason she was drawn there in the first place. She closed her eyes and she saw them running hand in hand through the dark confined walls that were wet and slippery as they were still today. She could actually feel the moisture in the air in her lungs. She could hear him calling to her to come back, the same sound she had heard before. Kelly wanted to know more.

"Do you think I can go back home if I walk in here again?" she asked Jamie.

"I pray to heaven above that you won't leave me again, Rebecca," he said and she saw the start of tears in both eyes as he spoke to her. He was begging her not to leave. "You see, I have missed you so and now that you are back, I cannot bear to go through that again. Please think about it and then make the decision." He spoke so solemnly to her.

"But I know that you know I am not the Rebecca you want. Surely you have not forgotten last night already," she said to Jamie. "You know that I am not her."

"I don't know what to think. I know you act differently and talk differently and you even smell differently, but I don't know how I can possibly let you go, because I have enough of her in you and enough of you in her. When I put it together, I only know that I want you. Whoever you are. If you are really Kelly, I will accept that and never mention it again. If you are not, I will not question you about what happened to you on the kidnapping again, ever. Just please do not leave me again, Rebecca or Kelly, whatever you want me to call you now. We have been together since we were children. I cannot ever forget or think all those years are gone."

He looked so helpless. The great big blond hunk of a man standing in front of her could whip an army, but he could not face letting her go. She felt the pull and she felt the joy and the love, but she was a two thousand and six girl, just beginning her life. So she made a decision. It was not going to be easy. As of right now, she knew it would be difficult to say the least. What will I do she asked herself. Jamie was standing there waiting. He had straightened up his stance and, although he was very confused, he was a man and a great warrior, so he had to be strong for himself. The well-being of every person in the castle depended on his good judgment and his common sense.

"Jamie, let's go back now. I am not sure that I want to go home just yet. But I will only need tonight and then tomorrow I will do whatever I have to do to make sense out of this experience I have been thrown into."

"Here, take my hand and let me help you out of the doorway. Watch out for the spiders and such as they tend to run in whenever the door is opened."

He stepped out into the sunlight. He remembered closing this door and it was right after the summer solstice last year. He never thought that they would want to open it again. Their life was perfect. Married and happy as they were, it made no sense to him to leave it open. And now everything was wrong. Rebecca was not Rebecca. Kelly was here, but who was Kelly? What a mess, he thought as he walked her to the castle.

Chapter Twenty

Had she waited for him? Had this all been planned a long time ago? Kelly had sent word to Jamie that she would meet him on the battlements after the noon meal. She had decided to take a long needed walk and think about this situation, to think about the consequences if she never returned to her world, to Arthur, to her mother and her father. To central heat! At that thought, she laughed so loud that Jamie heard her as he was climbing the wall turret to get to her. He burst out on the walkway to her.

"What are you laughing about now?" Jamie questioned her and her mood.

"I was thinking that if I don't try to go back where I came from that I might just freeze to death when the winter winds come and winter sets in here." She was still laughing.

"How do you keep warm in your time, my love?" he asked Kelly. His curiosity was growing.

"Well, you see. We have central heat and there are vents all through the home in each room. The furnace is in the basement and blows air over red hot coils and the warm air then goes directly to the whole house." Her eyes told him she was waiting for the next question.

He stood silent for a moment then he asked her three questions at once. "We have central heat, too. The massive fireplace in the great hall heats us all just fine," he told her. "Now the word vents leaves me thinking and I come to you for the answer to that one and to this question. How do red hot coals float in the air like you said?"

"Jamie, I am not laughing at you, but I said coils, not coals. Coils are pieces of wire and I am not smart enough to explain it. Vents are holes in the floor or ceiling where the fan blows the warmed air to all parts of the home."

She watched his face for a reaction to this answer, but he just looked at her and shook his head. "Actually you have vents of a kind in the castle ramparts and you told me that was where you shoot arrows when you are under siege. Vents are small openings and now I see that you are not so far behind in some things, but we don't have sieges and battles in my time. We all live in peace, except for the holy wars and the wars when a president had to declare war on another country to keep our peace in the United States of America."

On top of the old castle, she felt at home. She had made friends, of a kind. She wanted to stay here.

"Please tell me what you would wish for if you could have anything you wanted," Jamie said to her in a hushed voice, as if he was afraid to hear her answer. He moved closer to her and took her in his arms.

She felt complete and wanted, as she had never felt before, not with Arthur or even her parents. She shuddered to think that this might be where she needed to be now. And the castle had pierced her heart with love. The tall old building looked so different from where she had disappeared that morning. Now it felt like so long ago that she was in her time. Maybe a week had gone by here in her dream. She was not even thinking about dreams anymore and she wanted it to be real. She was so surprised at herself to even think such irrational thoughts. Decisions had to be made, and soon. Her fears that her parents were hurting and that Arthur might think she had run away were so hard to bear. But leaving here was even harder. The thought of going back hurt her so badly now. What hold did this place have on her? What secrets were waiting to be revealed to her?

"I waited for you. I will always be waiting for you. I have spent my whole life loving you and even if you are not who you say you are, even then I will wait. I will wait for an eternity if I must for you to remember all that we meant to each other. Can you remember our wedding, Rebecca?" He spoke as if in pain to her questioning eyes. "Can you remember the beautiful dress that your Lady Mother made for you? This is something that I find hard to understand, Rebecca. I cannot picture you any other way. I can't imagine why you talk the way you do now. I can't see you any other way, just the Lady Rebecca that I have always loved." His pain was visible to her. He was hurting and he was trying so hard to make her see that everything that had happened was real to him.

"If I could make a wish and it would come true, I would wish for the truth. The truth in where I belong. The truth in who I am and who you are. The truth in the walls of this castle. The truth is what I need. Why I am here. How I got here. Why you call me Rebecca. And let me tell you that if we did not have this relationship and I did not feel love for you, I would not work so hard to try to help us understand all this. But how could I feel love for a man I can't remember? I was married not so long ago in England to a wonderful man and his name is Arthur. When you asked me if I remembered my wedding dress, I felt faint. My heart was beating so hard. Because when I married Arthur, I found a wedding dress in an antique shop and when I saw it, it pulled me in the shop. I bought it and from that day on, I had visions of the gown and I saw it in a different style. It had been changed and altered. It was old, too. But I loved it so much. It meant something to me and I did not know why."

"Let me take you to the round room and show you the day we were married. Your dress is hanging in your wardrobe right now. Let's go see it. Together we can make this wish come true." He wanted so much to help her to remember. But as every day went by, she was remembering two worlds, two men and now two weddings.

Their wedding day had been captured on canvas. The painter was marvelous. The painting was so beautiful that she could not contain her enthusiasm.

"Oh, Jamie! Is this us?" she asked him as she stared at the two people in the painting. At the moment, all she could see was the wedding dress. Her eyes were huge as her mind raced with memories. It was the same dress that she had married Arthur in. They were outside and the day a sunny day. There were flowers in all the gardens and the two people standing by the rose garden looking into each other's eyes were so happy. She saw dogs lying around the table and she saw another picture of the bride and groom by a huge cake.

"Why on earth did we have such a big cake?" The picture was much smaller and the only other painting hanging in this room.

"Do you remember the custom of being able to kiss over the cake on the wedding day?" Jamie asked and then waited for her to answer the question. "The bride and groom reach across it and try to not disturb it." She had made sure the cake was large for the guests and sure that she could reach over it and kiss her new husband. She had spent hours making the cake with her mother. Jamie could not understand how she could not remember this day, but her wedding dress she remembered.

The second painting had the two people with a blue piece of fabric on their arms. "What was the blue band for, Jamie?" she asked. It looked out of place to her.

"The new bride and her husband wore them as symbols of faithfulness," Jamie told her. He was shocked and saddened by her questions. His mental state right then was not proving to be very good. He wanted her to remember, but she didn't seem to be able to admit that she could.

"What custom did you mean about the cake?" Kelly asked him.

"We were to be able to kiss over the cake and not move it from its position. The larger the cake, the more fun the couple had trying not to move it from its pedestal." He watched her face. He watched her movements and her eyes for some kind of remembrance. There was none. But Jamie was sure he could make her remember something about this day. So he kept on trying. The wedding dress had brought back her memory, so he went back to the dress.

"Tell me what you remember about the dress, Rebecca."

She opened her eyes wide as memories came to her. "I had a beautiful blue sapphire for a wedding gift from you, didn't I?" Kelly asked.

"Oh, thank the Good Lord above and yes, my dear. I gave it to you. It was a necklace with a large stone surrounded by smaller ones. It is in your jewelry collection in our rooms. Do you want me to go get it for you?" Jamie wanted to know.

Kelly could see it. In her mind, she saw him reaching around her to fasten the unusually large clasp he had had put on it for safekeeping. "Yes, I do remember it. Please take me to see it again, Jamie," she said. "I need to feel it and put it on. I feel like it is the key to my remembering."

Together they went up the castle's stone stairs until they came to their rooms. Jamie went in and went straight to the wall with the book case on it and fingered around the left side of it until it opened. She saw her first real secret passageway, a real secret opening in a real castle. She stepped back. Jamie went behind the open door as she watched him. He turned around and came back with a large wooden box in his hands. It was made out of mahogany and was a deep brown polished treasure box.

"What is that you have in your hands?" she asked him.

"It is your jewels that we protect from thievery. When I showed you this room so long ago and we opened the secret passageway together, we decided to keep your jewelry here. No one knows about this room but the two of us. Look here," he said as he pulled out a bunch of dried flowers. These were in your bouquet. You put in herbs for fertility and love. It was your own herbs that you grew outside the garden walls." He waited to see if she remembered.

The wedding gown was hanging in the wardrobe. She opened the door and took it down. It had been sealed inside a cedar cloth bag. She knew it was the wedding dress, but she had no idea how she knew it was in there. She laid it on the bed and unlaced the stitches that someone had put in the cloth to seal it up. Stitch after stitch, she pulled the silken thread out. Finally she saw it. The way it should have been. Not the way she saw it on her wedding day to Arthur, but the way it was in this time, beige and lace and handmade flowers, tiny flowers, mini flowers. A train to make you die for, twenty feet of train, trailing down from the neck line and sewn on the inside with tiny stitches the naked eye could barely see.

The arms had puffs on each shoulder going down to stitching she had never seen before on the elbows, going all around the elbow and down the arm to the wrist where they had sewn on white pieces of rice. She guessed it was rice because she did not have a clue to what else it could be. In the front, it had ribbons running down the side seams and more fancy stitching on the bodice. The fabric was silk and the colors were beige and white and pale yellow with gold thread in the collar where it went up to the hairline in the back of the dress. Gold threads went down the arms and down to the end of the train. It had changed through the years because she had seen first hand what time could do to a beautiful antique wedding dress.

The handmade gown made her cry. Her tears were falling and he wanted to comfort her. He took off his sword, which he never went without, and reached her side in two strides. He picked her up and carried her to the side of the bed where he laid her down. He lay down beside her and tried to comfort her.

She told him again about finding it in the antique shop. This time she knew why she had wanted it so badly. It had belonged to her in another time. But she had no memory of that time. Now, thanks to whatever fate had in store for her, she knew a lot more. She turned towards him and held him tightly so he could never get away again.

Jamie could feel the closeness this time. His heart was beating slow and easy. He felt her returning to him little by little. He was sure that if she gave herself time, she would remember everything. He was content and he was happy. His fears were almost gone. He had a feeling that time would bring it all back to them.

"On the morrow, I want to take you to the fair outside the castle grounds. I want to buy you some trinket from the fair and it will be a reminder that you were here and are here now. Let's forget about the time thing. Can we do that?"

"I hope we can," she said as she pulled his arms tighter around her body.

The castle stood atop the hill. Waiting, she stood outside hearing the sound of old ghosts and spirits in the air. She had seen the ruins in her time, but what she saw today was not ruins. It was a great fortress standing tall and proud over the lands. Waiting. Waiting. The whispers of fairies and the memories seeping into her brain. How could she ever leave it? The castle she visited was never so vibrant, never so charming, never so real. Her schooldays of history books about castles could not compare to this. How could she ever leave? She knew now that she would never, ever leave.

Chapter Twenty-One

The morning came with the sea breezes blowing the tapestry hanging in the slit Kelly called a window. Lying in Jamie's arms, she held on tight so he would know her intentions were in his favor. She was remembering last night. They had made love until they both fell asleep in each other's arms. He was so attentive to her every need. She was new to this kind of sexual intimacy. She had only been married a few weeks and she had had no experiences with sex before Arthur. Her time with Jamie was a revelation to her. He had such deep rooted feelings for her that she felt them in his every touch and in his kiss, which was different from Arthur.

He knew her and that knowing fact made it hard for Kelly to not love him back. She felt the touch of lightning when he made love to her. She felt the beat of his heart. She saw the stars and the sky light up with his touch. There simply had to be more to this than a trip back in time could provide.

Her whole body was on fire for Jamie. Her brain screamed out his name to her. Her body remembered his touch. She knew that it had happened to her before, but it was not Arthur that had given her these feelings. It had to have been Jamie and it had to have been in another time. Her face was in the painting. Her portrait was in the great big hall, hanging as if she had always been there. She knew this was wrong, but how could you prove it to these people?

Kelly leaned over to kiss his lips a hundred more times before the morning got away from them in a flurry of food and servants, and animals to feed and knights in armor took him away to practice their strengths.

There was a real Medieval Fair in the village and he had promised to take her this morning.

"Jamie, are we still going to the fair?" Kelly asked him.

"Yes, when I make a promise, I keep it. And that is something you should know from our past, Rebecca."

"Please remember that I am not Rebecca, Jamie," Kelly told him as she scooted up close to his side and began to rub his neck like she had last night. "I wonder if your neck is any better this morning?" she asked in a sultry voice still filled with sleep and lovemaking.

He smiled at her inquisitive eyes and said, "Yes, and I do not for the life of a Lord know what you did to make that pain go away."

"You know, in my time we say 'for the life of me'. You just used a two thousand and six slang saying." She was laughing at him.

Jamie pulled up the feather filled coverlet that had slipped down from her shoulders and pulled her so close that she could hear his heart beating. He covered her with his body and pulled the coverlet over them both. He took her to the stars one more time before they started off their adventure today. Kelly knew there was surely something here that she had to recall. Something that she could remember from all the stories he had told her.

She made herself a promise. She would find a private place and think over all that had happened to her until she came to a conclusion she could live with. But for now, he was all she needed. She made love to him with a new soul inside her brain and body. She loved him in ways that shocked even her. She did not want this man to ever forget she had been here. That is, if she should decide that she had to leave, which she would not even let into her mind yet.

She kissed his whole body. She saw him bewildered by her actions. She felt the awe in his body when she crawled down to kiss him from his waist downward. She kissed his feet. She licked his big toe. She tickled his feet and then she took his manhood in her mouth and felt him stiffen up from the shock of her most intimate move.

When he could stand it no more, he went with it and spiraled to the stars this time alone. She reached out her hand to his cheek and saw that he was almost in tears.

"What is wrong?" she asked him. "What did I do that made you cry?" Her eyes were full of questions.

"I know that I was always happy with Rebecca, but I know now that you can't be Rebecca. And I am so confused. Rebecca was very shy in our marriage bed and even later she was reluctant to make love the way we just did. I don't know what to think. I don't know who you really are. Can you explain this to me once more? I will listen and try to understand all that you tell me. I have a need to know more about Kelly. You really are Kelly, aren't you? But how? How did this thing happen to me? Why did it happen? Have you any answers for me this morning after we just had the most wonderful night of my life last night. Even last night, I was beginning to worry that I might be wrong. I felt it in my soul and knew something was just not right and I did not know what it could be. I only know that I love you and I always will love Rebecca, too. But where is Rebecca now? Has something happened to her? Because even though you look alike, I know you are not her. I know it as surely as I know who I am."

"I have a theory, but you won't like it and I feel afraid to mention this to you. Are you sure you want to hear my thoughts on this, Jamie?" she asked him with her eyes downcast and her voice so quiet and still.

"Yes, and I am ready to accept whatever it is you have to tell me this morning in our big bed, where the life I know is going to change with your very words. Go ahead, Kelly, and tell me what you think happened here." Jamie sat up in the bed and stared at her face while he waited for her to begin.

"I have read about a thing called time travel," she said. She saw his face full of doubt. "I saw a Hallmark movie about it also and then I saw a time travel movie at the theater. I wondered about it, but I didn't really think it could happen to anyone. I love fiction and I always went to this type of movie when my friends wanted to go out to see a flick."

"What is a flick, and a movie? I do not know either." Jamie looked like he had more questions but she stopped him.

"Wait until I am done and then I will answer all your questions. I know how it must sound, but you took the other things I said better and I want you to be able to accept what I am about to tell you. Because I can honestly say that there is no other way this could have happened, Jamie, at least no way that I can think of."

"When I fell in the doorway of the side wall of this castle that day, I was in the year two thousand and six. Now I am in your time. I must have traveled back for a reason. And here is what I think happened. But remember, Jamie, that I am only guessing at this," she said earnestly.

Rebecca must have been killed by her attacker and, as she died, I fell and hit my head at the same time in my life and went back and ended up in her body. We joined souls because someone higher up must have know that you needed her so much that you could not survive without her in your life. I must have taken her place," Kelly said.

She waited for a couple seconds then asked him, "Can you imagine this? Is it possible? Did I take over her life here? Tell me, please, what you think happened. Because I cannot tell you any more other than I am here and I do not know how I got here anymore than you do. We must never tell this to another person. I am afraid that the people here will think I am a witch and have me burned to death. If this is too hard for you to accept, let me try to go back through the door I came here in. Your face tells me a lot, dear Jamie. I see fear, sadness and no hope, but no resolution in your mind. What do we do now?" she asked with tears in her eyes.

"Kelly, first I want to call you Rebecca. Is that okay with you? I hope you cannot fault me there. And anyway, the people here see your face and they know you as Rebecca, too. We cannot upset the whole castle with this strange happening. Can we? And I want to have time to come to terms with Rebecca's death, which makes me want to go out and kill whoever did this to her. I have to find whoever did this. Kelly, you must know that I could never let this go unpunished," he told her.

"But, if you go looking for Rebecca, what will people think? Be careful what you do, my love. It might backfire on us both."

"Backfire?" he questioned her word.

"I will explain it later, Jamie."

"I have lost Rebecca, but I have found you. I have Rebecca here, but she is not the one I loved. She is so different today. But I cannot forget her. Can you accept that I find Rebecca in you and you in Rebecca? Can we live that way? Will I be enough for you? Arthur? What about Arthur? There is as much to keep us apart as there is to keep us together. What is your heart telling you now, Kelly?"

"It is so strange to hear you call me Kelly. I had begun to like being called Rebecca. I have heard it for the whole time I have been here. I cannot see me leaving now. I think our relationship is forged in history. We have history. Why? I don't think I can explain. But for now, let me go. You are holding me so tightly that I can hardly breathe goof ball."

"May I ask what a goof ball is?" he asked with a giggle in his voice. "I am sure I have never had a goof ball in my lifetime. Where can I get a goof ball? You talk about goof balls quite a lot, My Lady."

"It is some more of that slang that I mentioned before, just a silly way to make conversation. There is actually no such thing as a goof ball." She tried to make him understand the slang of her time.

"I have tried to picture what a goof ball might look like, but it is a strange word. I do not want to keep you from breathing, if you do not breathe, I will die also, My Lady."

Kelly changed the subject. "Okay, what about the village fair? I want to go so badly. I want to compare it to the fairs I have attended in my world. Can we still go?" she begged him.

"Let me have someone get the horses ready for us. There is a jousting today, but it might be that you won't want to see anyone hurt. It is a very diligent battle atop a horse. The winner wins the favor of his lady. The ribbons will be thrown before the tourney starts and the winner gets his lady. What do you think about it? Do you want to do that, too? I want to buy you some trinkets and some fabrics for a new gown and anything that you see that you might want."

"I'm happy today that we will spend it together again. These past few days have been like magic for me."

Jamie was thrilled to hear her coming to a decision about where she will go, home to her time or as he hoped to stay in his. He had come to believe that she really did come from somewhere else. He just chose to not think about it any longer. It was mysterious and he did not understand at all. So it was better to hope she stayed forever and that nothing would ever change for them. Ever.

There was a loud knock on their chamber door. In came the servants. The day started with a hustle, the Earl shouting orders here and there, water coming in for a bath, which was so unusual for their time, but heavenly for Kelly.

Bathing had been one thing that she had dearly missed. When she had asked for hot water the first time, they looked at her like she must be sick. They fretted over her for a time until she finally made them understand that she needed to bathe quite frequently. Jamie noticed the difference in her right away. His Lady Rebecca never asked too much of any of the servants in the castle.

The Earl came for her and took her hand in his and they descended the winding stairs of stone together. The day was a beautiful day with the sun shining brightly on the meadow outside the castle walls.

As they headed towards the village meadow where the fair was, she felt so alive and needed. More than she ever had felt before. It was very different than the way she accepted each day in her life before the time travel backward. Each morning when her eyes popped open, there was excitement and an eagerness to get going and spend her time in this new world. Each day brought her something new to learn, see, smell, taste, feel, and hear, experiences that she loved.

The trade stands came into view. She stared at them, not believing that she was really living proof that this fair was real. The carts sold all kinds of things. The ribbons were in many different colors and they were hanging from metal poles in the air. The wind was blowing them this way and that way. She could smell the horses and she saw the ring where the jousting was about to begin.

Jamie led her toward the benches and made her a seat. He bowed in front of her and took her hankie for his good luck.

"What are you doing, Jamie? I don't want you to fight for me. I am already yours. Please come back." She called to his retreating back. She was so upset now that all she wanted to do was go back to the castle.

She was seated by three other ladies who saw her nervous state.

"Why, Lady Rebecca, you were never upset about your Lord when he jousted before. He almost every time wins your favor. He even knocks the young men off their mounts. Is there something we should know about the Earl? Has he been hurt? Is he ill? Does he need to fear about his talent today?" They were gossiping amongst themselves and she turned her head away from the ladies. Then she fixed her long skirt and sat demurely watching and waiting for the Earl to come out on his steed.

When he appeared, his horse was wearing a heavy mantle of metal and screen. He had colors on of green and blue. The horse also had green and blue on his head and in his mane. He stepped out onto the field like he was already a winner. His horse had evidently done this many times before. There was no fear in the horse or rider today.

The horns were blowing the beginning of the tournaments. The jugglers were on the field and everyone was having a wonderful time. But in Kelly's mind, all she could think of was what would happen to her if he died and she was left in these terrible times alone with no one to look out for her anymore. Maybe Jamie had forgotten, but someone had kidnapped his Rebecca. And Kelly felt like she must be dead.

If that was the reason she appeared in this time, then something must have happened to Rebecca. What if those persons saw her here today and tried to kill her again? She felt very real fear now. It was the first time she had thought about it that way. The closest she had come to worrying about her safety was when one of the chamber maids made remarks about her acting differently. She saw an adoring look in the girl's eyes whenever Jamie was around. The maid did everything she could for the Earl.

Kelly had forgotten about it, but she wanted to ask Jamie if there was anything between this girl and himself, because she could feel it. It was in her stance and in her face each time he came to dinner escorting Kelly to the table. When she served him, it was with a proper swish of her skirts and a smile from ear to ear. Now the day was taking on a different meaning. She was afraid.

The music blared loudly and the horses and riders began to fill the field. The cheering from the crowds was loud. People of all kinds were here today. When the Earl came onto the field, they cheered him so loudly that she had to smile. He rode over to her bench and bowed in front of her. She did not know she was to stand and give him her ribbon, so when the ladies next to her started to talk and she overheard them, she jumped up. He smiled a special smile and winked, for her eyes only. She had seen that smile before. In their bed chamber after the most wonderful sex she had ever dreamed about.

She bowed her head and took her seat. He rode into the middle of the field and someone ran out to give him his lance. He took it in his hand like she would take a spoon to eat ice cream. Trying to put her fear away, she tried to take the thought of the ice cream and remember how to make it. She would surprise Jamie tonight. She remembered that all you needed was milk and ice and flavoring and salt. She had seen everything but ice in her short time here.

The trumpets were blaring and the horses started to charge towards each other. The first blow was given to Jamie's opponent. Jamie thrust the lance out hard and almost knocked the challenger off his mount. They circled and lined up. The trumpets rang out again. They charged. This time, Jamie knocked him off and he hit the dirt hard. Jamie rode up to Kelly and she bowed to him. The horns were loud. The music was not to her liking, but it was after all the best they had.

She got up and he jumped off his horse. His boy took the horse and his heavy mantle and walked away. Together they took a cool drink of Mead and she was giggling so hard that he took her silver cup from her hands and replaced it with water.

"You have a liking for our Mead, don't you, Rebecca? This might be more suited to your fancy than Mead. It is a hardy drink that many soldiers can't handle. I was surprised when you drank the whole cup full, My Love."

"Jamie, after sitting there and watching you put your life on the line in front of my own eyes, I think I need a Vodka Collins and maybe even a Singapore Sling to calm my nerves down."

"Excuse me, My Lady, but whatever are you talking about? I have never heard these words before."

Her eyes twinkled as she said, "Let's have some ice cream, my big man."

He was so startled by her language that he did not know what to say next.

"Look, Jamie, a Vodka Collins is a drink unlike any you have here. I don't usually drink at all, so I guess I am pretty drunk, right?" she asked as she took his arm and held on tight.

He smiled in appreciation of her situation and walked her around so she could get her feet back on the ground.

"What is ice cream?" he asked her a little later, after she seemed to be back to her old self.

"Ice cream is the best, Jamie. Can we make some tonight?" She saw his blank look and decided to keep the ice cream for another time.

Chapter Twenty-Two

The festivities had all but worn Kelly out. The day had been a day to remember. She had seen so many things that day at the fair that she had read about back in the future. She loved the jousting. Her adrenalin was flowing. The excitement was in her every move. Her eyes were so bright and her heart was so happy. Her fear was there, too. But as in the books of old, the bravest knight always won, so she was not too worried about her Jamie at the moment.

And she loved the trinkets they all wanted to buy. To her it was just junk but the people at the fair thought they were needed things to live a good life. Kelly had no idea how anyone in this time could live a happy life. These times were hard times.

The air fairly sparkled with anticipation in the games. The people were so energetic and enthusiastic that it showed in their every move. The day was positively a day to remember. Kelly walked fast to keep up with Jamie. He was reaching out his hand to move her toward the wagon with all the fabrics and ribbons of silk, in all colors and lengths.

Kelly went straight to the vivid pink ribbon. She put her fingertips on it and reveled in the feel. There was nothing in her other world that could even touch this silk, so very soft and fine. The color was so much brighter and vivid and although she had not conquered the money of the time, she knew it was rich and would cost a lot. But Jamie bought her the whole roll.

She was shocked and surprised that her thank you was mumbled in the midst of all the people watching this transaction go on. For a moment, Jamie thought he saw two dirty ruffians staring at Kelly, but he put it all down to the amount of coin he had put out for the ribbon. And they walked on.

Next he took her to get a piece of dried meat that they could only get at the fair. It was something the merchants had cooked up themselves and at every fair, Jamie would get a large portion for himself to devour. He took a bit of it and gave her a taste. He explained to her that he loved it from boyhood, that his father took him to the summer and winter fair each year if he had worked hard in his training and proven to his father that he deserved to go. He actually thought that his father would have taken him no matter now good or bad he had been, but he never mentioned this to his father as he grew up to be the meanest and strongest knight in the area, which encompassed a great, large area.

Kelly took a bite and immediately rendered it the same beef jerky they had in her time. She chomped on it and ate it quickly. This was the first food she had been given that was as good as home food was, since she had turned up in this era.

It was a warm, humid night. Kelly was standing on the battlements and her mind was made up. She was staying here with the Lord. The battlements were heavenly, but she needed to be able to move around, so she decided to leave the roof line and explore outside the castle walls. It was late and no one would be watching.

Kelly went back down and out into the night. She wanted to walk and then her mind could be clear and her thoughts would all be reasonable to her when she considered staying here forever with Jamie. Jamie made her heart beat fast. Jamie made her days full and exciting. Jamie was everything to her now. She could not imagine going back to her previous life and even leaving her family now was not so hurtful to her mind.

She could feel the wind on her face. She could taste the salt on her lips and the surf was smashing against the rocks below. There was a change in the air. A storm was brewing and she loved storms. She stood still and she could feel the castle getting ready for the storm. This mighty fortress had stood its ground for many battles with the sea and the elements of the night. Tonight would be no different than any other night when a good storm was brewing out at sea somewhere.

Kelly was thinking about who might be getting the worst of it right as she stood on the edge of the cliff looking out to the lightning flashing off in the distance. The thunder was getting louder. The wind was not just restless anymore, it was furious. The clouds were rolling and the wind was so strong that she could hardly hold herself upright when the wind hit the rocks behind her and bounced to hit her squarely in the back. Her eyes were watering from the little bits of sand and pebbles blowing in the air.

Getting out had been a little tricky. She wanted to be alone. She did not want to feel the pressure she often felt when he was there because she could see the begging in his eyes. She could hear the silent "please" in his mind.

From time to time, she hugged herself and looked around. She thought she had heard something behind her, but looking back, there was nothing to see. No one was outside in this kind of weather anyway she told herself. Still, the feeling persisted that someone was watching her the whole time.

When she got to the lookout point on the cliff, she found a dry log and pulled it over to the edge. She sat down for a while and let her thoughts go to where they wanted to go. After about thirty minutes, her behind was feeling wet. She gathered up all the dress she had on and imagined what the people back home would think if they could see her now. A big smile went all over her face at the thought, but at the same time remembering Arthur and her parents brought a sad look in her eyes. While she stood there, she remembered the jousting and the fair she had seen that day. The weather had been good then, but now it was going to get rough.

She stayed for an hour. She could see the lightning in the sky off in the distance. She prayed that her life here was going to be a good one. Even a better one that her life in two thousand and six. She loved Jamie and he loved her. She was staying. Now she had to tell him.

Her decision made, she turned around and headed back to the castle and to Jamie. Hugging herself close to keep out the rain that had started to come down in buckets, she raced for the safety of her new found home. Once she got under the cover, she turned once again to see the lightning and rain racing down from the sky. Standing there, she knew what happiness really meant and that her happiness was the thing that was made in the past, not the present. Why, she did not know yet. But she was as sure as a girl could be that this was no dream after all.

She turned around and stepped toward the huge door that had kept the storm outside. All of a sudden, she felt the presence of another person. She had no fear that she would be harmed, but she had not heard a sound before and she was surprised that someone else would be up here and she had not heard them come in the creaking door when they opened it.

Looking about as she walked to the shadows that the castle ramparts made, she did not see the two men come out from under the rocky ledge of the roof line. One man called her by name. "Lady Rebecca!" he called. The other man told him to shut up.

Kelly turned quickly and was caught by the rope around her waist. She struggled to get free, but they were too strong for her. One of the men said, "Ben, gag her quickly."

Ben was not a name she had heard around the castle before. Who could he be? He thought she was Lady Rebecca. Ben took out a dirty rag and put it in her mouth, tying a nastier one around her face and eyes, but not before she saw the other man.

"I got 'er, Tom," he squawked out to his partner.

Tom, another name she had not heard before. What was happening to her? They thought she was Rebecca. Kelly kicked and tried to bite the men through the rags in her mouth. She had no luck. They tied her arms behind her back and then she felt a hard knock on her head. All she could do now was be quiet. Maybe they would not kill her if she acted unconscious and was very still. She heard the branches crunching under her captors' feet. She heard them mumbling, but whatever they were saying, she could not make out the real words.

The smell from the men made her almost toss her cookies. Just remembering that familiar phrase that her mother had always said made her tremble. When she was freed from this nightmare and these horrible men, she wanted to try out this phrase to Jamie, and she put the rest of this ordeal out of her mind trying to imagine what he would say to "tossing her cookies." She tried to force a smile and his face in her mind, but she remembered no more.

Chapter Twenty-Three

When the evening meal was ready, a maid was sent to fetch Kelly for the dinner meal. The meal had been brought out and put on the table. All the servants were surprised that Kelly did not show up. Jamie had been sitting there for a few minutes when he noticed the servants whispering to each other. He had not had time to think something might be wrong, but when she did not show up, he worried. Jamie sent several of them up the stairs to find out what was keeping her. He told them to go to their room first, but when they returned without her, he went running outside.

The weather was bad now. This storm had been in the air all day and his first thought was that she might be on the battlements watching whatever it is that she watched from the highest point on the castle.

Running as fast as he could, he reached the ramparts first. Looking all around and in the places where she might be out of the rain, he only saw black empty places. She was not there. He was mad with worry and he could not imagine where she was. He ran back in the doors, asking everyone had they found her. No one had seen her.

Knights searched the whole of the castle. Twenty people running everywhere, even to the out buildings. He questioned everyone about her activities during the day since he had left to go settle a quarrel in the lists that afternoon. She had been in her room when he left and everything was normal.

He was frightened and he wanted to find her and put his heart back to beating again. What did he do now? Where was she? He went up to the battlements to see for himself.

He pushed hard on the door and raced out into the rain that was now coming down in sheets, pelting his face like stinging needles. She was not there either. He turned around and put his hands inside his woolen cloak to warm them. Then he saw a ribbon on the gravelly rocks of the floor of the castle. It was pink. It was one of the new ones he had bought just yesterday for her hair. She had had it in her hair this morning when they broke their fast.

His fear was overwhelming. He remembered her saying to him just a day or so ago about Rebecca, the fact that if someone saw her and they had tried to kill Rebecca, they would come after Kelly thinking she was Rebecca. And thinking that she knew who they were would make it more important for them to kill her for good, a second time. He had mentioned that whoever they were, they would not be looking for Rebecca if they had actually killed her already, but he was worried then and now he knew what had happened. Someone had seen her at the fair. The word had gotten around and they had come back to see for themselves if it really was her. What they saw made them come back to get her again.

Chapter Twenty-Four

All at once, she heard a hard tug on the door and heard a chain rattle. The door was being opened. She tried to sit up, but she couldn't. Her tears were flowing like rain and she knew that if it were the bigger of the men, she was in for trouble. He had already told his friend that she was his and he was going to sire a bunch of babes with her and no one would ever find her when he got to where he was going.

She was so scared that she couldn't talk. If this was him, she was as good as dead anyway.

But where was Jamie? She knew she was right when she thought he would be looking for her everywhere. What was taking him so long to find her? But then, even she did not have a clue as to where they had taken her. There had to be clues left behind. She only prayed that Jamie found them in time.

But she knew that he did not know about CSI and he had no good clues to follow, because she had heard the two men talking about how good it went and there was no one behind them, even after three days of traveling.

It had probably been five days now, but she slept so much that she didn't know for sure how many days had gone by. Everything was just a big blur to her. She knew hunger and she knew pain and she also knew she had a fever. Now that must be why she never got cold lately. At first, she was so cold and then she got warm and kept going to sleep.

The man walked over to the heap in the floor and began untying the rope on her hands and then the fire raced up into her hands and fingers. The circulation had been cut off for a few hours and she remembered when it started. When she tried to turn over, her hands became tangled up in the rope and she had no way to untangle them. So that must have been about an hour ago. Thank God he was doing this now. Otherwise, she might have lost her hands in time, being tied like that. He pushed her over and grabbed a handful of hair which made her stand still. She looked up at him, but her vision was blurred and it took her a few minutes to clear them up. When her eyes finally adjusted and her hands stopped burning, she felt a renewed strength building in her heart. A strength that might keep her safe for a while longer, until Jamie found her and took her home again.

Kelly was so sick and her body ached all over. She felt like she had been punched with boxing gloves and someone had been careful to not leave any cuts or wounds that might bleed. It was almost like time had stopped for her. She did not have any idea how long it had been since her captors had taken her away from the castle.

In her mind, she tried to imagine that Jamie was on his way and she would soon be found and taken back to where she belonged.

In the background, she heard feet coming towards where she had been placed in a tight little space where she could not even straighten out her feet. She had been laying on her side for so long that she had pins and needles running all up and down the left side of her body. Kelly knew she must be quiet and she closed her eyes to the overwhelming blackness that she had become used to every time she opened her eyes.

The sound kept coming and at last she could hear voices, the same ones who had taken her away. Those horrible men whom she wished a painful death on were there talking about her like she wasn't able to hear them.

"I have made a bloody decision, my friend, and I don't care whether you can go for this or not, but as you can see, I have the deciding factor in my right hand."

His partner in this kidnapping had all but forgotten how he could not trust him. So when his eyes saw the sword sticking out from his side, he almost fell backward.

He got hold of himself and answered, "Hold on. You 'n me, we be in this together. What are ye planning to do with that pistol?"

"I am taking control of our satiation."

Kelly could not help but hear the terrible grammar when they spoke to each other. And now in this instant, Kelly got frightened. She felt it in her brain and in their voices that the odd man was planning to take control and he would kill the other man without so much as a blink of his eye.

She heard some scuffling around her, but she couldn't hear any words. Silent as she was, maybe they thought that she was already dead. Maybe she better move or moan or something just to let them know she had heard them talking and was not dead.

A loud crunch and the sound of a heavy body falling made her jump and scream. All went silent. Not a sound did she hear. She strained her ears and then she heard a dragging sound and scuffling shoes scooting away from her.

"Stop! Stop!" she cried out. "Come back and let me go to the bathroom, please," she cried again. "I need to go before I wet myself." Not a sound answered her back. "I'm so hungry I could eat three Big Macs."

All at once, she heard a set of feet coming back to where she was yelling from.

"Big Macs? What are ye talking about, ye deft lass. The Macs are people, not food. I will feed ye soon. Just keep silent fer me. I need no one to hear ye, do ye kin?"

"Kin?" she yelled back. "That's my cousin you are talking about. Shut up your mouth and let me out of here now."

"What is that all about your kin? I need ye to be still and then I can get some food fer ye. But if you bring in some more strangers with all that screaming then I guess I will have to shoot some more people tonight and it will be all yer fault. Do you hear me? So shut up," he told her.

"No, I won't and I don't care who you kill, but I have to go to the bathroom now."

"Och, I don't know what a bathroom is, lass. So ye better dry up that mouth and be quick about it. Do ye hear me?"

"Do you want me to wet on the floor and get all my clothes wet so I will die from sickness?" she said very patiently to her captor. She remembered the large one who seemed to be in full control and she hoped that the smaller man was still alive, but she only heard one voice now and it was the man she thought looked like the dangerous one of the two of them. Everything went silent when she heard the door shut quietly somewhere.

Chapter Twenty-Five

The sound was bothering her. The bee was buzzing right alongside her ear. But she was half afraid to open her eyes to see what it was. She had been sleeping so well. She remembered now that she had not been sleeping that well in a long time. She kept her eyes closed. She heard him snoring. It was a great thing to plan an escape now, but she knew that she could not get anywhere without him now. She had been counting the days since she had been kidnapped and to her mind it had been almost two weeks since she was taken.

In the beginning, she had thought that Jamie would find her. It was surely just a matter of time. But time had come and gone and no word from him. They had been traveling in the nighttime and sleeping in people's fields at daylight. In some obtuse corner where there were so many trees for cover that no one would ever check there for any reason.

She realized that she was lost forever in a world unknown to her. Oh, she knew she could fake it, but her captor was uncivilized. He wanted her for his own pleasure and he probably slept with one eye open to make sure she didn't run way. Sleeping in the daytime was really hard for her, because she had also been sleeping as they rode along through the long, dark, damp and sometimes wet nights.

He had a chain holding her horse and there was no way to get away from him. Through the nights, he had been kind enough to her. She figured that he thought she could never retrace her ground, but he knew that she would remember the castle and anyone she might ask would guide her there. So the chains were a must. He could not lose her, because he had plans. Putting out the word that she was alive and could be found for the right amount of money was out of the question. They would find him and kill him first.

So, through the long nights, he began to speak to her in a decent kind of way trying to get her to warm up to him. Food for her did not work, nor did the kind words. Even the extra blanket was no good. She was still silent. He knew she heard him and in time she would begin to get used to him and they would make a new life and he would have the beautiful woman he had wanted from the first time he had seen her when they had thought she was dead and had gone to see for themselves.

Lying so still, not moving and breathing quietly, one eye slightly opened to see if the dark of night had come again to the vast emptiness of her life. She saw the bee. A big yellow and black bumblebee was sitting on a piece of purple clover right beside her nose. She hated bees, but she did not move even an eyelash. The bee flew away and she let her breath out. Her fear came back swiftly when she saw him moving around at her feet.

It was time to run again. Her body was not used to horseback riding for nine hours at a time. She wanted to cry. She wanted to ask for a break in the pace they were keeping to each day or night as it turns out to be. But she would not give him the benefit of her voice. She kept silent.

The man had more guts than she had imagined. He was up and packing the horse bags. Then he gave her a shove with his dirty old boot and she sat straight up and gathered up her blanket and got up. She looked at him for her next move. He always told her everything to do and what not to do. He grabbed a piece of stale brown bread full of seeds of some kind and put it in her hand.

"Eat this as we ride. It will keep you warm inside and it is good for you." He turned his back to her and relieved himself in front of her as he had been doing all along. Then he asked her if she needed to have a minute of privacy for herself. He had finally figured her out and knew she would not go in front of him, so he gave in.

"Go ahead," Tom said slowly and sweetly. "Just don't run, because a bear or who knows what, maybe even a wolf will have your for dinner tonight if you do. And you are not worth a fight with a wolf, my Lady Rebecca."

She looked all around the area. Where in the world was she?

"Let's get going," she heard a voice say and it seemed like the man was talking to her. She picked herself up off the ground and walked over to where the man was standing with his arm out in front of his body. "What is keeping ye so long, girl?" Tom said to her. You know we must get going now. Darkness is coming on soon. I want to make tracks this day."

"Who are you, sir?" Kelly was surprised at the rough look of the guy in her way as she tried to walk around him.

When he did not move, she stopped and said to him again, "I asked you, who are you?"

He reached out his hand and grabbed her wrist. "Get on that horse before I show you what will happen if you decide not to do as ye are told, girly." His voice commanded her as if he was her boss or something.

"Where are we going? Wait a minute," she said. "Who are you and why do you think I am going to do anything that you tell me to?"

Tom just stared at her. "And what might ye be talking like you don't know who I am? Are ye daft, girl? Get on that horse and be quick with it."

Kelly tried to get on the horse, but she fell backwards and the horse got spooked and took off in another direction. Big Tom was mad now. He took Kelly by the arm and slung her down on the ground. She fell hard, but her arm was under her body and she screamed. Tom knew she could not go anywhere, so he went off to find the horse. That horse was the difference between him succeeding in this kidnapping or not. It was very important to find the horse and quickly so they could be on their way. He was very careful to sneak up on him when he finally saw him. He walked back to where Kelly was laying on the ground and she was crying.

"What is wrong now?" he screamed at her.

"I think I broke my arm," Kelly told him.

"How would you know if you broke a damned bone or not? Can you see in the flesh to the bone?" He was visibly upset now. He tried to pull her up and her pain was obvious. He stopped and took in the situation. He gave her his arm and picked her up to put her on the horse. Through the night she was very quiet. He tried to talk to her many times, but she acted like she did not know what was going on. She even told him she was not who he said she was.

"Who are you talking about?" Tom kept tracking the path in front of him. His one remark to her about her precious Jamie went right over her head. She made no move to answer him.

"Jamie who?" she retorted.

"You know who I am talking about. Why are you playacting for me? He will never find you now. We have traveled about as far as we need to go. I am going to find a place for us to put in a note for home for us. I heard tell that there were lots of huts around and that is what we need. I know a man about here who will get me a daily penny. I can help him because I helped him years before in the black smithy."

Kelly still never spoke a word. They traveled until the sun started to peak in the eastern sky. When Tom helped her down and they sat down and made a small fire, he realized she was hurting. Her forearm was wet with sweat. She was staring straight ahead. She never made eye contact with him at all. He put the little piece of meat he had left on a stick on the fire and covered her with a blanket until he could get it cooked for her to eat. When he could smell it and hear it sizzling on the fire, he took her a piece. She just looked at him. He tore it apart and put a small amount of it in her mouth. She chewed it and then he made her a place to lie. He leaned her over and put the blanket on her again and she closed her eyes and was asleep sooner than ever before. He was getting worried about her. Why did she act like it was okay now for her to be with him? She was not right. He knew the difference. He watched her all day. She seemed to be somewhere else. Where, he could not tell, but something was wrong with this captured woman. She did not even know her name. At one point, she had said her name was Kelly, but he didn't let it sink in yet. What tomorrow would bring was a new day.

Tom put his saddle down and rested his head on it. He had a lot of thinking to do, planning to do and he was worried about his Lady. She was acting as if nothing was wrong. She was going along with whatever he said to her. She was certainly not a happy Lady, but nevertheless, she was no problem anymore. He was really wondering about her change in moods. What if she was really sick? What would he do with her? He might have to go off and leave her all alone if she had anything that might kill her and he had become used to her gentle smile that she rarely ever showed him, but when she did it was worth it. He had thought about her every minute of every day since he had taken her. He wanted her so badly. But she did not want him. She had wanted her Jamie. And now, ten days later and far, far away from the castle, she was acting so strange. He could not help but worry about her condition.

Chapter Twenty-Six

Kelly heard Tom moving around and it felt like normal to Kelly to get up from her cold bed on the ground and begin to get things ready for a departure again when the light was failing and dusk was upon them. At first she had hoped to sleep at night but they had to move in the dark of night and so Kelly had grown used to fighting for sleep in the daylight hours. It seemed to Kelly that the day was so long. Kelly slept a little every night but she had such bad dreams and her fever was going away which had Kelly thinking all night she was about to give up on Jamie. If he could have found her, Jamie would have been there before now. Jamie was not going to find Kelly because he had no idea where she had been taken and who had taken her. That thought had come lately with every waking moment she had. Kelly did not worry on it so much now. Kelly knew it would be impossible in these times to track someone so devious and evil in a few days so when two weeks had passed and Jamie did not come for her, she had given up the thought. Kelly had a terrible time remembering all of it anymore. She had flashback of Jamie and then she would see her life before all this happened to her. Her mother. The castle. And somehow she did not know how to put it together anymore.

175

As her memories faded of this terrible time and her broken arm mended day by day, it was apparent to Tom that Lady Rebecca was so much easier to get along with. Wondering what brought about this new turn in her personality gave Tom a lot to think about.

The bags and horses were ready to go. Tom walked over to Kelly and helped her on the horse. Her arm was mending and he did not want to injure it again. His help was accepted and she even smiled at him. This got Tom to worrying. It was the first time she had smiled in all the days they had been together now. He was sure she was not happy, so why the smile?

"Are you okay, Lady Rebecca?" Tom asked with sympathy in his tone of voice.

"Yes, I think so. My arm is not so painful today. Maybe it is healing up. And I did sleep very well last night. Thank you for asking."

Tom just put his hands in his pockets and was very uneasy. She sensed he was uncomfortable, but had no reason for it. She had been the best traveling partner he had ever had.

Tom realized that he had to explain to Lady Rebecca that he had a friend some time ago in a little village called Weil. A man Tom knew by the name of James ran a blacksmithy in the tiny village. All he needed to do was to stroll into the village and find James and maybe James could help him get settled. He was very tired of sleeping on the ground and traveling by night. The thought of a permanent place appealed to Tom at the moment and Tom knew Lady Rebecca needed a place to call her own. They had traveled many miles and Tom had no fear that he would be found or that Lady Rebecca would be recognized in this little country village of about 40 people.

The horses were moving slowly toward the village and Tom saw Rebecca stiffen in the saddle. Lady Rebecca asked Tom, "Where are we? We are going to go into this village and we are not hiding anymore," she said.

"I used to know someone here," Tom replied. "I hope that James is still here and he can help us. I have been traveling toward this with you for a while now and I know that it is time for us to stop running."

Lady Rebecca wanted to say, "What are we running from?" But she kept her thoughts to herself. Sometimes Lady Rebecca had too many things on her mind and she couldn't put them in place, so this would just have to be another one of her jumbled up thoughts.

Going around a bend in the road, they saw people and children and Rebecca could smell smoke from the chimneys. Looking around, she saw a castle on the hill, pretty far away really from the village. Tom gave the reins to her horse and she followed him to the blacksmith shop on the edge of town.

While she waited, Tom jumped off, went in and struck up a conversation with a strange-looking little man. She saw him slap Tom on the back and saw them shake hands. So she assumed this was the man he was looking for. Maybe they would have a place to stay by nightfall.

James was very helpful that day, seemingly very glad to see Tom again and, after hearing Tom's problem and seeing Tom's beautiful wife, he assumed, he offered them the use of a little room in the back of the smithy until Tom could find better quarters for them to live in. He also gave Tom a job.

Two weeks later, Tom received his pay from James and immediately went closer into the village and acquired a small cottage for them to move into.

Chapter Twenty-Seven

Kelly wanted answers. So she started to ask questions. Kelly could not remember too much about the journey. Kelly could not even remember why she was here.

The ache in Kelly's heart had now been transferred to her mind. Day by day, she tried to do whatever was called for her. She smiled and did not talk at all. If this man spoke to her, she always answered him and went on with whatever she was doing in the first place. She knew the day would come when she would be rescued and if she could only hold out everything would be restored to her liking and her life, no matter what she had gone through so far, would be good again.

Kelly did not want him to get too close to her. In the beginning weeks, she had told him that she needed time to get used to him. He gave her that. She saw a different man now than she had thought him to be. He had cleaned up. He had been nice to her when he had realized that she was going to stay there with him. She never tried to run away. She never actually told him she would stay, she just did. She made no new friends. She stayed to herself all day and in the evening she tried to prepare a man's meal. For her it did not matter. As long as she fed him something, he was content to just sit and look at her. His job as blacksmith was a hot and dirty one. He was kicked by the cattle and by the horses. He was jerked this way and that and Kelly believed that the reason he had not tried to take her to bed yet was that he was so out of shape he couldn't do it if he wanted to.

She had almost forgotten the past time in the castle with Jamie. Not really forgotten, but it faded with every new day. Her life had so many jumbled up pictures in her mind that she could not place them in the right order anymore. So the best thing to do was to forget it. She worried about her mind and her sanity. Things were not clear anymore. So how she got here was a thing she could not remember anymore.

The little building she now called home had a fireplace where she would cook the meat. It seemed that there was always something new to get used to that she had not known how to do before. She had garden vegetables that he would bring in to her every few days. She had a hard time learning how to make the bread they liked in this new time in her life. But she finally learned to make it and baked it like a pro.

It was not very big inside, one main room with a sheltered area where Kelly slept. It had a blanket hanging up to make it a room of its own. Since she only had the one dress, she had to wash it out once a week and let it dry overnight. The windows were small and Kelly had cleaned them the first day she got there. Her curtains were from an old wooden box he had dragged in for her yesterday. It seemed that some lady down the path had given her a few things for her little home.

Even though she had only been there for three long frightening days, she felt alone and afraid all the time. It was great that she was free now and did not have to ride that horse anymore. No more days on the ground and hot food to eat each day now even if she had to make it herself. It was a fear she kept out of sight.

Today she wanted a break from the confines of her tiny abode. She wanted to go for a walk in the sunshine, feel the wind on her face, and smell the fresh air. There was something odd about the way her home smelled. She had not been able to figure out why she felt so out of place there. She had looked around her and saw there was nothing any better than the old castle way up on the high cliff overlooking the stream that ran beside her home. She has chills when she looked up at that castle. She felt as though it was standing there for her, waiting for her. But why? She had no memories of a castle that she could recall. Home was also a funny word now, because home was not what it should be. She knew that much but she could not put it in her mind, why she was not sure about the place she now called home.

There was a lone tree standing inside the broken down log fence so she went outside to sit there today, to change the pace for her. Every morning she had done the same thing, carry water in, cook, and make bread, while she had fantasies of being rescued. Rescued where and by whom she had not a clue.

She could see the water in the river that ran through the small village. There were little boats that went by the village every now and then. There was always a man rowing the boat and the boats looked like they had vegetables in it, as it floated by on the tiny ripples in the stream. The stump was hard to her backside, but the air was wonderful. She could see where Tom worked from there. He was sweating and running here and there for his daily pence.

Kelly could not imagine Tom working at all and to see him like that, it made her wonder why. She knew he wanted her. But he had been so kind to her that she hoped he would leave her alone for a long time, at least until she was able to figure a way out of there for her. When she thought "out of there" she then wondered where she wanted to go. She did not know. There was a lot she didn't know anymore. And it did not matter. She was okay. And when she thought, "I am okay," she wondered why would I not be okay? Another strange thing that had been happening to her. The sun was going down and she knew she had a pot of soup from yesterday to heat up, so she got up and returned to the cottage. The dishes were just wooden trenchers and she had boiled water to clean them. She did not want to get sick with some germ she had never heard of. Germ? What was that? Where had that thought come from?

She knew Tom watched her every move and questioned anything out of the ordinary that she did. Her answers must have been good, because he never bothered her.

"I have good news," he boasted as he opened the door and came in. "Today the Earl came down through the village. He stopped by the smitty and while we checked the horses' feet, he was asking for a few good men to come up to the castle to work for him. I heard him ask Edward if he knew of anyone around that he could get. So I stepped up and asked for an idea of what he needed. He told me he needed a strong man to help him with his fosterlings. He needed a knight to train with them and I said I wanted to try it. He also needs a man to take care of his horses. I told him I needed a place for me and my lady. He told me if you wanted to help in the kitchen, he could provide that also.

And I found out the reason he needs people is because they all got ill up there and are now dead. He told me it had been about three weeks since the last one died and it was all good in the castle now. How does that sound to you? I want to do it. Lady Rebecca, please say yes."

She saw the way he was working his hands and he was twisting in the chair. This was a surprise to her and she thought he would have made that decision himself.

"I wonder why you are asking me?" she asked him in her gentle proper voice.

He loved to hear her speak. Her ways were a marvel to him. He would never get tired of her. "I wanted to be fair to you. If you like the idea, I think it would be better for us than here in this small space we call home. We might have a better place to stay up there."

His eyes were really big and he was really scared she would say no. Kelly saw it in his eyes. And she wondered again why he felt that way.

As the days were getting shorter with each passing fortnight, Kelly had finally grown accustomed to being called Lady Rebecca and her memory dimmed to the things of today and tomorrow and she eventually stopped being able to remember Jamie at all. She did know her name was not Rebecca. But why bother telling him that? The idea of moving to the castle seemed to make Tom happy so Kelly thought, "Why not?"

She approached him late that evening and told him that if he wanted to move, it was okay with her. She had been trying to remember how she cooked at home. When she thought of home, she got so confused. Which home? What year? Where was she going now?

The confusion was growing day by day. Leaving Kelly lost in her world of today. Tom was very happy.

"I am going to walk up to the castle in the morn and tell the Laird that we want to take the job offered to both of us."

He waited for a look from her telling him it was okay for her to go to the kitchens. She made no move as to okay it or not.

"Well, what do you want to do?" he asked Kelly. "Do you want the kitchen cook to let you come in her kitchen and be her help?"

"Okay," she replied.

All at once she had a vision of her mother's kitchen. And reality came back to Kelly with a swift kick in her mind. She kept her face the same. Kelly tried to make her smile look real. Even though she was really upset, she pulled it off without a question from Tom about anything.

"On the day after tomorrow, we can get the cart from the castle and we can go about moving our few belongings," he told Kelly in a quiet kind of tone. Tom could see the anxiety on her face. He realized that she did not understand anything he said. So he kept talking and took hold of her hand to get her back in the small abode they now shared.

Walking inside made Kelly wake up and she asked Tom what they could have for their meal tonight. Kelly never knew where the food came from, but she knew he had never let her down since they got together.

Kelly tried to remember where she first met Tom, but her mind could not make sense out of it, so much of the time when she thought about different things in her life, mainly about time, she had no answers at all as to where or when this had all occurred. But in the meantime, she tried not to have these thoughts at all during the daylight hours. At night it was another thing entirely. Kelly knew Tom had always been nice to her. At least she couldn't remember any bad times lately. He was always there for her. He provided all her needs. And he was very kind to her. When she had tried to ask him questions, he had always answered her immediately, so when she could not remember, she felt secure knowing he was there.

He had become her companion and she counted on him now. But some days, when she was all alone and things were very quiet, she did go back and forth in her memory trying to remember something. It always eluded her but she felt kind of like there was something she needed to know. Although it never came to her, she wondered quite often about her mysterious past.

Chapter Twenty-Eight

Kelly was up and dressed before the roosters crowed.

Tom had gone for a little while, so she was going to cook some eggs for him for when he got back. All at once she thought about making him some toast to go with his eggs, and then she couldn't imagine where that thought came from. Kelly murmured, "toast," and scratched her head wondering how on earth she could make toast in this place. Memories come and go. She had been trying to keep them at bay, but they intruded at the worst times. Kelly had a huge loaf of bread she had baked the day before. While she wanted to get it warm for Tom, she only had to place it on the hearth to heat it. For a quick fleeting moment, she wished for a toaster.

That was when her thoughts got mingled up and she did not remember enough to put any sense to her visions. Although she did know what a toaster was, she did not remember ever having one. Time was making things easier for Kelly. The one thing that really bothered Kelly was the name Rebecca. She knew there was something there also that she needed to remember but it was long gone for now and Kelly did not question her moments of reflections for very long. Kelly took each day as it came and she was satisfied with her life, so why try to remember whatever it was when it was not there.

Tom came in and put down some cloth saddle bags and told Kelly he was going to pack up some things before he ate and while she waited if she could find him some string or rope to tie these things down it would be a great help. Tom mentioned that it was a long ride up to the entrance of the castle and he really did not want to have things rolling down the hillside. Kelly knew exactly where to get the rope he needed. Tom had put a large bunch of thick rope in the barn behind where they kept the horses.

"I already have you something to eat, Tom." Kelly pointed toward the makeshift table and he could see it was getting cold, so he went straight over to the breakfast and ate it like a hungry starving person. Kelly laughed when she came back and saw him already finished with his makeshift breakfast. Tom smiled at her and she felt like it was going to be a good day.

Together they put everything in the bags and Kelly went back for a second look. She found nothing to remind anyone that they were ever there in the first place.

With the two horses and the heavy leather bags, the two of them had a lot to put on the saddles and even more to load on the old broken wooden cart someone had loaned Tom for the morning trip to the castle.

They made good time. The hill was steep, but the horses were very surefooted and got them up the hill in no time at all. Kelly had a feeling of loss when she looked back at where they had been staying for the little time they had been there. Wondering why made Kelly talk to herself and she scolded herself for going there in the first place. Kelly kept telling herself not to worry about the past, only to make the present feel good.

The huge iron gates were a surprise to Kelly when they finally got to the entrance. There was even a moat and the water around the old castle went running downhill to the stream where Kelly had washed out their meager belongings a time or two. It was where she had met a couple of other ladies and they had been her only friends. Kelly knew it was time to make more acquaintances and the castle was full of people running all around the inside of the great walls that were fortifying in times of war she supposed.

Once they were received inside and got their bearings, both Kelly and Tom headed toward the back entrance to find a small but warm and comfortable place they could call home. Kelly was smiling and she felt the inner peace of a woman who had things together at last. Their home was a huge room and had a fireplace in the east wall.

Kelly could imagine how it would feel to have the small wooden table and roughly made chairs placed all around in a homey way. To Kelly, things were looking up at last. After a few hours, they had the place the way they wanted it, everything in its place.

There was nothing else to do but walk back around the grounds and find the Earl. Hoping to find him and get his jobs lined up and also to introduce Kelly to the Earl, Tom was in a happy mood. Kelly was thinking about one thing though.

Back in the other home, Tom had slept on the floor with his blanket and never complained. At first, Kelly remained afraid that he would try to get to her bed and she had worried a lot. Then when he never did try anything with her, Kelly had not been afraid of him anymore.

Now though, Kelly was wondering if tonight might change things for the two of them, she felt herself tighten up with those thoughts and so she asked Tom outright, "Tom, will you be sleeping on the floor here like you did before?"

Tom was caught off guard. When he got his thoughts together, he responded to her challenge in the polite and mannered way he had always been with her since she could remember. "Yes, Rebecca. If that is what you want, then that is where I will sleep."

Tom had never even thought about rushing her. He had her and that was what he wanted for now. Just to be around her. Just to know that he had a beautiful woman of his own. No one needed to know about their private life. And marriage was too personal for anyone to ask them. It was assumed that they were married and that was all he could want for now. Tom knew the day would come when she would have many questions for him and he had decided to wait for that day to come. Until then, he would be happy.

Coming up to the group of men in the center, training with their swords and helmets on, made an impression on Tom. Here he could begin a new life. Here things would finally come together and he would be living the kind of life he never thought he would ever have. And the beautiful lady was his to keep. She had begun to think he had always been there and he let her.

A man walked up to Tom and introduced himself as the person in charge, telling Tom where to go to get his helmet and then showing Kelly the way to the kitchens.

The kitchens were three rooms together, all dark and hardly any kind of light except for the big fireplaces. There was a door to the outside where they were growing all kinds of herbs and then vegetables were in the very back of the huge garden. Kelly thought about whom in the castle would take care of a big garden like this. There was not a single weed in sight. There were tall sunflowers growing against a rock wall and she saw a bench seat there. Thoughts of a sunny afternoon somewhere else popped into her mind. But the clouds were there and it never cleared up at all.

Her mind would try to remind her of a certain thing or time or place, but it was never very clear to her, so she had almost begun to stop even trying to remember. Then she said to herself, remember what?

Once again Kelly had to learn a new beginning to the life she was living. It did feel as if she had done this many times before, but there were no recent memories to call on so she was content and went straight to the bench to sit down and wait for Miranda to show up and show her around the whole castle.

Sitting there she saw a huge bird fly down and sit on a rock at the top of the wall. The bird had red eyes and they were looking straight at her. She did not make a move. And the bird kept inching closer to her. Somewhere in her mind, she thought to speak to the bird.

"Hello," she said. The bird did not move. "Where did you come from, beautiful big bird?" The bird just watched her. "Come closer to me, my first friend I have made here," she called in a sweet soft voice. The bird watched and cocked his head a little to the left as if to say I need to hear you better, but sat so still it unnerved Kelly.

"Okay, little friend, I guess we are both quite lonely and scared. Are you afraid of me?" she asked the black falcon. There was no answer. But the falcon moved three paces closer to her. It made her happy to see the bird was getting closer and not flying away from her.

In the background someone was coming. The black bird made a cute sound in his throat and flew away. Kelly called out, "Bye, little bird." She turned just in time to see a big burley lady walking toward her. She had her hands in her pockets and a frown on her face. Her walk was quick and she seemed to be out of breath.

"Here you are," the lady spoke as if she was annoyed with Kelly. "I have been looking for you in the kitchen and no one seemed to have seen you, let alone knew who I was looking for. You never need to wander alone here because it is not proper to be alone."

"I am so sorry. I just walked out to see the sunshine and I really did not know where to go or whom I was to meet. I do not get into trouble, Ma'am. I am a good worker and I mind my own business always." Kelly smiled at her and got quickly up and walked toward where the woman was standing in the gate entrance.

"Follow me, Rebecca, and let me start showing you what to do in the Master's kitchen. We cook the best for his tables and the rest is left over for the servants in the house. You will not eat here and you will not be able to take food to your rooms. Do you understand so far?"

"Yes, Ma'am. I certainly do understand and I would never do anything like that while I am working for you."

"You do not work for me. You serve the Master of the castle. I'm sure you know his name. And you will never be allowed to speak to him. Only through me do you get your orders and follow my instructions and we will get along good."

Kelly's reaction to the stern woman's voice was to smile really hard and make sure that she knew that she was manageable and would work hard.

"My name is Miranda. I am the head cook and housekeeper. You will work with me daily. The first thing I want you to know is that we are in the kitchen at 5 o'clock sharp. The Master breaks his fast early and ends his day with a large meal at 8 o'clock in the evening. During the day, you help with all of the work in the castle and you will have time to go to your dwelling and prepare for your husband. After that, we return to the kitchens to heat up all the evening meal and then we serve it. Have you understood all that I have told you?"

"Yes, ma'am."

"We make certain days of the week easier than others. Perhaps you can understand when I say we make soap on Monday and we weed the herb garden on Tuesday and Wednesday. We beat the rugs and sweep the ruses in the great hall. The Master is very clean in his abode making it very hard on us and very detailing in our daily scheduling. I hope you will be able to keep up and we can get along cheerfully working side by side."

"Yes, ma'am. I am very eager to please you and at work very hard for you. My days have been somewhat exasperating lately and I haven't even been able to tell where we were in relation to region and countryside."

Seeing the raised eyebrows, Kelly immediately knew she had spoken out of the norm and was ready for the next question.

"Excuse me, but what did you mean? You sounded like a person slightly crazy to me. Can you explain that to me right now? I must speak to the Master before I get a chewing out over you. I must be on to all of my help."

"I'm sorry. I guess that did sound weird. I meant that I had been ill and I think I broke my arm three weeks ago. It has set now, but before that I was very ill also. I will not give you any trouble at all. You ask and I will do it. I will be the model housekeeper."

"Model? What do you mean? I do not know that phrase."

"Oh my, I only meant that I would model or copy the other ladies and be a good worker for you."

"Okay. That is better. But do not try to confuse me with new words. I will send you back down the hill to wherever you came from. Now go fetch me two tubs of water from the stream. We must begin to clean the Master's chamber before he returns from his travel."

Kelly was actually glad to have something to do. She kept getting into trouble without knowing it and was on edge all the time. Finding someone to tell her how to go about this chore was her next problem. Miranda did not look like she wanted any questions at the present time.

Chapter Twenty-Nine

Many weeks had now passed and Jamie was relentless with his search. He had sent men in ten different directions with the order not to come back without her or some information to help them find her location. He had asked and searched for two weeks and no one had seen anything and not one person saw a lone rider or two traveling together in the day or night.

He questioned all the places they might have stopped for the night in his mind and then he made straight for all the pony stations and each little pub in every town he came through. Several times he heard stories that could have been about her, but they failed to be true after all his questions were asked.

At night, they stopped in little villages and while they ate and drank a pint or two, they listened to the conversation all around them hoping to hear information about a wayward rider with a beautiful woman coming through the village.

Once they heard some men talking about coming upon two men in the woods during the day and he heard that they were sleeping and when they stopped they had discovered that they were drunk and had not even a horse between them. So they moved over to the fire and waited for someone new to come in that they could listen to.

Jamie figured that he and his men were about one hundred miles from the castle and that tomorrow they would head in a northerly direction. They had been both south and north and now it was time to change again.

Jamie paid two farthings for a bed for his men and himself and about midnight they retired to their rooms. On the way upstairs to the small room in the attic, he heard some men arguing in a room at the back of the house. He stopped to listen and he heard a man say, "I tell you, I saw him take a woman and rush into the cave when we came around the bend and headed to the tree lines to watch for the next wagon to come along."

Another man said, "How do you know it was big Tom? They were out of our sight before we got there."

"Because no one has arms as huge and he had red hair. How many men could look like him after all? I saw him as he looked back out to see who was coming. I can't imagine why he was in the cave, but he was always up to no good. I know he took any kind of job. I remember he would kill for a song. I also remember that he was paid handsomely not too long ago to capture and kill the Mistress of Dunraven."

"Do you know the Earl? I heard that he went mad when they never found her. I wouldn't want him after me. I thought that maybe the lady we saw was his wife, but I heard they killed her and anyway that was a year or more ago now. It couldn't be her. I wonder who that was and I wish I had checked it out, because if it was her, there was a huge amount of coin for her return. I could sure have used that. You know Tom was a loner. He had no woman and no wife. The more I think about it the more I wonder who the lady was."

"Are you sure about what you saw?" one of the men in the room asked.

Having heard that, he motioned to keep quiet to his men who were standing toe to toe with him at the door with their ears pressed to the wall. Together they all had the same thought at once. Bust down the door and find out the location where they saw this man and how long ago it was.

Jamie reached out and motioned to the men to follow him on upstairs. Once they got to the top of the stairs, he spoke in a quiet voice so that on one else could hear him.

"I want one of you to keep watch on that room. When you hear the men up and moving around, come straight away to get the rest of us. It is already almost 1 in the morning and there is not much sleep time left and I want to be alerted if you hear anything else. Meantime, the three of us will plan a scheme for the morrow and at breakfast time we will have arrived with a plan. Remember to keep very quiet. Pray do not let them know you are outside the room. Else, something worse might happen to you when I find out. Now go."

Once inside the tiny room, they talked about all that they had heard and decided that in the morn they would go down and pretend to be hung over really bad. Maybe they could find a seat by the men in the room where they had heard the men talking earlier. They could bring up the subject of the Mistress being killed and no one would possibly know who they were this far away from the castle Dunraven. He hoped anyway.

Slowly the stars faded from the sky into a cloudy morn. The sun was not to be seen, but this morn Jamie had the tiny piece of information that he had traveled far and wide to find. He hoped to learn more.

In the late night, he had prayed so hard and he knew he was on to something. He only needed a little more information. His prayers were about to be answered, but not the way he had wanted them to be.

The fat meat in the greasy frying pan was smoking up the room when at last his man had come running to tell them the men had wakened and he had heard them say they were starving.

By the time Jamie got to the dining area, they were the first ones down. They had messed up their hair and then rubbed some black coal dust on their faces making them look like the most disreputable men in town. They actually looked a little scary to the buxom waitress who sauntered over to their table and asked what they wanted to drink.

"The coffee here is really black and good, they tell me," she said. "My name is Amanda and I will be here to serve you. Let me know that you need," she said with a quick wink towards Jamie. Even dirty and worn out, he still made a fine spectacle of a man. Several times she rubbed by his knee and winked at him brazenly. He took no notice, but the other men saw it and made mention to Jamie, as if he cared. They knew he had only one thing on his mind and that was to find his precious Rebecca.

The only thing that bothered all Jamie's men was that they really thought she was dead and they really figured up until last night that her disappearance was not only final, but they had not even a single clue to move forward with this plan until last night.

They heard the men climbing down the stairs long before they saw them. They were arguing over something and so loud that Jamie jumped up and pretended to run into them so he could apologize and make them like him. He told them to come to his table and break their fast with him and his men.

"Sorry, my mate. I did not see you coming down the stairs," Jamie told the dirty looking, greasy man. "Are you okay?" he asked, brushing off the torn brown shirt that was all but hanging on the man. "Come on over here. I see my friends have a table and I am starving after trying to sleep in this nasty hole. How can a man sleep with all that fighting and arguing all night under your head is what I want to know? Was your night any better than mine and my men?" Jamie asked in a big bold voice while slapping the horrible man on the shoulder.

"We were so full of the foul-tasting mead they serve her in this hole that I can't remember a thing about last night. The meat was so greasy I was sick when I went upstairs to the loft," the strange man replied to Jamie's questions.

Jamie had to figure another way to get into his mind, so he asked about his group in the eating area last night. "I saw you last night and I overheard you talking about Big Tom. I know that scoundrel from way back. He was a murdering lout. Did I hear you saw you saw him with a woman the other day?" Jamie questioned him carefully.

Robert studied Jamie before he spoke. He was being very careful with his answer because Jamie noticed that he was thinking before he spoke. His words came out in a question. "What woman did I mention? I tell you I was so drunk I do not remember talking about any woman." He looked at his mates and winked before he went on.

"Oh well, my mind was so numb from the greasy food I had to swallow and the stink in here was almost too much to stand, I can't remember what you were taking about to tell the truth. I thought I heard you say Big Tom killed someone. A woman. But you know I might kill someone before this day is over if I don't get out of this stinking hole." Jamie tried to come through the conversation in another direction by changing the subject.

Pushing the dirty man beside him out of his way, Robert agreed with Jamie that this was indeed a nasty place to try to rest. Jamie thought the man was on to him, so he went with the topic at hand and seeing Robert's attitude toward the man who was following behind Robert as they came down the stairs and before Jamie ran into him on purpose, he picked up on this man. Wanting a new conversation about the lady they had mentioned the night before.

"Come on over here and sit down and let's get some food before we all die of starvation. Hey!' Jamie called out to the woman. Amanda was replaced this morning by a much more talkative person. Jamie had high hopes that when the group with Robert left that a few sweet words would get this lady talking. She had been there the night before. Maybe she heard something he had missed. She was a looker and she probably would spill everything for a touch or a pinch or maybe a kind word and some flattery. Jamie knew exactly what to do. And he knew when to make his move. After the others were drunk or gone, whichever came first.

Jamie tried his mead and offered to pay for the rounds. He had not expected these grimy looking men to hold so much drink and not start talking. Time was slipping by fast and an hour had already passed along with six trays of strong mead. Jamie was getting very nervous. He was watching his drink and had to be careful not to drink too much himself. If he could not think he would not be able to pry answers out of the intoxicated men at his table.

The pot belly stove was boiling right beside him. His stomach was aching and he had a knot in there with the nasty tasting food still there from last night. He watched the time and as the minutes slowly went by, he made conversation very casually. Being very careful not to bring up anything about last night, he mentioned he had heard about a bunch of thieves that were robbing people and that he and his men were passing through the same area where they had been looting. No one had names but a few of Robert's men told about stories and different things they had heard. Then at the last minute before Jamie had decided to stand up and tell them he hand his men needed to be on their way, this last man on his right who had just come down an hour ago and joined in spoke up.

"You know, last night we were talking about Big Tom and I bet you he is in on that. He is a scoundrel and has even been brought up on two killings. I heard a month or so ago that he had even killed his partner over a woman." He grabbed his tankard and took a stiff drink.

Jamie's head came up and his eyes brightened. But his mind said not to seem too interested or Robert might be smart enough to catch on to him with questions that might lead to Rebecca. He took a long drink out of his cup and crossed his legs. He cleared his throat and then he said to his men, "Well, we must be getting on. We have a long way to go to bet back to the business that brought us here."

With that, all of Jamie's men started at once to say something, but one look into Jamie's eyes told them what they needed to know. Shut up was written all over his face and mouth. They took turns talking until one man brought up the woman again. Jamie listened with his ears open for a clue. Never did he join the conversation, but he had heard enough to get him going and soon he asked his men to get it together and they had to be leaving. All men stood up and stretched and no one mentioned the woman again.

As they started to get on their coats and get their bags, the man whose name was Jack spoke up and said, "Good to know you, Laird Dunraven."

Jamie turned around surprised that anyone would know this here in this new territory. Jamie tipped his hat and left. All his men behind him, they made an impressionable absence in the tavern.

As soon as they could get their horses saddled up, they headed north again. After about an hour had passed in complete silence, Jamie pulled his horse over to the side of the forest road they had been traveling on.

Gathering the men close, they discussed the words they had heard in the tavern less than an hour ago. Jamie asked them if anyone had picked up on a location from the conversation they all had listened to.

The big burley red-headed giant, that had been Jamie's faithful guard and friend for the most part of his life, leveled his eyes straight to Jamie and spoke up quickly. "I did."

Even though Jamie had been a kid when he first met Sven, he had always trusted him and as he had grown into manhood, Sven had grown older and wiser, but still remained his bodyguard when he traveled.

So now Sven had an idea and was going to spell it out for the rest of them. All the men looked at him and waited. "Robert said he had been in the courtyard at Freswick Castle and the lady was going to have new help soon. I heard another man say aye and it would have to be the lady friend of Big Tom because he saw them in the village talking one day and they both went into a small dwelling together, but Tom was pushing the lady in front of him and he had a hard hold on her. He never could tell if she had a feared look on her face because by the time he saw Tom, she had turned around. But she was moving very slow, kind of like she was sick or in pain. So I think it may have been Big Tom and the woman he has with him might be her, my Lord." At that, Sven lowered his head.

"Where is this Freswick Castle, Sven?" Jamie questioned him.

Sven said, "They talked like they had just come from Wick and that it was about seven days ride, my Lord."

"Stop with the Lord stuff, Sven, and get to the point. Can we get started now?"

He shouted to his men and all the men jumped up and went to working packing the horses down and in no time at all they were on the road again tracking down a castle they had never heard of before.

It was about noon and everyone was jumpy because they were in the woods so far off the main road that they thought they might be lost.

"Which way is the sun shining right now? We need to keep to a northerly direction," Sven yelled out as they all pulled up behind him and Jamie.

All through the morning, Jamie had been thinking about Rebecca, wondering how this had happened and thinking that maybe it really was his fault. Showing her off at the Medieval Fair that day had brought a whole new kind of terror and worry to his life. What had happened to his love was incomprehensible because he was really not sure if Rebecca was Rebecca at this time and this thing happened because he had not listened to her.

They passed through the deep forest, crossed over a racing stream where two of the men almost lost their seat. The water was cold and black with a smell that reminded them of fish because they were getting hungry again. The sky was turning dark. Night was coming in with a rush of cold wind. Cold chills washed over the men. All huddled up in a group, trying to figure out which way to go, they saw a puff of blue smoke go up in the air just a short pace in front of them.

"Wonder if we should check this out?" The voice sounded like teeth chattering.

Jamie put his hand to his mouth to keep them quieter, made all the men look around as if there was someone there that they could not see. "Shhhh!" He made the word with his lips, no sound escaping from his throat.

The trees moved in the wind and all at once ten riders passed them by moving at a fast pace as if they forgot something or maybe they were chasing someone.

Hidden deep in the trees, standing back off the track, they had been following, hid Jamie and his men from the ever watchful eyes of the intruders as they passed. No words were spoken for a long time. Then after about three minutes went by, they eased themselves out onto the road again and began heading north into the cold night wind.

After about an hour, they pulled up and Jamie and Sven began to discuss the night ahead of them. The horses were tired and so were the men. Along with the cold and the pace they had kept up this day, they were truly not fit to go any further.

The men began to unsaddle the horses and bed them down with a little grain they had brought with them. Building a small fire to cook the meat they had took some doing. All the wood around them had been wet to the touch and harder than that to get a nice size fire going tonight.

Grumbling men and noisy horses met the night as it came down on them. Finally after they had put down the blankets and gotten some dried bread and cheese to eat, the meat was done. The men hungrily chewed the meat and went straight to sleep with no talk of what or where they might be headed on the morrow.

Sometime in the night, all the men slept soundly, awaking to a more pleasant day and to a warmer wind this morning. They traveled in slow procession towards the castle keeping in the shadows at all times. Not wanting to be noticed, they were also very quiet. No one was talking unless they pulled up and stopped in a group setting.

Chapter Thirty

Rebecca had made a few friends here and was going through the days more content. She had no problem making the new head housekeeper like her. She worked hard and never opened her mouth except to say yes ma'am and no ma'am to Miranda. She washed and cooked and cleaned, put up foods and made more soap than she would have ever thought could be used. It was good to have a purpose again.

Tom was so happy to be with Rebecca that he forgot they had never talked about what had happened, about how Rebecca got kidnapped, about the treatment of the other man. Today he was trying to calm down a horse so the smitty could shoe him and while he worked holding his wild horse tight, his mind was whirling. He wanted to talk to her tonight. There were some answers he needed to give to her. He knew what he wanted to say, but he was nervous, too.

Rebecca wiped down their little table and wiped the sweat from her forehead. Even though it was cold outside, it was not in the little room they shared. Rebecca fried some meat and boiled some potatoes and beans for their meal.

Walking to the window, she moved the curtain to see if he was on his way or not. He was Tom. He was all she had to hold on to. He scared her at first, but since they came to the castle, he had seemed so careful of her that she wondered when he was going to try to sleep in her bed. That was what she worried about the most during her long days. She had long ago given up wondering about Jamie. She had almost forgotten him.

It all seemed so long ago now. Her attitude had changed, too. She was more congenial and actually was not depressed anymore. That made her think, maybe the memories that came and went daily were only that, just memories. She had a hard time thinking about the people in her thoughts anymore because her life had changed so much. She had very little time to remember things anymore.

Jamie was a clear memory, but maybe he had been hurt or even killed. She hated to think like that, but times were hard and people died for all kinds of things. She had begun to believe that she was going to be all right. And then she would open her mouth and out would come statements that she was not sure she remembered saying. She knew the meaning but tried to think before she made those mistakes. She had put herself in many a predicament by not thinking at first. Now she was good. She did not do that anymore.

Her food smelled too good. She hoped Tom would get home soon. She had made some bread, too. Turning around, she went to the table and reached out for a chair. Sitting down gave her relief from her hard day at work.

Soon she heard him coming. Rebecca got up and opened the door.

"Did you have a hard day, too?" Rebecca asked as he came in and sat down with a loud thump.

"Yes, I did and tonight I am starving. I did not even eat my lunch you packed for me last night and I was thinking I would eat it for my meal now, but something smells so good that I want to eat both things," Tom said with a smile on his face.

Rebecca liked the way they had settled in to feeling comfortable together at last.

"I made biscuits, too," she beamed up at him. As they both ate, there was a happy quiet in the room. Both of them eating and sharing the meal.

When they finished, she washed up again and went in to stir the fire up a little before bedtime. In the night, the little space they had got really cold if the fire was not going strong before they went to sleep.

She had borrowed a book or two and liked to read. Things in these books were so old and she loved ancient things like these stories told. Reading had been her way to pass the long evenings lately.

Tom pulled up a chair in front of the fireplace and asked her if they could talk. Rebecca wondered what but said sure to Tom and so he began.

"I want us to share the bed, Rebecca," he told her looking straight at her for an objection or a look that would say he had crossed the barriers they had put in place in the very beginning. She did not answer him and he got a little upset. "Well?" he said wanting an answer to his question.

She knew this was coming. But she was not ready to go with it yet. Her little mouth worked but no words came out. She twisted in her chair. She was really afraid to say anything.

Tom wanted to hear her say it was okay, but she did not open her mouth. She just looked at him and closed her eyes. In her mind, she heard Jamie say, "You know how much I love you, don't you?" She opened her eyes and she knew now was not the time. But it was closing in on her and she knew it.

Chapter Thirty-One

Jamie was getting a nervous feeling in his stomach as he saw the castle in the distance. They all saw it in his face and the way he was getting jumpy as they got closer to the place where he thought his Lady wife was being held captive. He was full of furious emotions and he wanted to kill the first man he laid eyes on. Thinking on it, he knew he had to control himself. That was going to be a hard thing to do.

The horses were jumpy and he was, too. He could hear a lot of noise in the castle yard ahead of them. People were going every which way. There was a lot of smoke in the air and he could smell food cooking. In his mind, he had to come up with a plan to get inside without making anyone suspicious of their entry to the castle.

All the men were clustered together talking as Sven came up with a good plan. "How about this horse of mine comes up lame and we need a place to rest the horses and ourselves for a few days. We ask to speak to the Lord and maybe he will invite us in and give us a place to rest for a while. If he does, we can check it out." He seemed to be really pleased with his story and to be truthful, Jamie liked the idea a lot.

They proceeded to the front gates of the huge old keep, all men eying the guards on the wall. They made a motion to invite them in and things were going well so far. As they approached, they asked the first man to reach them about the Lord and whether he was in at this time. They found out he was in a nearby town and would return tomorrow. They also asked if they wanted to wait for his return. That was lucky for the group of angry men and they all smiled and moved forward again.

Looking back and forth, Jamie saw no one that looked remotely like his Rebecca. This did not deter him at all and he jumped off his horse and pretended to be worried about Sven's mount. He hobbled the horse in like he was really injured. They fussed over the horse and the blacksmith came out to check him out. When he found nothing wrong with his inspection, he told Jamie that it must be a muscle and the horse needed to rest. They got a stall and fed and watered all the horses and then they took the men to the castle.

Inside the Lady in charge took control of all the men. She had a roving eye and saw a hunk in Jamie. She went to him and told them to sit by the roaring fire until she could get the cook to make them some food.

In the kitchen, Rebecca was kneading the dough for the evening meal. She was thinking how glad she was she did not have to stay and serve the evening meal. The Lord was a bit too friendly with her during the mornings. She had to hide from him on several different occasions. He had touched her back many times when she was walking by him at the table and he had stopped her.

Lord Brentwall was interested in her. She had seen him watching her from a distance. She had also seen the look on his wife's face.

His wife did not care for her at all because the upstairs maids had heard her say he had brought a woman here who thought she was better than everyone else. And she was too attractive to belong to Tom. She had told them there was something mysterious about Rebecca. And she was always close by when Lord Brentwall was at home.

Rebecca was thinking to herself that it was almost time for her to go to her room when she heard footsteps walk up behind her and the heavy wooden door to the back of the castle slammed shut very loudly. Almost as if someone had run in and slammed it behind them. She turned quickly to see what or who was in the kitchen in the early afternoon because usually she was always alone here doing the baking for their supper. If someone was here, it was not good. She had a feeling and it was also bad.

There he stood in all his glory. Or that was what he thought, Rebecca told herself.

"How are you today, Mistress Rebecca?" Lord Brentwall questioned her.

She had to be careful how she answered him and so she replied, "Very well, thank you. Can I help you? Because if not, I am really busy baking today for your evening meal time." She waited to see if he would leave then.

He had moved in closer to her. "How is it that you come to be with the likes of old Tom? He is certainly not what I would expect of you and he is not the type really to have a woman of your caliber. So tell me, where did you come from, honestly? There is no way I can put you with him."

Rebecca was appalled by his remark and after thinking for a minute, she answered with a question. "Why, sir, did you not know we were married for a long time now? Tom is a fine man and you really should not talk to me like that. I already see the fire in your Lady's eyes when she is around me. Please, I must go now."

Rebecca moved carefully around the Lord and went out the swinging door as fast as her legs would take her. She knew she could not tell Tom about this. He would do something horrible and one thing she did not want to do again was move around and have to find another place to live.

Tom was not that well liked among the people at the castle and she tried to make up for that by being kind and helpful to all around her.

Lord Brentwall was surprised by her agility and made a mental note to be quicker next time. He had had an eye on her for a while now. She was so different from all the women he had ever met in his entire life and he wanted to get to know her and find out how she came to be with that scoundrel, Tom.

Lord Brentwall found it hard to keep up with Rebecca. He would catch her out on the grounds and by the time he got to where he had seen her, she would be gone. One afternoon he was returning on horseback to the stables when he saw her go into the castle front doors. He jumped off his mount and threw the reins to the stable help, giving them a few orders as he walked hurriedly toward the castle.

Opening the door, he saw her skirt go around the corner up the stairs to the north tower. He was surprised to see her up there and went up the steps two at a time, almost twisting his ankle in his hurry to find her. She had been on his mind since the day they moved their belongings to the castle room they had been given.

There was something about her that made him think of a lady amongst them. He had tried to get it out of his mind through the months since they had arrived, but never had much luck. Each time he forgot about her while dealing with some other problem in running the castle, she would walk past him or she would have been asked to serve the evening meal and he would be in constant turmoil, because she made him want to touch her. It was an eerie thing. He could not put it away.

The north tower? Why there, he thought to himself. Everything was so quiet there. No one had stayed in the tower in a long time. What on earth was she doing up there? His questions were unanswered at that time.

Going down the hall and staring up at the winding stairs that he knew went to the turret room where there was no one and nothing, he heard her voice talking to someone. No way, he thought to himself. The hair on his neck was standing up and he had chills running down his back and arms. What was going on? Walking up the winding stairs, he had a feeling that he should turn around and now would be a good time to do it. All of a sudden, he did not hear anything. It was all too quiet. His fear took over and he turned around and left.

Hurrying down, he almost felt the chill leave the air. Warmth was all around him as he got to the bottom floor. Deciding to fix himself a drink to chase away the nerves, he took the jug down and started to pour when he saw Rebecca in the room next to the courtyard. He shook his head and took his drink and walked over to the opening between to the courtyard and spoke to her.

Rebecca jumped when she heard his voice, but kept on washing clothes in the wooden tub. The maids had been bringing her clothes all day, she had been working at this since sunrise. She had not known he was in the castle. So now she had to be scared again. He gave her a frightening feeling.

"How did you get down here so fast, young lady?" he questioned her. He saw the way she looked at him and he had a feeling she had spoken, but he had not heard her. "Well?"

She still did not open her mouth. He saw the look on her face. It was one of fear. He wondered what was going on in her head and why she looked afraid. But there were no answers coming forthwith, so he just stared at her beautiful face.

Finally she choked up a little and she spoke to him. "I have been in here washing clothes for my Lady, sir, probably for half of the day. I don't know what you mean, sir?" She lowered her head so as not to see his eyes on her.

"I saw you go up the stairs a few minutes ago and when I called out your name, you disappeared around the corner. So I went up the winding stairs to talk to you, but when I got up there, you were gone again." He spoke like he was upset with her.

She had no idea what he meant. So she spoke up and looked at him as she did. "I was here, my Lord. Not upstairs or anywhere near those areas of the castle. If you do not mind, I need to get back to my polishing." She dismissed him with that and he did not like the feeling at all.

He turned around and went back to his drink and his thoughts. His thoughts were going crazy because he had no idea what or who he had seen. He knew it had been a woman. But what strange woman was in the castle?

Some hours after Lord Brentwall left the castle to see to his help in the fields, Rebecca made a quick trip back up into the turret room. Almost instantly, Rebecca felt it, a cold wind blowing on her back seeming to push her up the stairs. She ran up the last ten steps, almost slipping on the slick stones in her haste to find out where the icy wind was coming from.

The handle on the door to the only room up there was cold to her touch, but swung open when her hand merely touched it. Jumping back from a case of nerves, Rebecca surveyed the room and she saw a large opening high up in the ceiling of the room. Standing there, she wrapped her arms around her body, feeling afraid but not knowing why.

She was so startled when the big black falcon swooped in and down towards her, that she jumped back against the wall, almost falling down. The bird landed on the top of the huge bedpost in the middle of the room. Remembering the falcon from the village, she tried to talk to him. "Here, little friend. Come down and let's talk. Where have you been? It has been a long time." She reached out her fingers and touched the falcon's back.

The bird looked at her with his little red eyes as if to say I am coming closer, moving all the while towards Rebecca's arm. He chattered away and Rebecca continued to talk to him. All at once she felt her fear disappear. Whatever was the bird doing in the turret, she wondered. Asking him again, "How did you find me? What are you doing here?"

He preened his head toward her touch as if to say something, but Rebecca did not know what. Rebecca held her arm out. "Here, come to me so I can pet your wings." The bird squawked loudly and moved to her outstretched arm. Rebecca had seen falconers working before, so she knew he needed stroking. Falcons carried messages in those parts of the country, making Rebecca wonder why he had searched her out again. Slowly moving her other arm to his head, she stroked him and he closed his eyes and so did Rebecca. Rebecca heard a soothing voice in her mind say, "I am Robert and in time you will be saved from Lord Brentwall's terroristic reign. In time all will be revealed. Go now and watch behind you."

Chapter Thirty-Two

Rebecca looked out the tiny window in her room. She could see the evening was setting in and the rain was not far away. She guessed it to be a little before 7 o'clock. It was past time for Tom to be back in the yards outside. She did not see him out the window. It made her wonder where he had gone.

She decided to put on the kettle of water. She needed a hot drink. The coffee was boiling and she was finally calming down. Tom still had not come home. Rebecca took her sewing basket and sat down in front of her fireplace and got out the sweater she had been mending for Tom. It was torn in the neck and she knew he did not have another warm sweater and it was getting cold out these days.

She was working when she heard feet coming toward her door. Thinking it was Tom, she went to open the door for him. Putting down all her mending on the small table, she reached out and opened it just in time to see him coming her way. He was a dirty mess.

Outside she heard a tremendous loud clap of thunder. The rain was coming down in sheets, making her glad to be inside the warm cozy room. She poured Tom a cup of coffee and gave him time to get off the dirty clothes before she questioned him about being so late tonight.

"What happened to you, Tom?" she casually asked him. "You are two hours later tonight than usual."

Staring at the fire and holding his coffee cup, he replied, "The master came down this afternoon and sent me to the yard to remove some small trees that were growing in the field where the men practice their sword fighting each day. It was muddy and the roots were deep. It took longer than I thought it would because I had no one to give me a hand. You know if I had not done it the way he wanted it, he would find something equally as hard tomorrow to show me who was in charge of my life."

Tom had a hard look in his eyes. It was very plain to Rebecca that Tom was not happy. All evening he talked about how he had to go out there and leave the horse he had been shoeing before the Lord had come out of the castle.

"I don't know why he chose me to do the work. He usually has nothing to say to me at all. It was not right to put that on me."

Tom was still mad. When he was talking, Rebecca had thought it strange, too. Then she remembered that it was the same time he had come into the kitchen and followed her around. Rebecca hoped that was not going to be the thing now, to get Tom away or tied up so he could harass her. Chills ran down her spine.

Chapter Thirty-Three

Jamie had the reputation for being savage when he had to be and today was no different. He was in a fury. He had just spent the night in the castle where he had hoped his Rebecca was being held captive. So far this morning and the night before, all he saw was a rough meal of meat, bread and cheese and some very good wine. And today, the feast for breakfast was in front of him but he still had not heard or seen any woman that might be his Lady wife.

Conversations were quiet all around the huge table. The Lord was at the head and he and his men were seated very near to the Lord. So close that he could hear every word spoken around the table. His Lady had been mentioned and he wanted to find her.

Jamie had not even given much thought to the fact that what he had heard was only a rumor passed by men who were equally as drunk as they could have been when he heard the gossip that night in the inn on their search for her. Jamie would never give up looking for her. He dreamed that she was waiting for him and he would find her. He would never forget the look in her eyes that day at the fair when the rough lot of men had spied her. She had known it and he paid no attention to them at all. The thought that someone would come back after her was not something he wanted to think about. So in his deliberate refusal, he had actually been the reason for this painful attempt on her life. So far they had gotten away with it. But now he could almost smell her. He knew she was here. He could feel it in every bone in his body. Why had he not heard about a woman there that worked there maybe or a woman being held for some odd reason? He had heard nothing at all.

The evening before, he had spent the time working his way to every table and every man there. He talked, introduced himself and still heard nothing to lead him to believe there was anyone there that did not belong there.

Breakfast was good. He ate until he could eat no more. As the men finished eating, they all left to go outside the castle and meet up so if anyone had heard anything they would share the information.

Rebecca was making the bread for the evening meal. She had flour everywhere. The air was white with a cloud of flour. She sneezed and dropped the cloth she was holding to move the dough with. As she bent over to pick it back up, she saw a man go by the corner of the dining room who looked like someone new in the castle. She moved her head out of the bend it was in so she could see who it was. It was too late. He was gone.

Back to the baking, she thought, giving the stranger no more thoughts. Millie came rushing in saying the master was on the way to the kitchen. Rebecca ran into the cellar where she stayed very quiet until Millie came back to tell her he was gone. It seemed like a long time to her, so she stuck her nose out and he was right there talking to Millie about her. Millie gave no hint as to where she had gone.

Finally Millie came down and told her it was safe to come back up. Together, they went about the normal duties of the kitchen staff to get ready for the lunch and evening meals.

Outside, the men went to the lists to exercise with the knights at the castle. At about noontime, Jamie was ready to go in, so he told his men he was going to go check on the horses. As he was walking off, he managed to hear two men talking about personal things in his home. Jamie hunkered down so they thought he was working with his boots and listened.

"Well, I am not surprised at all to hear that." Fenwick said to the other man standing there. "The master always goes after the beauty in the kitchen. And I cannot believe that Tom had the good luck to catch a woman like that anyway can you?"

"No, I do not know how he did that either. But I see him with her and he is always the gentleman to her. She had a strange way about her, ye know? Quite different from the ladies I 'av ever met. I think it was a miracle, I do, that Tom has such a lovely woman for a wife."

They moved on out of earshot. Jamie stood up and his heart was beating madly in his chest. This was what he had hoped to hear for two days now. Finally a clue. But how was he to find this woman? Where in the castle was she? Why hadn't he seen her yet?

So many questions and Jamie was sure now that she was here. Rubbing his forehead, he moved a lock of hair out of his eyes. Climbing the hill to the stable, he kept thinking how he could find her. He had to find her soon. They could not stay here much longer on the pretense the horse was lame when anyone with eyes could see he was fine.

The sun was going down and the wind was blowing hard. Rain in the distance was closing in on the castle high on the hill. The winds buffeted the walls, but all inside were warm and safe except Rebecca. The master had come looking again. He knew dinner was ready to be served because he could smell it. He made a move to go into the kitchen, but Jamie came in behind him saying, "I'm so hungry, sir. I can smell the fine meal about to be served and I couldn't wait any longer. So I thought I would get me a seat and wait." Jamie laughed as he sat down, but the Lord of the castle was not laughing. He was put off again.

Taking a seat to the left of Jamie, he said he had been ready to eat also. So the conversation started and Jamie kept it going until the rest of the men came clambering in to eat with them.

The mead was first and then the food was served. At first Jamie did not believe his eyes when he saw her come in and set down a big platter of meat on the table to the back of the dining room. He squirmed in his seat and wanted to catch her attention, but she never lifted her eyes to the table, not once. He was so happy he could not think. He just wanted to plan her escape. His men also saw her at the same time.

The master got up when she entered the room and went over to her. Jamie heard him ask her if she needed any help. She had a frightened look on her face. Jamie had seen it before and now he felt like there was something she was afraid of here in the castle. It made him worry about her. But what could he do? Nothing until he could talk to her in private. If only she would look up. But when the Lord came up behind her, he reached out and touched her shoulder in an intimate way, but Jamie saw the revulsion in her eyes before she turned her face downward. It hurt him so much that he choked on his own pain. He jumped up and started to go to her, but Sven grabbed hold of his sleeve and stopped him from making a scene in which Rebecca would be the one who suffered.

"Keep calm, my Lord," Sven said quietly in his ear while he turned Jamie towards the doorway out of the dining room. All the men saw it and followed him outside. They went to the stables where they could talk. Everyone wanted to talk at once, but Jamie stopped them with a slap on the stall door. Silence fell and Jamie took the floor.

"We have found her now but we have to be careful how we make our next move. I have to get her alone and then I can begin to understand the moves we must make next." No one said a word because they all knew he was right. "So in the morning at breakfast, I will try to get her attention and then if I can get her alone for a minute or two, she can relax knowing we are here to get her back home again."

Everyone nodded their heads in agreement with Jamie knowing that they had to be careful now that they had found her at last. Together they all walked back to the castle. Entering the high doors into the massive hall, Jamie saw her go around the corner with another big giant of a man holding onto her elbow, almost as if he owned her. He was guiding her somewhere in the castle, and Jamie was right on them. He followed them to a door where they both went into and he heard the bolt slide shut, as if they were locking someone out. "Did they sense that I am following them?" Jamie wondered out loud as he retreated back to the great hall for some wine to sooth him until morning came.

Chapter Thirty-Four

Sleep that night was impossible. Jamie had dreams of her and her strange way of talking that had endeared him to her in the first place. Later he dreamed the big man took her away and he could not find her anywhere. Then right before the sun came up on the foggy morning outside, he heard her call his name. He wakened with a start and saw it was Sven standing by his small bed waiting for him to answer him.

"Come on, My Lord, the sun is up and we need to break our fast in hopes of seeing her again this morning." Smiling at Jamie all the while, Sven took him by the arm and helped him rise. Dressed and ready to go, they hurried down the corridor. The food was being served as they took a seat.

Looking all around, he saw not one sign of her anywhere. The fireplace was roaring and the shadows on the great walls were an amazing thing to watch. Especially since he had to act like he was eating the scrumptious food being placed on the table by Rebecca. Again she never once looked at the men eating their breakfast. Jamie actually coughed and acted as if he were strangling.

Just then, Lord Brentwall came in and, as he went to have his seat, he saw the strange men who had arrived a couple of days ago sitting at the huge table by the roaring fireplace all in a scramble. Three men had grabbed for their leader as he coughed and spewed and as if on cue the great big bearded man he had heard called Sven hit the leader on the back and watched as if he had saved him from whatever catastrophe had been going on when he had been about to take his place at the table.

Thinking that they had been in the castle long enough, he rose from his chair with a thoughtful look on his face. Sven saw him first and tried to let Jamie know the master was walking around the table in their direction. Sven wondered what this could be about.

At the same time as Jamie turned his puzzled face around to try to find Rebecca or see which way she went, he saw the Lord right in front of his chair. Lord Brentwall was bewildered and asked him what was going on.

"I got choked on a piece of stringy pork and my men were trying to save me, I guess." Jamie turned to Sven for back up. Sven smiled and made sure that the lord knew this was exactly what had happened.

Taking his seat again, Jamie began to place his napkin in his lap as he spoke to Lord Brentwall. "Please excuse me for all the noise, my Lord, but I never expected to be choked nearly to death on my breakfast this morning, sir." With that, a laugh escaped his throat and the Lord walked back down toward his chair to eat his food.

"By the way, Jamie, how is your horse coming along these days?" he wanted to know. "I will accompany you this morning down to the stables and see how it goes with your mount, after we fill up on this good smelling food, if you want me to." It was almost a question, but not an order.

Jamie could see the look on his face. The Lord was waiting for an answer.

"That sounds good to me, sir. I noticed last evening he was improving enough, but I am not yet ready to make the journey with him, sir. I want to make sure he is well enough to cover a lot of ground and in a hurry since we have been held up here for a few days. I am heading to London and, as you well know, it is a long way on horse flesh and the horse must be in perfect condition to make the trip in a timely manner. I will need the utmost speed from him, sir."

Jamie hoped this would buy him a day or two at the most. Smiling, he started to eat, taking his time. He had been hoping he would see Rebecca again very soon. But no so lucky after about forty minutes, he decided to search the castle for her whereabouts.

He cleared his throat and Lord Brentwall looked up as he also made to leave the room. Sitting back down in his chair, he said, "Yes Jamie, what was it you needed from me?"

"I want to know if I could have one of your servants who are not too busy this morning for a tour of the castle. Can that be arranged, sir? It is so big and so well fortified that I might be taking a thing or two home to my own castle. We are raided so often anymore from the clans who can't seem to settle anywhere for long enough that they can have something of their own. They always want to fight and take what they can't have. I am sure you have the same thing in this part of Scotland just like we do, am I right, sir?" Jamie leaned back and waited for a response from his host of the moment.

"Yes, of course. I'm sure I can spare someone to take you around the castle, Jamie. Give me a second, because there is someone I need to catch before she goes about her other duties in other parts of the castle and I can't abide looking for a servant when they should be around when I need them."

Jamie wondered if it might be Rebecca whom he wanted to see but for fear of arousing suspicion he did not mention it. "Thank you, sir, and I will wait right here for you to make the arrangement for me and for Sven also, if that suits you okay."

"Sure, this won't take too long. I find a beauty working here and I have need of some information from her. Up 'til this day I have had no luck speaking to her at all. If you ask me, she seems a little high and mighty for me and I have a need to find out where this comely attitude comes from."

Jamie wanted to ask more questions, but Sven made a look as if to say, "No, Jamie, enough."

Jamie settled back down to wait. He had a fear that Lord Brentwall was looking for the same woman he was looking for, his lady. But he shut his mouth and sat there to wait it out.

In the same instant, there was a noise in the hall. Lord Brentwall almost ran head on into Rebecca. He stopped abruptly and let her pass. She was on her way to bring in the food from the tables.

"Excuse me," Lord Brentwall said in his rasping voice, "but I have a need to see you in private for a moment please, if you will."

Rebecca looked up at him and it was plain to see that she was afraid of him. Rebecca looked all around the room trying to make her voice clear enough and show no fear in it. When her eyes met with Jamie's, she had a moment of shock. Then she went right on with the conversation.

"Please, My Lord, I need to remove the food before I am called down on my lazy work. But if you will give me a minute, I will be right back." Somewhere in her mind, she thought she knew the man at the table with the Lord. But she was so upset at the moment that she could not get it into perspective. What with the fear of being raped by the Lord and trying to get out of his way, she nearly lost all thoughts of the stranger at the table.

"Excuse me, Ma'am." Jamie stood up to interrupt the scene playing out before his very eyes. "I would like a tour of the grand castle and the Lord has granted it for this morning. Would you be able to do this after you speak to the Lord?"

Jamie hoped he was in time. Trying to stop a nasty scene from happening, he moved over to where Lord Brentwall was staring at him.

"Sir, I would like this servant to show me around. Do you mind if I pick the person I want to do this for me?"

Lord Brentwall was so shocked by the effrontery of his guest that he did not know what to say. He turned to see if anyone else had heard the man make his demand. No one looked like they had even noticed Jamie in the room, let alone talking to the Lord. Most of the people in the dining room were eating or talking to someone beside them and were not the least bit interested in the Lord or his guest.

With his guest staring him in the eye, he had no other recourse but to answer him. "Certainly, that will be all right with me, but on the other hand, I am not so sure the girl will allow it. You see she is married and her man watches her from afar and she does naught to antagonize him. I can not even get a word with her because she is always running here and there doing the odd chore in the castle. Good luck to you, Sir Jamie."

As he told Jamie about the lady, he walked out of the room abruptly, heading toward the servant in his conversation. Jamie watched him until he was out of sight. His worry was that Rebecca did not recognize him. From what he had seen so far, she did not bat an eye as if she did know him. And hearing that she had a husband had totally sent Jamie into a cold sweat. How could they have gotten married so fast? It had only been close to a month or maybe five weeks since she had gone missing from his home.

After the shock of Jamie's request, Rebecca had immediately looked down so he could not see her eyes any longer. She had waited for the Lord to dismiss her, but he had instead taken her by the arm and led her out into the corridor to have a word with her, why she did not know, but she had a terrible fear of the man. His touch was cold and she was shaking with fear.

"I want to have you take care of some things in my rooms this afternoon. I will expect you at three o'clock and be prompt." He let go of her arm and retraced his steps back inside the dining room.

Rebecca, trembling from his touch, ran to the kitchen where the cook saw the look on her face and began to question her as to why she was so upset. Reaching into her big pocket, she pulled out a cloth and went to the water supply and dipped it into the water and carried it over to her and wiped her eyes off.

Chapter Thirty-Five

Mara, the cook, wanted an explanation for her tears. "Who did make you cry, Rebecca?" she questioned her. "Was it one of those rough boys in the yard? Come on now, child. Get it out of your head and calm down for me. Talk to me. What's it going to be?"

Wringing her tiny hands together over and over, she finally looked up and choked back a sob while trying to get her voice to speak to Mara. "The master, he has been giving me a hard time and now he wants me to report to his rooms at three o'clock today," she told Mara with tears fowling down her beautiful face. "What can he want with me, mistress Mara? I don't like him at all, you know. He has been touching me and I hate it. What can I do? Will I have to go to his rooms, Ma'am?" Shaking her head, she was very distraught.

Rebecca saw the look because the old woman knew what he was about to try with Rebecca. The master had always been after the new girls when they first came to the castle to work. Most of them bowed down and let him have his way because they did not want to lose their position working inside the castle. And, after all, they told Mara, one at a time, as they came and went, he was the master and they all thought he loved them after they gave it to him.

Mara was very worried about Rebecca. Mara had seen Big Tom and the talk around the courtyard was how mean and tough he was. He could take on three men at once. He could swing his axe harder and faster than any man there. Her thought was if she went home and told her man, he might kill the Lord and if she could prevent it, she must try.

Rebecca was staring at her now as if she did not even see Mara. Taking hold of her arms and shaking her a little bit, Mara was able to bring back the alertness she needed to try and talk to her. "Rebecca, please listen to me. I have been around her for nigh on to fifty years and I have a few ideas that might help us out."

Rebecca just shook her head and stared into Mara's eyes like a little trusting kitten might do.

"Whatever we do, we mustn't let him know we are on to him and his perverted ideas of being in charge of you just because you work here. I think you should go to his room and, when you get in there, stay as close to the door as you can and tell him this. 'I am not interested in you, my Lord.' Also say this and I might add that I know a lie is a bad thing, but this might turn his mind another direction if he thought you were pregnant, Rebecca."

Rebecca recoiled from the thought of him being anywhere near her, but the idea was a working one. She had to think that this would work or else she might cause Tom and herself to lose their lodging inside the castle. And Tom needed his work right now. It was all they had. She would not want Tom angry with her.

Seeing that Rebecca liked the idea, they spent the next hour talking about how to pull this off and let her get back to Tom for protection. Mara told her over and over again to not mention this to Tom. The fear of the problems a confrontation with Tom and the Lord was not something Mara wanted to be a part of. Walking back and forth and talking constantly about what she might put into action with Tom coming after the Lord was not a pretty thought.

The knights would of course kill Tom in the fight and then she would have no protector at all. What Mara did not know would not hurt her, was what Rebecca was thinking about her so-called husband. She was almost sure they had not been married, although she had been in a bad shape for a while thinking back and there were no memories because she had shut them out.

She had blank spaces in her mind and no matter how hard she tried to remember the past; it would not come to her yet. But if they had been married somewhere, he would be sleeping in her bed at night and he was so careful not to upset her about that part of their life that it made an impression on Rebecca that remained in her mind about being not married to him. Where did she meet him? She did not remember that either. Why, she wondered so often, were her memories so blurred and distant? Why can I not remember anything about Tom? She questioned herself a lot lately, but it did not help at all. She was at a loss as to the whys and the wheres right now.

"So if I back up to the door and tell the Lord that I am pregnant, he might back off? Is that what you really think will work?" Rebecca asked her as she turned and walked toward the windows looking down on the courtyard below.

She saw Tom holding up a horse's leg and knew he was enjoying his new job in the smithy. She decided that was what she had to do now and she would meet him in his room at 3:00 as planned.

"Thank you, Mistress Mara. I will do as you suggested and now I am supposed to be showing the men in the breakfast area around the castle for the Lord. I am better now. Thank you so much."

"These new men in the castle seemed familiar to me, Mistress Mara. Do they look like they have been here before to you? I have heard them talking in hushed voices and I am wondering if they are trying to do something right under our noses?" Rebecca smiled as she tried to get herself together again. But her uneasy feeling about the man they called Jamie was getting to her. She kept wondering why he looked so familiar to her. There was something about his voice and when she looked into his eyes, there was a question there. It bothered her to not be able to figure the new man out and that was very unnerving to Rebecca.

"No," Mara said in a whisper as she saw the Lord coming down the hall towards the kitchen. "You best run now. I see the Lord on his way to find you."

Rebecca turned just in time to get to the dining room doorway as the Lord came bustling in to the kitchen.

"Where did the girl Rebecca disappear to, Mistress Mara," he asked. Seeing that she could not lie to him, she replied, "Rebecca has gone to show the men around the castle, my Lord." Turning away, she hoped he would go out of her kitchen.

Mara could never get over the fact that Rebecca was so polished and well mannered. She was nothing like any other girl in the castle that she had ever come into contact with. There was something about her that Mara liked. The girl was a joy to be around. She worked as hard as anyone and never complained at all. Mara was shocked when she had first met with Rebecca. Sometimes when they were together, Mara felt like she was with a lady and not with a maid.

Mara had asked a few questions of Rebecca in the beginning, but never quite got a straight answer. She thought the girl was hiding something sometimes and then again she couldn't decide. Mara had grown so fond of Rebecca that it showed amongst the other maids in the castle because there was talk in the kitchen and Mara heard it all and saw the rest.

There was jealousy in the eyes of the other girls in the castle, especially when they had seen the Lord going in Rebecca's direction and leaving them alone. There was nothing Mara could do because a day without Rebecca was like a day without sunshine. And as Mara had grown fonder of Rebecca, she had requested her help more often than the others that had been there a long time. And in front of her inside the castle workings, they should come first. At first they noticed that Rebecca got the best jobs, the easier jobs, the cleaner jobs and they did not like it at all.

A few of the girls had shoved her in the winding rock stairwell once almost causing her to lose her footing and fall. She did not know it was a push on purpose and regaining her steps, she apologized for being so clumsy and almost making them fall with her. The girl who did it was so shocked by Rebecca's kindness that she ran on away and Rebecca went on to do her job in the large turret on the east side of the castle.

That particular part of the castle did not appeal to Rebecca in the least. She always felt like she was being watched from every turn she made up there. She only went there a couple of times a week and that was to clean the rushes on the floors, because the knights slept there around the huge fireplace when the weather was cold and the dogs made such a mess that she cleaned it on her own and no one, not even the Lord, knew she was doing it. Sometimes she wondered why she did it because no one else seemed to bother about the dirt and bones and cups and troughs that were thrown all around, but it did get on her nerves. So she took it on herself to accomplish this task for the Mistress Mara.

There were other times the girls were nasty to Rebecca but, being the kind girl she was, she never noticed it. Rebecca thought the girls were aggravated by something or someone. Then, on her way to Jamie and his men to do the tour, she heard Lord Brentwall. The hairs on her arm stood straight up. Chills ran down her back. Feeling her heartbeat quicken, fear moved in.

The Lord came around the corner and ran face to face into Rebecca. She saw him and leaned into the wall and, bending over, she stuck her finger deep into her throat. Immediate vomiting came projecting out of her mouth. She stood up and wiping her face, she turned around and pretended the sight of him was shocking to her, as if she did not know he had been there.

Keeping her eyes down, she said really loudly, "Shit! Being pregnant sucks." Then she touched her tummy and had a maternal look on her face that she was sure he would see and then looked up straight at the Lord. She pretended she had not seen him and spoke up quickly, as if to cover up her actions.

She saw the disgusting look spread across his face. Secretly smiling inward to herself, she immediately said, "Good morning, sir. I did not hear you come up behind me. I am sorry, I did not mean to be rude." Later in her room that evening, she had no memory at all of what she had said. But from the look on his face, it had worked. She spoke up, "Pardon me, but your new guests are waiting for the tour, as you told them I could do it. Thank you sir, but I will be on time to your room at 3 o'clock as planned."

Looking into his eyes, she saw revulsion, not lust. Silently praying thanks to God, she ran in the other direction quickly to get out of sight. Making a stop at the kitchen on the way, she had a bounce in her step and she ran straight calling, "Mara! Mara! Mara! It worked! It worked!" Mara came around the corner and hugged her tightly. Rebecca felt like she would burst from relief. Rebecca also felt a love in her heart for Mara who had helped her in a way that Mara would never know.

Chapter Thirty-Six

Rebecca remembered the new men were waiting for her to take them on a tour. Hurrying back, she met up with Sven. He was coming back in the doors in the front hall.

"Here ye are lassie. We have been waiting for ye to come back and I got to worrying about where you had disappeared to when ye did not come back for so long. Jamie sent me to find ye. He will be so happy to know ye are ready to show us around. Come with me, lassie. I feel better now that I have found ye."

Rebecca was startled to see Sven and had no idea why he was sent to find her. After all, she had other duties here at the castle and her promise to show them around was easily given and soon forgotten by her. So to see these expectant faces awaiting her made her happy once more. She could not wait to see Jamie once more. He made her feel so elated. She did not have time to think about that part of the feelings that he evoked in her yet. There was time for that tonight. Looking all around the room as she entered, she saw the delight in his face when Sven escorted her in.

"Here she is, my Lord," Sven spoke up first. "I found her coming from the back of the castle where I assume she

236

was put to work. While we waited, someone sent her on errands."

Jamie looked in her eyes and saw fear. He knew there was something going on here that was affecting Rebecca.

Oh God, he was so happy to have found her and now he had to make her come with him. But she acted as if she did not know him. How could that be? Searching her face as he walked up to her, he could see nothing in her eyes that said positively that she knew who he was. He was disheartened to think that now he had to kidnap her to get her back, because if she did not know him, she certainly would not go willingly with him anywhere.

Rebecca ever so slightly bent in a bow, as if to say, "My Lord", raising up straight as she placed her nervous hands in her pockets and her fingers tightened on the others as her nerves jumped in her neck for all eyes to view. Her nervousness was very apparent to the men gathered together to take their supposed TOUR of the castle. Sven looked at her hard and, to his eyes, she did not recognize any of them yet. That made for a problem in itself. How to get her to go with them if she had not a clue as to who they were?

Turning his back to Rebecca, he watched Jamie's face as he did the same thing, searching her eyes and her body movement for a slight recognition. There was a blank stare when she looked into his eyes at last.

Feeling very bad for Rebecca, Jamie reached out his hand and tried to get a grip on her own hand as he moved closer to her. She stood still. Jamie spoke up first. "Here, give me your hand." Then he let her know that he and his men were ready for the tour.

"Well, we are ready for the trip through the castle. Thank you for agreeing to show us this old Keep. You know, I am Lord of Dunraven Castle in the far north of here. Have you heard of it?" he questioned her, still searching for any sign that she knew him. He did not want her to respond to him in a too knowingly way if she were to remember him or the home they had been sharing before this kidnapping happened to her, so he was very cautious in his words to her. "We are ready now."

Rebecca had a feeling in her gut; but why, she did not know. She felt so humble in this man's presence, not afraid, very safe she thought. This man only wanted to have a look around and she could do that and it would keep her away from Lord Brentwall and his groping whenever he was close enough to touch her. But Rebecca felt maybe the Lord Brentwall would not be so into her anymore. Only time will tell, but she felt better now that she had played her part so royally.

Her smile lit up the day. Jamie wondered why she smiled at him in particularly. With hope he followed her.

Moving in front of the men, Rebecca headed towards the old curving stairs in the middle hall off the front of the castle. As they went up the stairs, Jamie asked her where her rooms were. Rebecca turned around and spoke up like she thought he needed to know something about her precarious living arrangements here.

"I live with my husband, Tom, in the back of the castle near to the kitchens," she smiled as she spoke like she really believed it herself, hoping to shut him up. She smiled again.

Jamie knew that she could not have married Tom knowing there had not been time for that, seeing that he had kidnapped her in the first place and wondered why she would say something so terrible like that to them.

Rebecca wondered why he was so curious about her and Tom. Thinking that maybe the Lord had told him he was taking her to his rooms for a little pleasure and maybe Jamie wanted the same for her. She had a foreboding chill race up her spine. That was all she needed now, another man trying to get familiar, too. Just the thought made her shiver again. Her smile faded for now. As she reached the top, Rebecca told them about the castle. She chatted on and on.

Jamie watched and listened but he did not hear anything that he wanted to hear. At one point, Jamie asked her again where she had her rooms. Rebecca looked at him thinking that he had already asked her that question a while ago. Even then, she did not answer him. So no, maybe, she should turn the tables and ask him why he wanted to know.

She thought about it for a short minute. Then she said, "Why, we live in the back of the castle, My Lord. We have a cozy little room that supplies us all we might need. The master here is very good to Tom and me."

Jamie wondered if he questioned her about Big Tom what he might be able to learn about their strange relationship. All the while he was prying there was no relationship at all.

"Where did you and Tom come from, Rebecca, before you came to live here? Were you an employee in another manor near this one?" Jamie waited with bated breath for her to answer him. Jamie knew if she remembered him, it would be hard for her to answer this question. And Sven could not believe his ears because he was baiting Rebecca, even if she did not know it. But then, what if she did? What if she was hiding something that she was afraid of? If she was, she would not tell them anyway.

Sven was angry with Jamie for not waiting and giving it a day or two more. Time for Rebecca to see them a few times and maybe she might remember them. Who knows? And you can't rush her, Sven was thinking.

"Dear, can we talk about the turret? I have never seen any lights up there since we first arrived and it would be nice to see the rooms up there. We have a large turret in Dunraven, but it is haunted and I was for sure that I saw a person in the shadows through the window one night here, but Lord Brentwall says it is not used. Is that true, Rebecca? Is this castle haunted, also? It is very old and I have heard some terrible stories from people about this castle. I also would not like to think someone was living in here that no one knew about, a thief or a desperate person finding a hiding place right under Lord Brentwall's nose. Do you know what I mean, Rebecca?" asked Sven.

Rebecca remembered being up there one day and hearing someone talking. She had also heard that no one was supposed to be up there. Rebecca also had chills every time she went into the west wing of the castle and that was near the turret rooms. How to answer that question so that the big man called Sven would be satisfied made Rebecca nervous.

"I have been up there, sir, and I assure you that no one lives in that part of the castle. I have been sent up there to retrieve things once in a while and I must admit it also makes me fearful when I do go there. But I have not seen any candles or tallows that could be used for light up there.

So I cannot tell you what you saw, sir. I suppose it could be haunted also."

Rebecca thought she had come up with a great answer and gave them all a big beautiful smile, a smile that Jamie remembered so well. It tore at his heart. It hurt and the pain was deep and hard to hide.

"My Lord, did I say something wrong?" Rebecca saw the look on his face and it sent a ripple through her heart. All at once she placed her hand on the visitor and tried to make him feel her need to make him enjoy his visit here in Lord Brentwall's home. If he told the Lord that she was not helpful, she had to fear again that he would strike out at Tom or corner her in the castle and make advances to her person. That she did not want to happen. Thinking that she made the visiting Lord angry made her think this day was going to be a bad one already, and it was barely even noontime yet.

Jamie saw her obvious distress. He did not want to upset her any more than she already was. So he replied, "Rebecca, it is okay. Do not be worried. We wanted to know if someone was here that Lord Brentwall might not know about, and we were wrong because it had nothing to do with you. I am sorry to have put you on the spot like that. Please continue on and tell us what you know about this castle. By the way, how long have you both been working for Lord Brentwall. You seem to not have answered us before?"

"Sir, we have been here only a little time. We were living in the town before the Lord offered Tom a place in the smithy. We like it here and I do not want to get into trouble with the Lord. If you tell him I offended you, he will take it out on me, I am sure of it. Or Tom, if not me. Sometimes

I think the Lord is on crack." It slipped out of her mouth before she knew where it came from. The look on her face was pure shock. "Oh my goodness, sir, I am sure that I do not know where that came from.

And when Jamie said, "Crack is a new word, my dear. What exactly do you mean he is on some kind of a crack?"

Rebecca shook her head and she also wondered where it came from. Thinking ahead, she said, "Oh, I'm sorry, sir. I meant no disrespect and I cannot tell you where it came from. I guess I'm just afraid I will do something wrong and Lord Brentwall will punish Tom for my mistakes."

"That man of yours sounds like someone you care a great deal for. I was thinking, how long have you two been married? You did say he was your husband, didn't you? I'm not becoming too personal, am I?" Jamie moved closer to her and looked down into her eyes. "I honestly am only interested because I don't hear many ladies talk that freely about their men where I come from."

Rebecca looked into his eyes and became uncomfortable in his stare. Something moved in her heart.

"I think we should go up to the turret and see if anyone might be there. After all, you told me, sir, it might be a thief in residence or, if it is a ghost, I surely hope it is not," she smiled a secret little grin straight at Jamie and Sven.

Trying to throw off his questions about Tom was working. She noticed that when she smiled at Lord Jamie, he had a look of someone who had just caught the prize. Now where did that phrase come from, Rebecca wondered. Sometimes it seemed that she had the strangest thoughts at the strangest times, but she figured that her situation caused her so much stress that her mind was unstable. Strange words worried her the most, because she could never guess why she had them.

The men followed her as she climbed the cold rock stairs and were murmuring to each other. She could not hear enough to know what they were talking about. Once she heard Sven caution Jamie about putting her on the spot about her man. Then she heard Jamie whisper back to him, "How will I ever get to know her otherwise, smart ass?" Swearing bothered her and she was shocked to think that the Lord was so haughty to his personal guard and friends.

Making small talk, she turned around and said, "Here we are." Waiting to see what they had to say now that they were at the end of the sightseeing around the castle.

Jamie walked into the room. Looking out the slit that let in the only light, he leaned into it and was about to say how much he enjoyed the tour when he felt a cold breath of air rush over his neck. His right hand reached automatically to his neck. Sven saw him and wondered what on earth he was doing. It looked like he was trying to catch something flying around his head.

"What is wrong, my Lord?" Sven spoke up too quickly for Jamie to get a reaction that would appease.

"I guess all those steps got to me. My back is hurting now." He reached back like he had a pain. Turning around, he felt the cold air brush his face. It startled him and then he heard a sound like a woman's voice in his right ear. "She needs protection." He jumped and looked all around the room. There was absolutely no one there. Looking upward, he thought he saw a black bird fly out of the opening.

The rest of them were talking and looking around the room. Jamie rubbed his head and then his eyes. He had heard it as if it was a lady in distress standing beside him. But he knew there was no one there. Maybe there "is" a ghost here he thought. But who needs protection, he kept thinking to himself. And then he heard it again. "The Lady Rebecca needs watching over. Harm is coming for her here soon." And then the cold air was gone as quickly as it had come.

"Okay, let's all get out of here," Jamie spoke up a little too loudly. He saw them jump at the sound of his words and they all filed out of the turret one at a time, but not before Jamie took Rebecca's hand and held her back at the end of the group of people heading down the steps.

"Did you hear that?" Jamie asked her.

Rebecca looked up at him and said, "What do you mean?"

Jamie said, "I distinctly heard a woman's voice speak in my ear that you needed protection," he stated in a hush.

Taking her by the hand, he led her out and down the stairs. When they got to the bottom, they turned and thanked Rebecca for her time.

Just then, they heard the Lord speaking in a loud voice as if to detain them. "Ho, there you all are. Lady Rebecca, I have need of a word in private with you now. If you will come with me, please."

Jamie saw her shrink back and knew what had just happened was a warning. He was the only one who heard it and now he knew why. Lord Brentwall was the problem. The ghost was trying to tell me something was going on here. And anything that concerned Lord Brentwall had to be bad.

"Lord Brentwall." Jamie was going to deter him until Rebecca could escape to her room. "Can you please go to the stables with me? I have a need to show you my horse's leg. I think it is swollen again and we did want to be out of your way as soon as possible, but now I think I may need a couple more days to enjoy your hospitality and the great food while we wait for Nelson to heal up for a long trip home." Staring into his eyes and watching for a reaction to his question, Jamie spoke up again, "Can we go now, sir? I'm sure Rebecca will be around when we get back. This will only take a few minutes of your time."

Lord Brentwall was so aggravated, he could spit. But he spoke directly to Jamie and said, "Yes, come on. Let's go see to your horse's needs."

When Rebecca heard that, she walked away before anyone could say a word more. Lord Brentwall saw her disappearing around the corner and was so angry he could hardly speak. He had to get these men out of the castle and soon. Not only was the high and mighty Rebecca pregnant, but he had a terrible time catching up with her. Each time he tried to catch her she was out of his reach.

When they reached the stables, Jamie took him straight to the stall where his horse was stabled. He opened the door and went in to his horse. His horse, Nelson, knew his master and began whinnying and jumping around. Jamie reached down and caught the horse by the ankle and started to squeeze it hard. The horse made terrible sound and Jamie told Lord Brentwall his horse was still a little lame. Hearing the horse and wanting to be inside the castle before Rebecca went to her room, he told Jamie that he could stay as long as he needed to. Departing the stables without another word, Jamie saw him stepping high toward the castle.

Pulling out a tip off of a carrot, Jamie stuck it into the horse's mouth and smiled as he nibbled on his treat. Nelson chewed as if he had deserved a treat. Jamie was thinking about the cold air and the voice. Now he was really worried because the turret that was not haunted was apparently very haunted and the voice he had heard was warning him to help Rebecca. He had to move quickly now. He had to get her out of there as fast as he could.

Chapter Thirty-Seven

Back in the castle, Sven cornered Jamie when he came in the doors at the back of the house. "What are we going to do now?"

"I think we have to keep a close watch on Rebecca. She was not too difficult to talk to today. Maybe in a day or two I can get her alone and question her about her future plans and then go on about her man, Tom."

Jamie had more things on his mind right now. Ghosts that talk to you were hard to find. And not only did he find one, but the thing talked to him and gave him a warning about Rebecca. The warning was not too much of a surprise. Jamie knew the Lord was after Rebecca in a bad kind of way. He was going to rape her if he got the chance, because Rebecca would never go to him willingly; of that, Jamie was positive.

Standing in the castle galley, Jamie decided to search out Rebecca and he told Sven to give him some time and he would try his best to talk to Rebecca and see if she remembered anything. Jamie knew her memory was almost gone and it had to be because of something Tom had done to her. Whatever it was, he did not really want to know. But it was important that he talk to her and try to get her mind in touch with his. He wanted to take her back of her own free will, not be tricked and kidnapped again. He was so worried about her frame of mind that he wanted everything to go smoothly so she was not ever to be afraid again.

Jamie's head had been battered around a lot in his life, but when she was there, he was so happy and he had to get that back again. Jamie turned and put his hands in his pockets as he walked in the direction of the room where Rebecca had pointed when she told him where they stayed in the castle. Sven shook his head.

His mind was spinning with all the turmoil going on in the castle. The Lord was obviously a man who got what he wanted and it was so apparent to all of Jamie's men that what he wanted today was Rebecca.

Sven wanted Jamie to go after her, but in a safe kind of way. They had to make a plan and they had to follow it to the end, bringing Lady Rebecca back where she belonged beside the Earl of Dunraven in her rightful place.

Staring at a beautiful painting hanging on the stone walls of the Keep, Sven hoped that Jamie would go about this rescue in the proper manner, keeping his head on his shoulders and not hanging from a gate outside the castle for people to see and remember that the Lord here was indeed the Lord and this is how people who get in his way will be handled. The peacefulness in the painting disappeared with Sven's thoughts.

Rebecca had gone running toward her room. Going down the long corridor her heart was racing. What could she do to make the Lord stop chasing her? There had to be something she could do. But even she knew that when the Lord of the castle wanted something or someone, he usually got it, one way or another. Praying had become second nature to Rebecca since she had come to be with Tom. Right now she was hoping Tom was still at the smithy and that the Lord did not have time to get to her before Tom came in from working, all tired and then he might have to protect Rebecca from the Lord, who Tom did not want to upset at all if possible. She hoped the act had changed his mind from raping a pregnant woman.

Rebecca knew this and worried. This was the first time in Tom's life that he demanded some respect. Rebecca knew it was because of her. She was such a real lady that people looked up to him and his supposed wife. She knew he liked the idea that she would be his wife someday.

Since he had not yet run into any of the men in Jamie's party, he did not have that to worry yet. But it did worry Rebecca. She knew that soon he would see the new men and wonder why they were there. If Tom saw how the Lord of Dunraven seemed to watch Rebecca, there would be another problem for her. Right now, she did not need another thing to worry about. Three men were more than she could handle in her frame of mind.

Finally reaching her doorway, Rebecca hurriedly opened the door and closed it with a loud bang and put the lock on tightly. Rebecca threw off her cloak, hung it up and looked all around the small abode. Deciding to make some coffee, she went to her little can and got it out. All at once, she thought how great it would be to get a mocha café. Startled by the strange thought, she went on to make the drink. When these thoughts clouded her mind, she mentally closed the door to the unknown. Mocha café. Wherever did that come from? She could see a chocolate coffee in her hand and a 5 dollar bill paying someone for her cup of coffee. Shaking her head, she cleared her mind.

That morning she had hung a huge kettle on the hearth pit with meat and potatoes in it. Stirring it with her wooden ladle, her thoughts returned to the man she had just had the strange conversation with. Lord Jamie. Ghosts were not a routine topic in the castle. So whatever he had heard, it worried her, because she was the target, so Jamie had told her.

Lord Brentwall went straight to her door and began to pound on it. Rebecca wished she had a back door to run out of just now. Once again, what in the world was a back door? Another word she did not know where it came from.

Rebecca tried to block out the sound. Holding her hands over her ears, she cringed and stood still. Lord Brentwall did not give up that easy.

"Rebecca, open up now!" he shouted at the back of the door. Red in the face, he turned and ran into Jamie with a thud.

"What is going on here?" Jamie almost shouted at the Lord.

Lord Brentwall, red faced from shouting, replied, "None of your concern, I am sure, Sir." Then he turned around and walked away. Jamie heard him say, "pregnant". His mind went wild with that thought. His mind was ruling it out. Out loud he said, "Impossible!"

Jamie was startled at the verbal abuse the man could let loose when he was annoyed. And annoyed he was today. Jamie watched him until he was out of sight. Then he knocked very gently to let Rebecca know the horrid man had gone and it was him at the door right now.

Standing with her hands still on her face, Rebecca moved them down a little bit and heard another voice outside her door. Hearing it was Jamie she went to the door and spoke through it to him.

"Thank you, Sir, for making Lord Brentwall leave my door. I was so afraid." Rebecca reached her shaking hand to unlock the door.

Standing there so tall and proud made Rebecca calm down quickly. She knew that the Lord would not be back today, but tomorrow he would return and he would be so very mad. Jamie had saved her again. What was that about? Where were these strange thoughts coming from? She shook her head and moved aside and bid him enter. All at once, she remembered it was time for Tom to come home.

Even though Jamie knew that Rebecca did not remember him yet, or their life together, he also knew that she would not ever willingly put up with Lord Brentwall manhandling her. She had a fierce temper and he remembered it vividly from many encounters with him in the beginning. He had to smile when he remembered her telling him that it was the year 2006 because he had tried to talk her into seeing the local medicine man. Those memories were all he had to cling to until he could get her straightened out and her memory recovered.

And the Tom thing! It was so hard for him to even go there. Rebecca was his and he knew without a doubt that she was not married to Tom and he prayed to the Lord above that she was not carrying his baby.

It was even harder to look at the big man named Tom whenever he passed him in the castle or courtyard, now that Jamie had heard the word pregnant come out of Lord

Brentwall's mouth. Thank goodness he had only had two encounters with him so far. The end was coming because he could not stand to see her hurting like that for much longer. He was constantly planning an abrupt departure from the castle with Rebecca firmly in his care. But he had a new problem now. He would not stop until he found out if she was with child. Someway he knew she wasn't but he had not figured it out yet.

Tonight he and his men were going to plan the escape from the castle. He was getting nervous just thinking about what he could do and keeping her safe was his first priority. And the thought of a child was constantly plaguing him.

"Thank you, sir, for your help once again," Rebecca told Jamie with tears in her eyes. Her hand was shaking hard when she reached out to press a thank you on his arm.

"You cannot let that man harm you, Rebecca, because I can tell he only has trouble in store for you. Please feel free to call me if you need me. I am always near, Rebecca. Can we talk for a minute until you can calm down a wee bit, my dear?" Jamie was going to try to press her for her past and see where that took them.

"Please have a seat, Rebecca. I have a few things to talk to you about, if you have the time." Jamie questioned her gently.

"But, sir, I do not have time. It is time for my husband to come home any minute and he will not be happy to see a man in our home. Can we talk tomorrow, please sir?" Rebecca was pleading. He could hear the anxiety in her voice as she pleaded with him to leave.

"Certainly, Lady Rebecca, I will leave this instant."

With a shocked look in her eyes, she spoke up quickly. "Why did you call me Lady Rebecca, sir? I am just Rebecca."

This was not something he had time to explain because he had to get out of there right now. He certainly did not want a confrontation with big Tom nor did he have time to explain why he was there. So with that, he reached for her hand, brought it to his lips to kiss and left her standing there puzzled by his abrupt exit.

Actually, Jamie had been a lifesaver to her. Never did a day go by that he did not show up wherever she might be and ask her for a word or two. It got to be the highlight of her day. She found herself looking for him wherever she went. Her moods were in full swing whenever she ran into him. It had only been a short while ago that he had arrived and she was sorely afraid that someday soon he would take his men and his sore lame horse, Nelson, and leave the castle. That would be a sad day for her now that she had become such close friends with Jamie.

Early in the evening just the night before, she had had a long talk with herself about this man named Jamie. First of all, she had begun to look for him. When her eyes opened early in the darkness of morning, her first thought went to this man, wondering where he would be today and if she would get to see him again. With her Tom away working such long days until the wee hours of the evening, she had plenty of time to consider his presence in her life here at the castle.

Tom had no time for Rebecca because when he came home he was so tired and hungry that all he had on his mind was food and sleep. That gave her a peace of mind that she had lost before as Tom continuously asked for her hand in marriage. And to sleep in the bed was a horrible thought to her now.

Jamie had changed all that. Why, she did not know. But she had a feeling that would not go away. One of a man she wished was hers.

But when she thought that, it bothered her like a headache in the back of her eyes. She had a tingling feeling and whispers in her head. Shaking her head, she went about her daily chores and then headed down to the kitchen to help prepare breakfast for the knights and the lord of the castle.

Jamie was getting tired of waiting for Rebecca to remember him. Each day he felt more of her coming his way but not enough for him to sit down and talk to her about who he was to her and the whole story. Maybe today he would get her to take him back up to the turret room where he heard the warning the first time he visited it. Getting her alone might help him talk to her about the situation that was burning him up. Big Tom made him think that he was mean to her and he hoped that was not true, because if he found out Tom had touched a hair on her head, then Tom was as good as dead.

Chapter Thirty-Eight

Walking down the corridor, he felt more in control than he had before in a long time. He had seen the look in her eyes when he reached out and took her hand. Then when he kissed her hand, she was startled at his touch. Her eyes showed her shock and her happiness all at once. Jamie put both hands in his pockets and he started back towards his room, but the word child was never far from his mind now.

Rebecca could never forget the look in his eyes. Who was this man? He had made her happy simply by his attention. Had she been that needy? She did not think so. But her life had been so upside down for so long now that she had tried to accept it and not think about it. Time was working its way with her. She was calming down and now she thought she knew why. This man in the castle was different. But then he was far different from Tom. Her heart was beating a different rhythm. Falling and rising once, twice, three times.

Rebecca thought she had better calm down again. Because she had no idea why this man, a perfect stranger, could make her feel this way. Shaking her head, she walked over to her little rocking chair and almost fell into it. She was so glad that Tom had not shown up and had a face-off with the man called Jamie.

The fireplace was roaring with flames as high as they could get. Her head was swimming with strange thoughts. Then she heard Tom's footsteps and knew she had to get up and put on a happy face, forgetting the turmoil of the hour before. Putting that behind her, she opened the door and smiled into his face.

Tom was taken aback at once by the smile on her face. This was certainly strange for Rebecca to look so happy.

"Why are you so happy to see me, Rebecca? Did something happen today?" Tom was curious.

"Yes, and I was so worried that I came back here and locked myself in. Lord Brentwall came banging loudly on the door expecting me to let him inside all alone with me. I know he has bad things on his mind and I am so afraid of him, Tom. What can I do? He leers at me when I serve in the mealtimes and he follows me around the castle. And if he catches me alone, I think it will be bad for me and in return for you. I think you should be asking around about his habits with this staff. If he has done any girl any harm, we need to know, Tom. And if he has, I think we should leave immediately. I have seen the look on his face and it is not good for me; I can assure you of that. Just the today, he put his hands on me and the new man was waiting for a walk through the castle and that was all that saved me from his lecherous looks and hands."

Now that Rebecca had told him, she stepped back and waited for a response. But there was none. She was surprised by his lack of words.

"What can we do?" Rebecca asked him almost holding her breath. Time stood still for a moment. Then he came back with an answer.

The blood raced through his veins and he had a murderous look in his eyes. But when he spoke, his voice was rougher than she had ever heard in all the time she had been with him, even when he did whatever he did with the other man.

His voice was tight with anger. "I will keep a close watch on him, my dear. An accident might be just what he needs."

Rebecca saw it in his eyes and knew without a doubt that he had murder on his mind.

"But while I am here alone, how will I keep him at arm's length, Tom? She was terrified about the next morning and how she would explain Lord Jamie being in her room. And she did not want to handle this alone. But from his words, she gathered that Tom was worried about his job there and her, too. Who would win Tom's favor? Lord Brentwall or Rebecca?

Chapter Thirty-Nine

Over night, Jamie had lots of time to rethink the Lady Rebecca departure he had in mind. But first he had to get her alone, then and only then could he work his magic and get in tune to her memory and nature. The nature of Rebecca was what he would plead, too. That warm, cheerful girl he had found a long time ago, who constantly told him he was talking to a girl from the year 2006. A big smile came to his face when he remembered that time and her things she showed him from her time.

Remembering the medicine from her time that did so well when he was hurt and other things she brought with her from her time, he finally came to realize that she had not been making it up at all and there was something ringing true when she told him these things. He had begun to accept her stories as truth and then the fair had come to the countryside and in the little village so close to the castle where he felt so safe and secure, he found another tragedy implementing itself in their life, the days and time and months they had spent putting together a perfect love was now terribly gone wrong.

The time had come to make a move and he was going to get out of that castle before anyone knew which way he was going. And he was taking Rebecca with him, that much he knew for sure.

When the first rays of sunlight came through the tiny slits in his ceiling, he jumped up and he saw the black falcon fly through the slit in the ceiling again. He was so surprised that he threw the warm covers to the foot of his sleeping area and pulled on his pants and his shirt and headed to find the whereabouts of the Earl this morning, forgetting the falcon again.

In the late hours of the night, he had lain there in his bed and planned the day to come right down to the time and place where he was going to meet Rebecca the next day, because he knew her daily routine around the castle. He knew where he could find her and he was on the first step of leaving there as he walked briskly towards the breakfast area. Smiling a big welcome smile, he stepped into the room to find the Laird eating and staring at Rebecca as she left the room for more coffee.

"Good morning to you, sir," Jamie said as he took his seat on the left side of the table so he could watch the comings and goings of Rebecca as she served the men their breakfast. Jamie thought it would have been better if she had been the cook instead of the serving person, because then she would have stayed in the kitchen and out of sight of one bad ass Laird.

Lord Brentwall was drinking his hot black coffee and when he put his cup down, he answered with a smug voice, "Actually, sir, I am doing far better than you are, I'm sure." Then he put his cup back to his mouth to drink again. Smiling he said, "What are our plans for the day, Sir Jamie?"

Jamie was taken back by the evil look in Lord Brentwall's eyes and wondered immediately if the Laird had seen him retreating from her room after first going inside to make sure Rebecca was all right. If he had stayed and hidden around the corner, then her problems were just starting and today had to be the day to get her free from this dangerous situation.

Jamie spoke up with his plan in mind and put the plan into motion. "I wanted to have Rebecca take me to the castle turret again and tell me the story she started to tell me the last time she took my men and me up there. I wanted to ask your permission first before I asked her. The last time she was acting strangely when she made us leave that part of the castle. Sir, you know in my home we have a place in the castle that is rumored to be haunted and I had the same feelings when I was up there in your turret. Have you been up there lately yourself? That is why I wanted to take my men around it again. We are very interested in hauntings from the past. They seem to be trying to tell a story or trying to prevent something bad from happening again in history. I was certain you would not mind me borrowing Rebecca for that reason and I would be trying to help you, sir, if there is something wrong here in your castle. I hope this suits you, sir, because I feel something is not quite right here and I think I can help you find out what is wrong in that turret. How does this sound to you for this morning's little jaunt up the stairs once again?

Jamie could tell that Lord Brentwall was terribly upset by his short but to the point little speech which had no quarter for a rebuttal from the Lord in front of all the men in the breakfast room that morning. Inside Jamie was laughing hard, but no outward sign was visible.

Jamie saw Lord Brentwall squirm in his seat as if he had worms and it took all he had to keep a sober face. Waiting for an answer was quite tolerable in spite of the mean face Lord Brentwall was showing all guests at his table right now.

The first thing Lord Brentwall said to let everyone know that he had been studying the question put in front of him was a satisfying and long awaited for, "Yes."

"Sir," Lord Brentwall spoke up at last. Removing the grimace from his face was not that easy to do. But nonetheless, he had accomplished it for now. "I have many pending things to take up the most part of my morning anyway, sir. So I give you leave to fetch the maid Rebecca and go on with your task at hand for the morning. By the way, Sir Jamie, isn't it time for you and your crew to be heading home soon now? I have given you my hospitality for far more than a senight and I have noticed that your horse is doing quite well lately. Am I to presume that you will be taking your leave of my hospitality soon, sir?"

Jamie was startled at the audacity of Lord Brentwall and made it quite clear how impressed he was with the stay they had been offered there at his castle. He in return did not give him the answer he wanted to hear, but he made a commotion in talking to his men and turned his head and focused his eyes straight on the Laird's eyes when he spoke again. Leaving no doubt as to what he meant, he stood up and told him in his own thoughts how he felt about being sent out on the spur of the moment.

"Sir, we have been treated so comfortably here that we want to leave you with a silence in your hall and help you get rid of the ghostly encounters in your abode. So we won't be leaving just yet. After we take care of the ghost, we will travel at first light and there will be no need to have anyone send us off. We will leave quietly and no one will be needed for breakfast in the morning. Just give us this time in the turret and after sustenance tonight, we will gather our belongings and be gone quietly and quickly. If that suits you, sir, I am off to find Rebecca and be on my way to rid this home of its longtime ghosts. Thank you, sir, for all you have done for us. My horse is also perfect again for the long journey to the east and home. It will take us nigh on to three weeks to get there, but I am eager to get home once again."

Jamie noticed his men turn to look at him when he gave the wrong direction to home and the men were al satisfied that the lord took it all to heart and they would not be bothered with his presence again today. But tonight would be the performance of a lifetime, if they could get away with it. If they did, they would all be leaving in the night without a trace of them ever being there in the first place. It was a great plan, but it would take some talking to get Rebecca to go with the plan. That was what he was going to do now. He was going to find Rebecca and get started with it.

Chapter Forty

In the kitchen, Rebecca heard the exchange at the tables and wondered why this man wanted to go to the haunted turret again. Thinking it would be better to be spending time with him than dodging the lord, she secretly smiled to herself and went on into the breakfast room with fresh hot coffee. Her hand was on the silver handle with a pot warmer cloth to keep it from burning her and when she reached out her arm to pour fresh coffee into the Lord's cup, he grabbed for her arm and twisted her fragile skin until she screamed out in protest. Jamie dropped what he was eating and jumped to her rescue at once.

Looking into Lord Brentwall's eyes, Rebecca realized that she had made a bad mistake and began to cover up the scream with words that made no sense at all.

"Ouch, sir, I am so sorry but the coffee burned my fingers and I thought I was about to drop the pot and I did not want to burn you, and the fear that I was about to harm the master scared me also and hence the scream. I apologize, sir. It will never happen again."

Lord Brentwall stared into her eyes and smiled at the lie she had just told to keep things normal at the table. He knew the next time he called her to come to him, she would do it without any backlash from the beautiful full pink-tinted lips he had been lusting after for too long now.

"I am asking you to help these men rid us of our ghost that has been haunting this castle since before my parents were born. My man Jamie here thinks he can take care of it and I am not so sure that you know about it, but two lovers were killed here and walled up in the west wing tower over two hundred years ago. Lovers who knew too much and someone got rid of them. That is the story I was told when I was a kid. Do you think you can take them back up there this morning and let them see for themselves? I will no be taking back talk from you, lassie, so do as I say and meet me in the dining room for an early supper meal. I have things to discuss with you and we will be dining alone this night."

Rebecca was shaking in her shoes. What had she done now? She had put herself at his mercy. Oh God, what would she do now?

She started to shake and Jamie saw it and took over the moment quite perfectly, if he did say so himself. "Excuse me, Rebecca, but let me see to your burn."

"She is not harmed. I can assure you of that, sir."

Jamie backed away so Lord Brentwall could stand and hopefully leave the room. Lord Brentwall removed the napkin from his lap and stood up very straight and tall. Looking all around him, he decided to retire from the breakfast room and made his bow and left them all standing there looking shocked at his abrupt departure from them without so much as a goodbye. Jamie was thinking fast and furious. His time was shortened by the private dinner plans the Lord had made in front of them. He must work fast now.

"Come with me, my dear," Jamie said in a quiet tone of voice. Turning to his men, he said in a whisper, "Follow me up three flights and then sit down and wait for me to descend the turret. Make not a sound while you wait. Keep an eye and an ear out for any trouble you think might be coming."

Sven looked up at Jamie when he mentioned being quiet and keep an eye out for anyone who might disturb them before he got the chance to talk to her and try to explain things.

"Jamie, who would come up there anyway?" Sven looked perplexed after questioning Jamie. He had never questioned his friend before.

Jamie shot him a look as if to say "do not question me". Seeing the frustration in Jamie's eyes, Sven caught the message at once. Jamie needed Rebecca alone and it was his friend's job to protect them, no matter what the reason. Sven looked down and began a conversation with the rest of the men.

"Conner," Sven spoke as if he had never had anything on his mind but obeying his friend, "come close and keep an ear out for anyone coming up the stairs. We have to keep Jamie and his Lady safe for a while longer."

Turning to Rebecca and seeing her visibly shaken, he decided to take her by the arm and lead her up the stone stairwell. She did not open her mouth, but she followed him up and up and up until they reached the turret room.

Opening the huge barred door, he ushered her inside. Closing the door again, he turned around and took her in his arms. At once she stiffened up and tried to step backward.

"It is okay, Rebecca. Please let me have time to talk to you. You should know by now that I won't hurt you. I am here to help you out of a bad situation," Jamie spoke softly. He relaxed his arms, but she reached down and pulled them back around her. It was a gesture he found remarkable in her mistreated frame of mind. He had hopes that she remembered him. But the next words that came out of her mouth were not the ones he was hoping to hear.

"Please, Jamie. Help me. Because I think I am in big trouble with the master tonight. Help me, please." Her words were almost cries of desperation.

Rebecca was wringing her tiny hands and Jamie took her arm and walked over to the window seat where he placed her down on soft cushions and then he started his part of the plan.

Questions first, then answers were the words he heard in his mind last night while he tried to plan and then he tried to sleep. But there was a voice calling out to his mind. He heard it plainly and loudly all night. "Help her, Jamie. It is almost too late for her. Help her now." And with that dream echoing in his ears, he made his plan. Now he only hoped it would work. The ghosts must be there to help him. "Oh God," he prayed, "I hope you are here now, ghosts."

She was looking out the window and the side vision of her face was too beautiful for Jamie to turn his eyes away. His words came out slowly. "Rebecca," he pleaded to her. "I want you to look at me and think hard."

She turned her pretty face to him and said the most amazing words he ever heard. "Jamie, I know I must know you, but I cannot remember you. Sometimes when you walk by, I seem to remember you from somewhere. How can that be, Jamie?" He turned to her and there were tears in his eyes.

"What happened, Jamie? Why are you crying? Tell me, please. I know you know something but I do not know what you meant when you said that I knew you."

Jamie stood up and put his arms around her. He rubbed her arm softly and then pulled her hair back from her face and looked into her eyes again, smiling. He said, "I want to tell you a few things, but I don't want you to think I am crazy. Will you listen with an open mind and not be frightened by what I am going to say? All right?"

She looked like a baby experiencing a new sight. She lowered her eyes and said, "Not a word, Sir Jamie. Please tell me what it is I need to know. I am ready to listen."

Jamie spoke softly again and as he did, her eyes lifted up to look into his.

"I know you, Rebecca. You are my wife." Seeing her stiffen up, he said, "Not yet, Rebecca. Let me finish, all right?"

She nodded and looked down again.

"Okay, it is like this. I know big Tom is not your husband because he kidnapped you from the medieval nights fair we were attending close to my home, Castle Dunraven."

At that, she looked up at him and said, "It seems like I have heard that name before."

Jamie pushed her hair around again and began to talk to her mind, hoping she was remembering. "How did you get here, Rebecca? Do you remember that?" Jamie asked in a hushed tone.

"No, I do not remember anything before I had a broken arm and Tom was with me. He helped me get around. I guess it healed on its own, but I have heard that if you do not set a broken bone when it is first broken that you will have terrible arthritis in your bones and the pain is awful. Tylenol will not help it at all."

Jamie was looking at her and wondering where those words came from. "What is Tylenol, Rebecca?" Jamie asked her.

Rebecca responded, "Jamie, I do not know what I said. Sometimes words come into my mind and I have no idea where they came from."

She looked so small and delicate. Her fear was running rampant in her eyes. She kept her head lowered and that was what made Jamie move on with the plans he had made in the middle of the long cold night. He had a plan and he had no fear that he could not work it out. He would take his precious wife home at last.

"We were married over a year ago, Rebecca. You are my true wife. You were taken from Castle Dunraven on a cold rainy night many months ago, right from under my nose in fact. I had the feeling they had killed you, but I kept searching and looking for a clue until I got here. When I found you, I did not know what to do to get you out of here. Tom is another problem. He is not your husband. Do you remember marrying him, Rebecca?"

Jamie was quiet, trying to read her thoughts again. All of a sudden, she looked frightened by something in the turret. Glancing over her shoulder, she quickly turned around. Looking all around her, she looked as if she did not know where she was. Jamie took her by the shoulders and lightly pulled her around to him. The first thing he noticed was her eyes. They were glassy. Blank. Staring straight ahead and at nothing he could see.

"Rebecca, what is it?" Jamie shook her this time. Still not a word came from her mouth. Her eyes going left and then right. She was nodding her head, as if she were speaking or rather answering someone. Jamie was very upset at the turn of events. How was he going to get her attention? He did not want to shake her because he thought he might frighten her again.

Taking her by the arms softly, he led her to the window seat again. He lowered her frail body to the cushions and sat down beside her, waiting to see if she was going to come back to him from wherever she had retreated to. Leaving him coldly and silently as she had done made for a bad situation for him.

Jamie knew that he did not have time for this. Quietly he sat there waiting for anything. He knew she had to see him. Time was all he had for the moment.

Rebecca felt rather than saw a mist forming behind her and turned to look. There it was. She could see it. She knew Jamie was there, but she could not speak his name.

Then the voice came out of nowhere, speaking to Rebecca and no one else. It pulsated and vibrated in all corners of the room. She felt the transition. The air was slowly rippling gently over her body and she felt comfortable with the changes in the room. She was not afraid at all. All at once she was surprised by the change and she felt like she had been there before. It all felt familiar to her.

"Rebecca? Do you know your rightful heritage? Rebecca? The soft voice of a woman came out loud in the cold room. Rebecca heard it. She said, "Yes, but I don't remember much. I do know my name is Rebecca? Where are you? Why can't I see you?" She was searching for the voice.

"I am here beside you," came the sweet voice again. This time Rebecca turned completely around. Somehow she knew Jamie was there but she could not make her mouth open and speak to him. She tried and tried again. Nothing came out. She knew that something strange was going on, and in that moment she felt her nervousness start to dissipate. In fact, she was quite calm in the face of the ghostly appearance.

"Rebecca," the voice came again.

"Yes," Rebecca said in a strangled voice. "What do you want with me? How did you know that I was Rebecca? What do you want?" Her voice was strained but remained calm enough to ask more questions.

"I have been waiting for you for a long time. You have had another life and I had to wait for you to come to me. I am sorry that I had to put you in this danger, but for things to come around again to the way it was supposed to be, I had no choice. When you married Jamie, I knew I had to get both of you here some way and out of Castle Dunroven and here to this one, Castle Doonfoot. You are the rightful heirs. But Lord Brentwall was as cruel as his ancestors and I waited and watched. Well, here we are and we are going to do to him what was done to you both."

Then there was a male voice and it was speaking to Jamie. Jamie stood up and turned all around as Rebecca had done, but saw nothing yet. He listened. The conversation was going on all around him. He heard a man speak all at once directly to him.

"Sir Jamie, do not be alarmed. You are where you need to be right now. I know you cannot understand what is going on, but I am going to explain it to you. Lord Brentwall is here because his family killed the rightful heirs over a century ago. His family took what was not theirs to have. I was the laird here, Lord Robert. Both my wife, Adrianna, and I were killed and walled up in the priest hole here in the turret. I want you to open the priest hole and bury my beloved wife and me in a proper grave before you take leave here. Everything that has happened to you both was for the sole purpose and reason of getting you back here where you belong to undo the injustice that was done so long ago. Trevor was our firstborn. Trevor was our only child and he was sent to Dunraven Castle to be trained as a squire and then turned into knighthood. Then he went off to fight the holy war. When he returned to our castle, Castle Doonfoot, he met and married your mother. Then Trevor and his new wife left here to go on a yearlong wedding trip. While they were gone, Lord Brentwall's ancestors invaded our castle and killed us. We have kept vigil over Trevor and his family and his descendents. You are our great great grandson."

"Jamie, I know you have your own castle, but I want Castle Doonfoot to be taken away from Lord Brentwall and returned to your next of kin to be held for your children when they come to you and the lovely Lady Rebecca in time. Do you understand? Can you do this for me in the short time you have left here? And do not worry. Lady Rebecca is not with child. It was a ruse to keep Lord Brentwall away from her, but we are not sure if it did work. We can only hope."

"I would have made myself known before now, but I did not want to scare you both away from the part of the castle where we have been buried. So I waited. The first time you came up here with Lady Rebecca, she felt it and so did you. That was when I knew it was time to catch up where I left off so long ago, cut down in my prime. All I had to do was wait. Now you have come and we shall work this out between us. I have a very simple plan. It will rid the castle of the scoundrel and make it easy for you to return to your life and your castle."

"I have waited to right this wrong for a hundred years. Your great great grandmother, Adrianna, is here and she has kept a secret potion hidden for over a hundred years. Here is the plan."

The voice stopped. Jamie looked at Rebecca. She had heard it, too. Together they stared at each other, neither wanting to break the spell that had come over them both.

Jamie went to her and pulled her into his embrace. She held on for a long time. Then she broke away and turned around in the room asking for Lady Adrianna to appear.

"Please, Lady Adrianna, where are you?" She spoke at last. What is it that we have to do?" Rebecca waited.

A couple of minutes went by in silence. Then Lady Adrianna said, "Here, my child." Rebecca saw her appear and looked into the brownest eyes, almost the color of smoke. Rebecca held out her hand. In a moment it was taken into a warm one and the clasp was strong. Adrianna led Rebecca to the priest hole and put her hand on the cornerstone into the exact spot she had left the poison so many years ago.

"Is this where it is?" she asked.

"Yes, pull out the stone. The container is there and is untouched. This is also the priest hole where our bodies have been left all this time."

Rebecca took the stone in both hands. It moved slowly. Finally it came out and left a gaping hole. Rebecca put her hand into the hole. She felt it immediately, a small container, round and rusty in her hands. She brought it out into view. Jamie took it and pried open the long rusted lid. The smell was unbearable.

"How can I use this?" Jamie asked in a hushed tone.

The words came out of the Lord Robert's mouth who Jamie could now see. Looking him over, Jamie wrapped his arms about his body and rocked back and forth.

"I am not sure how this is to be the answer." Jamie questioned the solid man now standing in front of him.

"Listen to me," the ghost of Lord Robert said.

"I am listening," Jamie replied.

"Tonight when you have your last meal, bring the bottle of wine with you that I will leave in your room in a little while. It will have enough of the poison in it to kill the horrid man who now claims title to this estate. You must be certain that no one else drinks from it. You must come to the great hall an hour before the rest of the castle comes in and it will look like you have been drinking for a while. Prepare to act intoxicated. Act accordingly. Place your hands around one of the serving girls. Pull another one onto your lap. You know the act. Play it well.

After you offer the third glass to him, act as though you are going to pour the rest of the wine into your goblet. I will knock it out of your hands. Since no one can see me, it will look like you did it. It will spill all over the floor and you can then ask Rebecca, who will be serving, for a fresh bottle for you and your men at the long table. Make sure he drinks it when you get your refill and make a toast to your long ride ahead of you. That way he cannot refuse to toast with you."

Jamie thought it all sounded perfect to him. Rebecca looked at him and some of her memory returned. She remembered a lot of things all at once. The look in her eyes told Jamie that all was not so perfect after all.

"Is everything to your approval, dear?" he asked with a worried look at her.

"Who is Arthur?" she asked Jamie. Many thoughts were going through her head. All of different men and places, jumbled up in her head. All of a sudden, she felt lightheaded. Pulling both hands up to hold her head, she rocked back and forth. She saw something in her mind. It scared her. It was in the sky. She was looking up and the biggest bird she had ever seen flew right over her head. She ducked and lost her balance. Falling backward, she hit her head.

Jamie rushed to his knees to help her get up. "What was that all about?" he questioned her.

"I don't know. I saw something in the air. A huge silver bird. I never saw a bird like that before. What am I doing? I feel like I am going crazy."

Jamie took her hands and lifted her back to her feet. "Let me help you."

When he at last got her up and they both looked around, the ghosts were nowhere to be seen. Now he was worrying about the evening ahead of him.

The sound of a feminine voice came back abruptly and both of them looked surprised. "Look." Jamie spoke to the ghostly voice. "What you have planned here is a murder. Do you really think we would commit to such a vile act?"

Stepping back toward the wall and looking down at his hand and seeing the jar still there made Jamie think. "Wait a minute," Jamie said. "I must be addled to try and poison the lord here but it might just be the diversion we need to get going and to take Rebecca with us. It will cause a commotion, but with the Lord almost dead, they will forget about us and Brentwall will need all the attention so we can slip out unseen and unquestioned in the dark of night. When they find out he is dead, we will be gone for good. It will be too late when they try to find us," Jamie said with a satisfied look on his face.

"Gone like thieves in the night," Rebecca added.

Jamie looked at her and asked, "What? Rebecca, where did you hear that saying?" Jamie was surprised by her words, strange words again.

Her eyes looked glazed, like she did not know why she said it. Shaking her head, she replied, "Jamie, I don't know why I said those words either. It seems to me like I am saying things I have never heard before. Do you think I am insane from all the drama here?"

Jamie looked at her and wondered where the word drama came from. But he did not say a word. She just needed to be saved before something bad happened to her. Jamie felt it was his job to step in and save her. And he was ready.

"Adrianna, do you think this will work?" Jamie asked her.

"Yes," was all that he heard and he saw the figure of a woman disappearing. The man was still standing there. He was waiting for Jamie to tell him if he was going to poison Lord Brentwall for him. The look on his face was incredible.

Jamie knew the plan would work. So he said the words the man wanted to hear.

"Yes, I will. But I need you to tell me which bottle of wine you will put the poison in. Yes, I will do it. The plan is a well thought out one. You have waited too long already and this will suit both of us when it is over. I will ask for a bottle to be brought to my room and that will be the one you will use. Okay? When I go down to dinner, I will act accordingly. Bringing the bottle with me and offering it to him for thanks for all his hospitality for all my men, and the stable for the horses and the grain for my horses. I think it will work." Jamie was so elated he could not think any more.

Jamie shook his head and took Rebecca by the arm and walked on up the remaining stairs. Placing her in a chair, he told her he would be right back and returned to the men in the turret. Seeing the contented look on her face, Jamie was at ease.

Jamie was going to get through this mess with Rebecca, no matter what. Jamie kept thinking to himself, "Say the right words, be calm, be tactful, but most of all be honest with her." And so it begins.

"Rebecca, sit here and wait for me while I go to explain to the men what we are going through. I only need a few minutes. I want to explain about the ghosts, about the bodies buried in the wall and how we found out about all this.

Telling them how I know about the bodies will bring many questions and doubts. And telling them I am a direct heir to Castle Doonfoot will make them even more curious. I need time to go into some fine details here. And I need them to help me remove the bodies and bury them. I cannot do all this alone. I do not want the suspicion to be put on you.

There is a lot of work and not a lot of time. I cannot do this alone and it is not something you can help me do. I need them and they do not know what we know, so it is up to me to make them see the right thing to do is to bury my relatives quickly and get out of here. I know they will have a lot of questions to ask, so just relax and keep an eye out for ghosts. I will hurry back to you."

Jamie waited to see her reaction. There was a decidedly rough edge to his voice. Rebecca heard it. Rebecca gave him a perfectly happy and contented smile. Jamie's heart was peaceful again with thoughts of getting her in his arms at last.

Jamie preferred to spend all the time with her, but it was not possible to do right this minute. Rebecca knew he was right. She also knew the men did not indulge in ghostly matters. It was something not talked about if you were a big man. And these were truly big men. She was sure the men would not like to hear about the ghosts. But if it had not been for the ghosts talking to her, then no one would have ever known about this tragedy.

Jamie had mentioned it to her and Jamie was almost sure a couple of them felt it. But they were too unsure. Because they felt the strangeness each of the three times they went up those steps. Jamie was pretty sure that the men already. Rebecca had heard them talking amongst each other. She had heard the men mention this to Jamie and he had always had a way of talking them out of the notion that something was wrong up there. Jamie had tried to keep the men calm and alert at the same time, while they were in the small chamber.

While Rebecca waited, she made herself search with her eyes all the corners and dark areas of the turret. Nothing was out of the ordinary at the moment. Rebecca heard nothing and saw nothing. Jamie was her husband, she had been told. So now she would think on it while she waited.

Now she could hardly wait for him to tell her more. She knew they would make a decision about the dead bodies walled up and she had high hopes they would decide something about the two of them. But right now, they had to take care of the bodies. And somehow they would finally be laid to rest. But then, out of the blue, coffin came to her mind. Rebecca wondered where that had come from. They would need a coffin for the bodies. Rebecca wanted more for them, a fitting end.

Sven was the first to notice that something was wrong with Jamie when he came back to them. "Jamie, what is wrong up there? Is Lady Rebecca all right with being there alone? You know we would have been all right if you had not wanted to leave her there to talk with us." Sven's voice was shaking.

Jamie had to get it going now. "I have to tell you men a story and it will not be easy to accept what I tell you, but I have knowledge that I must share with all of you. So take it easy and keep calm, because it involves all of us.

I know it will be hard to believe, but Rebecca and I have both seen and spoken to the past Laird of the Castle Doonfoot. You know you have felt it. I did, too, but I did not know what it was then. When I say past, I mean hundreds of years ago."

Seeing the astonished look that at once came over the men, Jamie at once made a huge smile come over his own face and that alone calmed them down. Just to see that smile that had been gone for so long made them happy and they would believe anything their Lord told them. Jamie saw the looks diminish. Each man was looking at him, waiting for whatever it was that Jamie wanted to tell them.

"The last time we went to the turret alone, we were both taken back by the spirit of Lady Adrianna and Sir Robert. After the first shock of seeing and hearing them, we both instantly knew there had to be a good reason for them to be up in the turret. When they asked us to listen to their story and told us they had been murdered by Lord Brentwall's ancestors. Then their bodies were walled up inside the priest hole in the turret, we were so surprised. We were both saddened to hear their terrible ordeal, but to learn I was directly related to them brought another emotion as well. Now we want to help them. I hope you can understand how we feel and will want to help us do this last thing before we leave here.

Their story was a terrible one to be sure and we are going to bury them once we recover the bodies from the turret. We must do this quickly and not let anyone know our business. Do you men think we can do this quickly today and not be seen or found out?" Jamie waited for his answer.

Jamie's answer was quick in coming. Conner spoke up first and then the rest of the men nodded their heads in agreement. "We have no problem here, Sir. Go about your business and we will guard the tower steps for your protection."

With that taken care of, Jamie ran up the steps a second time, his mind going on and on with his plans.

Chapter Forty-One

Together they left the turret and talked as he walked Rebecca back to her room. He left her at her door with a word in her ear. "Do not worry. We can do this. We will let him drink and then I will start sending my men one by one to go to the barn and get ready to leave. We will act surprised when he falls out of his chair and hits the floor and we can then have his knights send for the healer. While they wait, we will be ready and leave them before he dies. There is no way they will ever know what has happened or that we were involved."

"Maybe I need to think about this first. It might look suspicious if we take you with us and you come willingly. We may have to grab you and run. Let big Tom come after you. We will set a trap for him and then he can be punished for his crimes and for kidnapping you. What do you think about the plan now, Lady Rebecca?" Jamie questioned her thoroughly.

Rebecca nodded her head as if to say she was not afraid. She took Jamie's hand and looked up into his eyes. Jamie saw she was very tired and the thought that Rebecca was now planning to help him kill someone might be a little much for her right now.

Rebecca was thinking what a terrible thing to be talking about! Even if that someone was the horrible Lord Brentwall, it meant to commit a murder. Her brain was trying to process the latest plan. Looking around the small room she was standing in, she remembered being in the turret in the castle where she had always felt a lonely cold dread fill her mind whenever she had been asked to go there. It all had looked so familiar to her. But she did not really remember why she had gone there in the first place. Jail, that was what was coming into her mind now.

"Jamie, if they put me in jail will you pay my bail?" she asked. "You will go to the bail bondsman and get me out, won't you?" The worried look on her face diminished as she waited for the answer she needed to hear.

"Bail bondsman?" Jamie asked her. "Please tell me what that is, Rebecca." Jamie questioned her. All at once the words felt so odd to her. Her mind was going in so many different directions that she could not remember why she had said that unfamiliar word at all.

"I do not now why I said that, Jamie. Let me think for a minute and maybe I can come up with the answer for you." Her head was down and Jamie could see the wear on her visibly in his eyes.

How could he have known that the haunted turret would hold all the answers for him? Just to think that it had been there all the time. What a mystery it had been and no one had ever tried to go up in that part of the castle because they said it was haunted. It was whispered about in the castle in low voices, even murmurs. But it had been so quiet and no one had bothered to listen.

Jamie was trying to think back right now and wondered if Lord Brentwall knew the history here. If he did, he would have been the one trying to stop them from going up there. Jamie did not think Lord Brentwall knew anything about it. It had all happened so long ago.

If they could pull it off, it would be a wonderful thing. But killing a real live person was not something a man could do without good reasons. Thinking again made it feel wrong. But it was surely the only way they would get out of there alive.

Jamie had it settled in his mind now and he turned to face Rebecca. Seeing the emotion in her eyes, he knew she was also worried about the outcome of the evening.

"Rebecca, calm yourself down a bit and let's think about how we are going to do this. I want you to go to your room and pack a few warm things. Nothing large, but warm enough to keep you comfortable during the ride out of here. As we head south to Dunroven, it will become a gentler wind and warm up a bit." He saw her face frown. "Dunroven is my home and yours."

The questions on her face and in her eyes were more than he could bear. He walked closer and asked her to sit in a chair by the fire.

"There are things I need to clear up for you. I can see you want out of here, but you have to be wondering what makes you feel so safe with me. We were married, Rebecca."

As he lowered her to her chair, she stumbled and he reached out to steady her by taking hold of her arm. Quickly and gently, he let her down on the goose down pillows. She leaned back in her chair and let her head drop. Her hair pooled out and she looked like an innocent babe sitting there on the pale rose cushions.

"This all seems so odd to me. To hear you talk like this is frightening me. But I am sure you can explain it all to me, Arthur."

Jamie looked at her and said, "Who is Arthur, Rebecca?" He watched her as she shook her head like something was just not right. "Are you aware that you just called me Arthur, Rebecca?" he questioned her carefully.

Rebecca did not know why she had said that to Jamie. Looking upward, she smiled and told him she had no idea why she had said it. The name Arthur meant something to her. She was sure of it. Staring off into space, it felt like she knew a man with that name. But she could not remember him. She closed her eyes and she heard his voice from somewhere calling to her. "Kelly! Kelly! Kelly!" Who Kelly was, she was sure she knew, also.

Jamie saw the perplexed look on her face. Her eyes were shut but he was certain she was somewhere else. Jamie felt sure that the day had been too much for her to absorb, so he leaned into her body and she instantly put both arms around his neck and cried.

"Jamie, I was married to a man named Arthur. I remember now. But it seems like another lifetime ago. I cannot remember much, but enough to know that I knew this Arthur. Please help me, Jamie. I am so confused through all this and then you tell me I was married to you. When was that, sir? How did I get here with Tom? Did you let me go? Was I a bad wife? Why did this happen? And more to the point, why did you not try to let me know that you were here to bring me home again a long time ago? Although, sir, I must tell you I do not remember being married to you."

Jamie was so sad about the present situation. He did not know where to begin. And Arthur was a shock to him.

In the corner of her room, a presence appeared again. The man was a shadow at first, then becoming more and more defined. At once he spoke up and his words were so softly spoken that Jamie was not sure what he was saying.

"Speak up, sir," Jamie said.

The wind was beginning to blow outside the window where Rebecca was seated. She turned to listen to the howling wind and she saw the man, too. He spoke louder now.

"Listen to him, Rebecca. He will tell you all he knows. There is a lot at stake here tonight and your participation is required to right all the wrongs. It took you a long time to get back here to pull off your part and you have undergone a lot of twists and turns to get here. Let us take care of the matters at hand for tonight and then all will be revealed to you at the end. Can you do this for us?" the man asked. Then she saw him turn towards a wall where Lady Adrianna was appearing. Her sad look brought Rebecca back to the plan at hand.

"Jamie, I will be all right. I would think a strawberry daiquiri might help me out, but I will do whatever is needed of me. And when we accomplish the end we are working to, I will be waiting to hear the rest of the story."

Jamie looked confused. "What may I ask is a strawberry daiquiri, my dear?" Looking blank, he knew it was another one of her strange phrases from the life she had told him about when he first found her in the tunnel wall. It all felt so long ago to him now. Thinking about it, he felt rather than knew that she had been through two lifetimes already and now this was making a third. Arthur being the first husband, then he found her and believed she was his lost wife, Rebecca. Then Tom took her and she believed he was her husband. Then Jamie came in to rescue her and now the ghost in the turret said she was his family. What she had had to go through so far was more than a mere gentle Lady could bear. Jamie just knew that he should be there for her and in the end he would straighten it all out for them both once and for all, once they returned to his castle.

"Well, sir, I am not sure why I said that. But it sounds like I need a refreshing drink of strawberries."

Jamie looked at her again. He shook his head, knowing that she should know the time for ripe berries was in the late summer. Not the early spring. But he let the thought go for now anyway. Things were getting more complicated each time she opened her mouth. Jamie needed her to get her mind ready for tonight.

"Okay, let's get ready for the showdown," Rebecca said. Jamie gave her a look but said nothing. Lifting her up, she put her hands in his and they walked toward the door so Jamie could go back to his room and get ready for the evening to come.

Chapter Forty-Two

The bailey was quiet for some reason this afternoon. Rebecca, looking out the slit in the rocks of her room, saw a number of the archers in a corner enjoying a talk about the next field day exercises. Rebecca knew it was time to leave for the kitchen. She grabbed her shawl and left her room, going down the long hallway and through the portrait gallery. Looking to her left and right at all the portraits of people who had once lived in this castle, she heard footsteps coming toward her. She looked up and saw Jamie walking toward her. She felt the need to talk to Jamie more about the plan and she could see in his face that he needed to talk to her.

Walking slowly and following a little behind Jamie, she was shaking a bit from the ordeal she had just undergone. Finding out that Jamie had known her and had not engaged in the details with her in all the time he had been here made her wonder if it was true. How could he have been so secretive when he had known how to get her out of there all the time? It was not big a problem for Rebecca, but it bothered her a little. So she decided to talk to him again. She wanted to know more facts and more whys about the situation. She wanted him to confide in her and help her process this information. It was a bit more than she had imagined it would be.

"Jamie," she spoke up all of a sudden, "can we go out to the gardens to talk? I have so many questions for you."

"Yes, my dear, we can go now," Jamie said as he nodded his head in the direction of the open doors.

Walking together, he picked up her hand. Looking around to make sure no one could see them he pulled her closer to his body. When he was sure they were out of sight from prying eyes, he laid his head on hers and she felt the emotion rush through her body for the man who had been so good to her while she had not known who he was, but had felt a need to know him better. He kept watching her face. He was also watching for anyone to come upon them.

Jamie's mind was terribly busy at the moment. He was trying to figure out how he was going to explain all that he knew to her and why he had waited so long to do it. Of course, he had many good reasons and the main one was that he was trying to keep her safe. He had worried so much in the past and it had cost him dearly. His nerves were jumping. His brain was whirling with information that he needed to share with his lady wife. But first he had to make her remember that she was his lady wife.

Bringing all that back to her was going to make the next step go as planned. Keeping her safe was his primary worry right now and he thought he had a lot of things to do and explain to her in such a short while. So he needed to start now.

All of a sudden he remembered that she had wanted to speak to him first. What could she have to say? There was so much for them to accomplish today. Time was slipping by too fast now.

Leading her to a stone bench in a corner of the garden under some big tall beech trees where the shade was perfect and the warmth from the sun would still keep them comfortable, Jamie let her down onto the seat. Moving next to her, he sat down and kept her hand in his. It felt right just holding it. The air was gently moving her hair. The sun was peeking through the branches. Her face was worried and he knew it was his fault.

"Rebecca, I have a lot to tell you. Let me start at the beginning. I am sure you are going to have many questions, but wait until I am through and then we can relive it together. Is this a thing you can do, my Lady?" Jamie waited and when she finally answered him, he took in a long breath and started the story from when he had first seen her. As he explained, he saw her face move into many quizzical looks. Still keeping silent, he continued with the tale.

At first Rebecca thought she was dreaming. But then there were times when he said things that made a memory open wide to her. Names she had heard before. Dunraven castle. The medieval games. She was remembering things as he told her word for word how she came to be his wife.

He even told her who Arthur was. He told her how she made the choice to stay with him and leaving her other world behind, they had let her take the place of his wife, Lady Rebecca, who had disappeared some time before Kelly had arrived bleeding in the castle walls.

The name, Arthur, brought with it a picture of a man she had loved. But her love for Jamie had grown and she could not leave him. She had made the choice and now she could remember the man, Tom, and how he had kidnapped her with that other man. Her fear of Tom came rushing back to her. She shivered. Jamie knew she was taking in a lot of news but it had to be told. When he eventually stopped, she smiled and he felt like maybe he had his Lady back.

Jamie leaned into her and kissed her on the side of her face. She turned in towards him and kissed him full on the lips. The joy that Jamie felt could not be explained.

"Dear Jamie, I feel as though I have been put through an ordeal that led me to this place and time just to be with you. Whatever happens now, we both must keep a vigilant eye out for Tom. I am sure we can get through this evening, but I must have a reason not to go back to our room here. Tom will be in late but he will expect me to be there. So I must go down to the field and tell him I am going to be serving tonight so he will not go looking for me and cause a scene that we cannot deal with. We need to go through this evening's plan right now. Then I need to go find Tom. If we can keep him out of the great hall tonight, this might work."

She shook her whole body and tried to stand up.

Jamie pulled her into his arms where she belonged and held her tight for a moment. When he let his guard relax, she stood up and they turned toward the castle doors.

Chapter Forty-Three

Nerves were tight. Jamie went to his room and found the bottle of wine waiting for him. There was also another bottle for him to drink from before he went down to dinner. Taking a drink from the bottle, he changed and dressed.

He left for the galley to tell his men the plan and for them to get packing. As he returned to the bailey, he saw Rebecca's skirt swishing as she went in through the kitchen opening. He hoped her nerves were better than his.

Jamie turned toward the dining hall. A couple of Lord Brentwall's men stopped him and talked to him. He watched as Lord Brentwall went into the dining room and took his chair at the end of the massive wooden table. Although Lord Brentwall was alone in the room, Jamie could hear his men as they were returning from the jousting exercises in the field for the day. Some slowly entered and went over by the large fireplace. Others bent down to ruffle up the dogs for a minute then they started to seat themselves at the table. Jamie was glad there were so many men tonight. His mind was working on the plan and to make sure the right man got the right wine tonight. Tonight was the most important night in his life. Everything had to go as planned.

Waiting for the rest of Lord Brentwall's men to come in from the fields to eat had been hard for him, so hard that he had begun to drum his fingers on the huge wooden table. Lord Brentwall looked at Jamie and remarked that he was very impatient tonight about something.

"Good man, Jamie, what ails you?" he asked. As the rest of the men filed in one by one and took seats by Jamie, he prepared himself for the comfort of their meal together.

Jamie spoke up. "Lord Brentwall, sir, I am most happy to be taking my last meal here tonight and that tomorrow I may be heading towards home again. I have been away a lot longer than I had predicted when I left. I am sure they are beginning to worry about my prolonged absence at my home. But to answer your question, I am not agitated at all. Let me offer you a glass of my wine before we eat. I brought it specifically for thanks for all you have done for my men and, of course, my horse, which has landed us here far longer than we anticipated. You have been so kind to my men and me. Have a toast to my safe journey home in the south of England. A long and tiring one to be sure, but I need to get home soon. It has been a pleasant stopover and you have been the ever vigilant Lord. Many thanks to you, sir."

With that, Jamie reached out a hand for his trencher. At first, Lord Brentwall was so happy to hear they were leaving that he did not hear all the rest. So as Jamie reached for the trencher, Lord Brentwall moved even closer to Jamie.

"Dear Sir, I am going to be glad to be rid of all these mouths to feed. And I need my privacy back. I hope you go with glad times. I will be ever so glad to drink to your safe return to your own home. But where might that be?"

Holding the glass out away from the table for Jamie to pour the wine for him, Jamie thought that maybe he knew it was tainted wine. Reaching out his own glass for a toast was the means to force the Lord to take drink up while Jamie drank his alongside the Lord.

Meanwhile back in the kitchen Rebecca was shivering with cold, the episode tonight ever present on her mind. The persistent chill invaded her mind. She was so uncomfortable in the kitchen that several maids mentioned her color had gone white, but eventually went on with the dinner service about to begin.

Turning away from the women, she picked up the pitchers and headed for the tables. With her arms full, she walked towards the men seated at the tables. Her eyes met with Jamie's at the same time. They both had the same thoughts and they both knew it. She lowered her face downward with no expression visible to the room full of hardened men.

The noise was overwhelming. Her fear was great that someone would guess their intentions that night. Her hands were shaking, her eyes were darting back and forth. But she never glanced towards Jamie.

As she poured the wine, she noticed Lord Brentwall reach for another mug of Jamie's wine. Lord Brentwall was already leaning in so close to the food that his hair was hanging in the gravy and she saw him try to right himself more than once. The more he drank, the more unstable he became.

Jamie was holding out his cup to her. He wanted more wine or he wanted to tell her something. When she got close enough to speak to him, he reached for her hand. She tried to pour wine in his cup and look at Lord Brentwall at the same time. Her fear was taking control of her.

The shaking of her hands told Jamie what he already thought he had seen. He was afraid that she would fall apart and someone would notice her attitude and service was not the same as her usual self on the nights before.

Taking her hand as she poured, he whispered in her ear. "It is almost done, Rebecca. One more drink or two and he will fall to the floor. When he does, just walk slowly to the kitchen and put the pitcher down. Tell the head cook that you need to go check on Tom and you will be back in a few minutes. No one will suspect that you won't be coming back and soon they will be busy taking care of the men and forget you are not there.

In the meantime, I will give him another drink. It should finish him off. When he falls out of his chair, he will be surrounded by his men trying to revive him and I will slip away in the middle of the activity. I want you to go to the stable. The men are already heading that way one by one. Three have already left. I saw them go. No one else saw a thing. Remember we are safe right now."

Lord Brentwall saw them talking and even though his eyes were blurred now, he did not want her talking to him for some reason. He could not remember why. Trying hard to speak to her, he found he had no words. He tried again but this time he had no voice and did not remember what he wanted to say to whom. His wine had never made him feel this way before and he was beginning to think that something was wrong.

Trying to pick up his mug, he slammed it down. The wine went all over the table, leaking between the timbers of the wooden table. It caused a commotion in the eating hall and Jamie used it for his escape.

He watched all the men rushing to Brentwall's side and he jumped up and went over there, too. Saying a few words that no one heard, he made his escape. Slowly he moved towards the doorway and slipped outside the room full of men yelling to each other.

He saw two men, laughing merrily, trying to pick up Lord Brentwall to a sitting position, but Brentwall fell backwards quickly. Jamie was hoping the deed was done. The men did not know it yet, but when they did, all hell would be running through the castle like evil.

Jamie made his way through the castle quietly, slipping through the corridors without being seen by anyone. Everyone who was anyone was in the dining hall trying to get to the Lord. He could hear the running feet and hear shouts occasionally as he made his way out the side door to the gardens.

Looking back and forth as he ran to the stables, he saw no one. That was good. Rushing inside the stable looking for Rebecca, his heart about to burst, he saw Rebecca sitting on a horse waiting for him.

His men were already mounted and as they threw the reins of his horse to him, he followed Rebecca's horse out the doors and the group slipped out into the dark night. The deep woods along the bank of the small burn was soft and wet, so the horses made no sounds.

Keeping the horses quiet, they made their way across the castle land and into the darkness of night, slipping away like they had never been there at all.

Chapter Forty-Four

Putting as much distance between them and the castle as Jamie could, they traveled all night and when the sun started to come up over the horizon, they slowed the pace and started to look for a secluded place to sleep for a while. When dark came again, they would try to put much more distance behind them.

Rebecca was so tired and stiff, she did not have any conversation skills left. The race through the night had all but done her in.

"Jamie, please stay with me while I rest," Rebecca said while she put her hands over her mouth and yawned.

"I will be right here," Jamie replied. "Our lives have been changed forever, Rebecca. No matter what happens from here on in time, and I mean my time, Rebecca, not your time, I will keep you closer to me than I had ever thought possible. It is alright, lassie, because I have got you safe with me now. Relax and sleep for a while. When you wake, we will move on toward the castle and when it comes into sight, I pray that all your memories return and my prayers will be answered.

The expression on his face said more than words. Rebecca knew he was still afraid that she would not remember him when the time came and they finally got back to his castle.

"Jamie, can you please tell me something about your home so that I may think about it on the way back to Castle Dunraven?"

"My hope is that you will remember on your own, my love. I do not want to think I put anything in your mind before you come to know things for a fact. I want you to know everything."

The rest of Jamie's men were bedding down across the small fire they built for warmth, hoping that the day would progress quickly while they took turns resting. Jamie reached down and put the blanket over her shoulders, tucking her in and with a gentle pat on the back, Jamie stood up and turned toward the fire. His shoulders were drooping and the men knew he was very upset about the way things had to end with Lord Brentwall.

He walked over to his men. Dark piercing eyes bore into those of his men. All at once, they knew there was a problem. Looking at the anguish in his eyes, they were all silent.

Jamie turned and walked away again. This time he had a murder on his mind, one that he had been involved in. He had killed before, but that was to save his life or the life of one of his men. He had been trained to protect his castle and his home. He would do anything he could to make his Keep safe from invaders.

But now he had killed a man or at least been a part of the plan to get rid of him. Who would believe that ghosts had led him into this situation? Who would believe that the Laird of the castle would take orders from two ghosts?

He could never be associated with this death. Looking up at the blue of the sky that was just now clearing off the fog of the night before, he made a prayer that the events of the past few days did not ever catch up with them. His main source of worry was Rebecca. When she had time to get back to her life with him, would she also remember their part in that death and would it haunt her? Would he lose her again? Jamie had a lot to think about today.

Turning around again, he stepped into the circle where his men were waiting to hear what was on his mind.

"Love is worth fighting for," he said to his men. "I will fight for her. Are you with me? How many of you know the part I have played in Lord Brentwall's death?" Jamie waited for an answer. Not one man spoke up. Then Connor, his oldest knight, stood up and spoke out for all the men.

"Sir, we know only that Lord Brentwall was very drunk and fell from his chair at the table. We were all there and you had naught to do with any of that mess last night. No more, no less. Is there some meaning you want us to hear from this? We all saw you drink out of the same bottle and eat the same food. That is what we know. Let us proceed this evening to our homeland and resume our lives the way they were before all this terrible kidnapping happened. Our Lady Rebecca will become settled once again and our lives will begin afresh, Sir."

Jamie was relieved to hear that they saw nothing amiss here. It also cheered his heart to hear the way they rushed to Rebecca's aid. They had been through a lot with Jamie and they were on his side all the way.

Rebecca was cold and tired. With the clouds so thick above, she wondered if the rain was far off. That would make for bad, wet sleeping arrangements today. The men were already trying to catch some much needed sleep. The night had been a long and fast run. She was really sleepy. But she had the fear of Lord Brentwall and his men coming after them.

Even though she knew or rather thought she had seen him die with her own eyes, she was afraid that at any moment a group of riders would ride into their secluded dark resting place.

It would be the loneliness of sleeping alone and the fear of not being alone that would keep her eyes open. Rebecca saw Jamie coming her way with some large round pieces of bedding. She wondered where he found that.

"What have you there, Jamie?" Rebecca's voice was so clear it rang out over the rest of the men. She saw a head or two lift at the sound of her voice, but seeing Jamie there, they all resumed their sleep.

Jamie wanted nothing more than to lie down beside her, but was afraid to make the suggestion. He handed her the blanket and told her he had it on the back of his horse so she could keep warm and dry if they encountered any bad rainy days on their ride homeward. Jamie could see the bright look on her face and knew he had made her happy with his thoughtfulness.

"Can you rest beside me here for a few minutes? I fear that I am very distraught with last night's memories and am afraid to close my eyes at the moment. I won't mind at all and I need a companion beside me." Rebecca waited for his answer.

Jamie's heart could not believe what his ears had just heard. Exactly what he had been hoping for came out of nowhere and he bent down to her and smiled, "Of course, I will be here until you sleep, my dear. I will always be here for you, Rebecca. Do not forget that."

Feeling so cheered, she rested her head on Jamie's shoulder and soon was fast asleep, never knowing when Jamie moved her head down onto the blanket roll he had placed for her to rest on.

Jamie had a man in the woods watching for anything strange that should occur and he had a man on the left side of the river watching also. He felt they were safe enough, so he moved quietly away from Rebecca's side and laid his head down a few inches from hers. Soon he was asleep, too.

Jamie's dream came fast. He was taking Rebecca across the river and her horse fell, dropping Rebecca into the racing stream of water. He reached out for her and her hand slipped into the air. Jamie saw Rebecca fighting the water. Then, all of a sudden, Lord Brentwall was there, grabbing for Rebecca. When he saw her look at Lord Brentwall and smile, he screamed out loud, "No Rebecca, do not look at him! He is going to hurt you!" Feeling at a loss, Jamie reached out to extend his strokes in and out of the water to get to Rebecca before Lord Brentwall got a hold of her hand.

All at once, Jamie felt pain. His eyes opened and one of his men was there slapping him hard, trying to wake him up from the horrible dream he was having. Rebecca was also sitting up by his side with her hands on his, trying to let him know that she was all right and his fear was only a dream.

Looking around him brought him face to face with Rebecca. He grabbed her to his chest and his hands kept stroking her hair up and down. At first she said nothing. Then slowly she began to speak in that soft tone that Jamie had grown to love. He could tell that his heart was okay now that he had her by his side.

"Rebecca, I thought I had lost you either to the rushing water or to Lord Brentwall. The dream was so real and I was so frightened. Thank God, you are all right. Here, my love. Move back to your blanket and let me lie beside you til darkness comes. I feel the responsibility of your safety greatly on my mind today."

"Please feel free to lie by me, Jamie. I too feel as if something is going to happen to us. Are the riders getting near to us, Jamie? Please tell me what to think today. I am so frightened when I remember what we did. How can we ever forget the part we played in the death of Lord Brentwall, Jamie? I know it will haunt me forever. I never thought I would be a part of a murder. I always wanted to be a CSI inspector but not on the opposite side of the law."

Jamie looked at her strangely. "What did you mean, Rebecca, when you said you wanted to be a CSI inspector? I do not recall that word at all." Jamie's face looked perplexed.

Everything seemed to be falling in on them all at once. Their fear. Their dreams were full of fear. Their love had to be strong to survive this. The trip ahead of them was still very dangerous and there was still a long way to go with no way to know if there were men from Lord Brentwall's castle searching the roads and forests for them at that exact moment. No way to know what was going to happen. This made Jamie very cautious and he knew every moment mattered from here on out.

Chapter Forty-Five

Jamie had visions of happier times in his and Rebecca's future. But sometimes the danger overcame the visions. He only wanted her to be happy and safe again in his own home. The thoughts of where she came from or who she really was were far from his mind these days. His memories of his wife, Lady Rebecca, were totally wiped out of his brain. His memories of her as his wife were hard to recall these days because all he wanted was her in his castle and in his life again, once and forever. No more would he take her anywhere if there was not a group of guards with him, protecting her at all times.

"Jamie, I really do not know why I said that. I also do not know what it means," Rebecca told him, dropping her head. She remembered that she quite often said things with no understanding of them even now knowing she was going to be safe at last and knowing that when they reached his abode and she saw all the people who supposedly knew her, things were going to become very uncertain for her when she first arrived back at the castle. She could not wait to get things back to the way they were before she was kidnapped. She had a lot to remember.

Rebecca wanted to comfort Jamie. She could see the emotions running wild in his face, from happy to sad, to real fear and then to dread when he tried to figure out how this would end. Would he have her back again? Would she remember?

Rebecca knew. He had asked her over and over again about the things she remembered and how she felt when she tried to remember him and the things that they had done together. He had also questioned her about her feelings for Tom. That had gone nowhere fast, because she had no feelings for the man who had kidnapped her and kept her prisoner. Although she did tell Jamie that she had come to rely on Tom because it was all she could remember and things had been so vague after she broke her arm on the trip when he took her. But no, emphatically no was what she had told him. She had seen the mask of doubt slip off his face when she said that. Rebecca knew he was worried about their relationship and she was equally as worried about herself, too.

When Rebecca had time to try and sift through all the things that had happened to her in the past year, it seemed almost too much to imagine. She had decided that she had been a victim of a haunting in the beginning. But the things that happened after the trip back to Dunraven Castle had been all related to Jamie and herself.

It was amazing to Rebecca that she finally could remember all those things. She had a dear spot in her heart for Arthur, but it was all a plan to get her to England and then to keep her there. She realized that all the things that had taken place, even the death of Lord Brentwall, had been planned by someone somewhere and it had all happened because it was supposed to happen. It was a miracle that they righted all the wrongs that had been going on for some hundred years or more. When they talked about it, it all made sense to the both of them. Rebecca's heart belonged to Jamie. Her life belonged there with him.

The only thing that she would like to find out, if she had a way to do it, was what had happened to the real Rebecca. She was planning to ask Jamie if they could find out more about his real wife. Just not knowing made it hard for Rebecca to go back again and step into his wife's shoes. Even though she had become his wife before, it might be harder now that she had gone through all the things that had happened to her since she had been taken against her own free will by Tom.

She had been a witness to his partner's murder when Tom had gotten rid of him in order to keep Rebecca for himself. She had broken a bone with no doctor to attend her. She had been lonely and she had lost her memory for some time. Then she had been accosted by Lord Brentwall. Then there were the ghosts that haunted her still in Lord Brentwall's castle. She had been through a lot. But her heart told her that she was going to be all right as long as she was The Lady Rebecca and Jamie was there to love her through all time.

After all, she had already been through many time warps and now knew her place in this new life. Rebecca could not understand all these changes back and forth in time, but the end had proven to be all she needed. Now maybe she could rest and go on with Jamie in his time.

Rebecca knew Jamie was not too sure yet, but she had been thinking about all of it and knew he needed her to be there. So now she was going to put everything behind her and move forward with Jamie. All she had to do was tell Jamie.

He asked himself one question all the time. Would things ever be the way they were before she was taken from his life? A man should never treat a lady the way she had been treated and he wanted to wipe it from her mind. His only prayer was that she had the strength to go back where she belonged. With him.

Jamie had no way of knowing that things were at last working out for the both of them and he was going to see a new Rebecca today and for the rest of his life.

Jamie's acute awareness of her nearness to him made him watch her movements.

"Jamie, whatever are you looking at?" Her voice smoothed out the air of confusion.

"Thinking back to when we were happier and times were not so strained, Rebecca." Workings his fingers through her hair, he turned to her with a sweet smile on his face. Seeing his smile made Rebecca feel less worried, she felt like the future would all work out in time. And they had plenty of time. Time was not of importance anymore. All that mattered was that Rebecca showed him what it was going to be like.

Her arms were up and around him in a moment. He took the opportunity to kiss her hard and she knew the timing had been right all along. Time had been her enemy once, but now time was her beloved......and yesterday's sunset was today's blessing......